Beneath

GILL ARBUTHNOTT

KELPIESTEEN

Kelpies Teen is an imprint of Floris Books

First published in 2014 by Floris Books
© 2014 Gill Arbuthnott

The publisher acknowledges subsidy from
Creative Scotland towards the publication
of this volume.

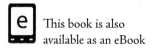 This book is also
available as an eBook

British Library CIP data available
ISBN 978-178250-052-0
Printed in Poland

Kathryn – this one's for you.
My goodness, you deserve it.

Summer

Chapter One

He stood in the shadows, breathing quietly, utterly still, watching.

Watching her.

He knew her so well, though he had never spoken to her. He knew everything he needed to know about her. He'd watched her with her family, with her friends.

He wanted her for himself.

Should he do it now?

He hadn't expected her to come here today. Should he do it now? He wasn't ready. And it was too soon after the boy. But it was such a chance. It might be a long time before a chance like this came again.

He would deal with the consequences.

Very carefully, he began to edge towards her.

Jess stood by the pool. It looked as it always did, brown water reflecting the sky, a rustling border of reeds, and birch and alder trees growing almost to the water's edge along one side, and a little boggy meadow of rushes at the other. She breathed deeply, glad to be away from the noise and bustle of home.

A couple of mallard ducks landed on the water nearby, disturbing the reflection of the clouds, and she moved round the edge of the pool to get a better view of them. She stood for a few minutes, watching them dabble for food.

She ought to go back. There were chores waiting for her

back on the farm, but it was so peaceful here, with no one telling her what to do.

Reluctantly, she turned to go. As she did so she glanced down at the ground. She paused. There were footprints – no, hoof prints, in the mud at the water's edge.

It took her a few seconds to realise why they looked odd. The horse was unshod. Strange… That would mean it was wild, and she'd never heard of any wild horses in the area, now or in the past.

A cloud went over the sun and the ducks flew up without warning, making Jess jump. Her heart beat fast. *Idiot.* They were only ducks, most likely frightened of their own shadows. But still, the familiar woods seemed suddenly threatening.

A twig cracked among the trees behind her. She turned sharply, scanning the woods for a sign that someone was there. The breeze ruffled the leaves and for a second she thought she saw a shadowy figure in the undergrowth.

Heavens, girl! Jess told herself. *Get a grip on your mind and stop imagining things. Just because Donald went missing doesn't mean the place is suddenly full of monsters.* All the same, she turned on her heel. *Best get home.*

There was a noise from among the brambles at the far end of the pool. She froze. Had she imagined that too? It had sounded like a growl.

"Hello?" she called, trying to keep control of her stampeding imagination. No one answered. Or at least, no one human. The growl came again. Surely it was too deep for a dog?

Genuinely frightened now, Jess edged towards the path that would take her home, never taking her eyes from the bramble patch.

She was sure she could see a flicker of movement behind the tangled stems. Something big; something dark.

As she reached the path and backed along it, the brambles

became silent and still. Jess took a deep breath. Whatever it was, it had gone.

And then, without warning, something crashed through the trees nearby. She caught a glimpse of a black shape leaping past her, too fast to see properly. Panic consumed her, and she ran blindly. She must have veered off the path; branches tore at her face and clothes, for a moment she lost her sense of direction. She saw the line of the path again and threw herself towards it, breath sobbing, terrified to glance back for fear of what she might see.

Behind her, a violent flurry of noise ended in a splash, then silence, and suddenly Jess was out of the trees and in open air on the heathery hill.

She kept running until her eyes were streaming and her lungs were raw. She glanced back every few seconds now. There was nothing behind her but the empty hillside.

The farm came into view. Jess forced herself to slow to a more normal pace, trying to convince herself that it was stupid to have been so frightened. After all, what had she really seen or heard? Something in the trees – well, that was most likely a deer. Something big and dark and growling among the brambles – a stray dog.

She opened the gate to the farmyard, then walked quickly to the kitchen door and let herself in.

She was safe.

The kitchen was empty. Jess downed a cup of water and told herself off for being foolish. Everyone was on edge, but she had tried not to be swept along by the tide of unease.

From the window, she spotted her father coming across the fields, and went out to meet him, hoping he'd have some good news.

"Anything?"

Ian shook his head. "Not a sign. They've called off the search." Ten-year-old Donald had gone missing from the neighbouring village a few days before.

"What could have happened to him?"

"He must be dead. Maybe a wolf took him."

"But wolves don't attack people – not here, anyway," said Jess.

"They might, if he was already hurt."

"But they wouldn't be this far down the valley in summer, surely?"

For a moment, she thought he was going to shout at her, but when he spoke, his voice was quiet. "Just leave it be, Jess. Likely we'll never know what happened to him."

He walked wearily off towards the barn, leaving his daughter staring after him, wondering what he wasn't saying. When she went back into the house, the click of knitting needles from the main room told her where her grandmother, Ellen, was. Jess checked her shoes for mud and went in.

"Hello Gran." She planted a kiss on the old woman's soft cheek. "Father's back."

"Is there any news?"

"No."

Ellen shook her head. "It's no wonder. Ian knows they've been searching in the wrong place."

"What do you mean?" Jess asked.

"The footprints, of course."

"What footprints? I thought there was no trace of Donald at all?"

Her grandmother drew in her breath sharply, as though realising she'd said more than was wise.

"No… no, of course not. Pay no attention, child, I'm thinking of the one that disappeared last year. What was his name?"

"Aidan. But I don't remember any talk of footprints when he disappeared either." Jess skewered her grandmother with a look and waited.

The old woman put down her knitting needles with a sigh. "The men found footprints leading to the water's edge down at Roseroot Pool."

Jess felt the hair on the back of her neck prickle. *Coincidence*, she told herself. *That's all. And an overactive imagination.*

"Are you talking about Donald or Aidan?"

"Both of them."

Jess digested this in silence for a few seconds.

"But Donald was a good swimmer. He and Ashe sometimes swim there. Used to swim there," she corrected herself. "And Aidan could swim too. Surely if they did find footprints they checked the pool?"

"I'm sure they did. But they didn't find anything, of course."

Jess was still thinking out loud. "It doesn't seem very likely, does it, that they would both fall into the same pool and drown a year apart when they could both swim?"

Ellen opened her mouth to reply, but at that moment Jess's mother, Martha, came in, and she stopped abruptly. Jess had the strangest feeling that Ellen had said something she shouldn't have.

Next morning after breakfast, Jess helped load the cart with the farm produce to take into Kirriemuir: cans of milk, eggs, butter, cheese, some smoked eels and a pail of blaeberries she'd gathered the day before. The berries were the most important thing as far as she was concerned: because she had picked them herself, she got to keep the money they brought.

Her mother came out of the house waving a piece of paper.

"You forgot the shopping list. And the money."

"No, I didn't. I was just coming back in for them. Anyway,

Arnor would have given me credit and I could have guessed what to buy."

Her mother rolled her eyes.

"Martha?" Ian's voice came from the house, calling his wife.

"Coming," she called back, then to Jess, "Get on with you then – and don't be all day. I know what you and Freya are like when you get talking."

"Yes Mother. No Mother. Goodbye Mother." Jess blew a kiss and flicked the reins and the cart moved off.

She let the horse choose its own pace, which could best be described as an amble. Peace at last. For the next while at least, she was in charge of herself.

The track pushed between the edges of the fields and joined the road into town that skirted the forest. Jess had thought she might meet someone else heading for Kirriemuir, but the road was empty.

Suddenly the horse stopped dead and Jess's mind came back to the present with a jolt.

"What did you do that for, you stupid beast? Get on." She clicked her tongue and flicked the reins, but the horse ignored her, raising its head to sniff the air and making a little whickering sound.

"I said, get on!" She tried again and this time the horse moved off as though nothing had happened.

Then she had the oddest sense that someone was watching her from the shadows under the trees. She turned round to look back, half expecting to see a deer.

Nothing.

Jess had this feeling of being watched from time to time in the woods and occasionally on the farm itself. She'd assumed everyone else had the same feeling until the day she mentioned it to Freya and was met by a look of blank incomprehension. She didn't mention it again.

"Fool," she muttered to herself now. "You're as bad as the horse." And then her eye was caught by a flash of movement between the trees.

Something glossy and black. The turn of a head. The swing of a tail. A horse?

Then it was gone.

Jess thought about the strange hoof prints by Roseroot Pool. Perhaps there really was a horse running wild somewhere out there. But surely someone else would have seen it?

By the time Jess reached Kirriemuir she had almost convinced herself she must have been mistaken about the horse. She drove slowly through the narrow streets, stopping to talk to people she knew, chickens fluttering out of the cart's way every so often. A blast of heat from the smithy washed over her as she went past, along with the reek of singeing hoof.

She tethered the horse to a rail in the square and went to see if there were any new signs on the big tree that served as a noticeboard.

There were two handwritten notices – a bull for sale, and a litter of deerhounds – and above those, a big printed sign.

By order of His Most
Excellent Majesty, James VI.
Each barony to hold three wolf hunts
this Year of our Lord, 1577.
A bounty of six shillings to be paid
by the Baillie for each wolf head.
This 4th day of June, 1577.

That was certainly new, though from the date, it had taken a while to get here from Edinburgh – it was nearly August now.

She'd better remember to tell Father. He'd want to take part. The wolves had been growing bolder over the last few wintersrs, even taking livestock close to farm buildings. Folk had started to bury their dead under cairns of stones – there were stories from further west about wolves digging up bodies. There had been one wolf hunt in the area already this year. No one would object to a couple more, especially if they paid a bounty.

Jess walked back to Arnor's shop. There was a wolf's head mounted over the door, getting mangier by the year – it had hardly any fur left on its muzzle now – but Arnor wouldn't hear of removing it.

It was known locally as the Summer Wolf. Twenty years ago, when Arnor was only nineteen and newly arrived from Norway with his parents, it had terrorised the area for almost three months. It had taken sheep and calves, killing for pleasure as much as food. Then it killed two young children, and every man in the area set off to hunt it down.

It was Arnor who had tracked it and managed to kill it – a huge, black-pelted male. His reputation was made. He'd killed other wolves since then, winter wolves, like everyone else, but the Summer Wolf was unique.

He came out now to help Jess unload the cart: a big man, with blond curly hair and a beard. He always reminded Jess of a friendly bear in clothes, if such a thing could exist.

"Good day Jess. What have you brought today? Plenty of milk, I hope. Eel – that's good: we're short. Blaeberries – they'll all be sold today."

"Freya!" he called into the shop doorway. "Jess is here. Stop admiring yourself and come out here to help."

"Coming!" came the reply from the depths of the shop.

Freya appeared a few seconds later, a tall girl with creamy skin, blue eyes, and honey-coloured hair in a braid that came halfway down her back: the local beauty, and well aware of it.

"Hello Jess," she said. "Wait until you see what the cloth merchant brought from Dundee yesterday." Then her attention was caught by something on the cart. "Mmnn… blaeberries. My favourite." She picked out a few of the biggest berries and popped them in her mouth.

Jess slapped Freya's hand in pretend outrage. "Stop it! They took *ages* to pick. You should be paying me for them."

Freya laughed at her and picked up the pail. Jess took the eggs, while Arnor brought in the heavy milk cans.

Freya pulled Jess to the back of the shop. "Come and see."

Jess let herself be towed along. She wasn't nearly as interested in clothes as Freya was, but a novelty was a novelty, and always welcome.

"Look."

The bolts of fabric set out on a counter at the rear of the shop caught Jess's attention properly.

"Aren't they beautiful?" said Freya in a daze of pleasure. "I want them all."

She gazed at them hungrily, as though they were edible: lengths of wool and linen dyed a clear red, and the green of new bracken shoots, and the startling blue of a kingfisher's wing.

Freya picked up a length of blue wool. "What do you think?" She held it against herself and walked over to the shop's only mirror to admire the effect. "Do you think it would suit me?"

"Yes, but then a feed sack would suit you," said Jess, noting how intensely blue Freya's eyes looked next to the wool, and how her hair shone against it. She was still right though: it didn't matter. People stole glances at Freya *whatever* she wore. Her body curved softly in all the right places. Standing next to her, Jess felt about as shapely as one of the smoked eels she'd just delivered. *Scrawny*. That was the word. She sighed.

"You try." Freya held the blue wool in front of Jess. Jess scowled at her reflection.

"Mmnn… maybe the red would suit you better," said Freya critically.

"They're wasted on me," Jess said. "I'll still look like a bundle of sticks, whatever you put me in."

They folded the cloth and put it back as Arnor came over with a handful of coins for the blaeberries.

"Spending or saving?" he asked as he handed them over.

"Saving."

"No new dress then?" He gestured to the counter.

"Goodness, I can't imagine I'll *ever* need a dress that fancy. I'd have to move to Dundee. Anyway, it would upset the cows if I went to milk them wearing something that bright." She grinned at him.

"I'll get your mother's order made up."

"We'll go for a walk so we don't get in your way," said Freya, steering Jess towards the door.

"Or you could stay and help…" Arnor suggested.

"No, it's all right. We'll be back in an hour."

As they emerged onto the street, Jess said, "How do you *do* that? I'd never get away with wandering off when there's work to be done."

"Well, there's more work on a farm. Anyway, he likes to do it himself really, and Lachlan's in the storeroom if it gets busy and he needs help," said Freya promptly.

Lachlan was Arnor's ancient assistant, so slow-moving now that if you asked him for milk you'd likely get cheese. Jess was unsure how much help he actually was, but he was as much a part of the shop as the floorboards or the wolf's head.

The real truth was, though, Arnor never refused Freya

anything. Her mother had died when she was three, and Freya was all that Arnor had left of her.

They strolled past the smithy and the carpenter's shop and dodged a bucket of slops being thrown out the back door of the inn. When they reached the arched bridge where the river flowed through town they stopped and sat on the parapet. The water was low at this time of year, and sluggish. As she watched it, Jess remembered the conversation with her grandmother the day before.

"Have you heard anything about Donald?" she asked Freya.

"Only that the search has been called off. Why?"

"You haven't heard anything about him drowning, then?"

"*Drowning?* Donald? He could swim like an otter."

"Mmnn… That's what I thought. It was something my gran said, but she must have been confused."

"Hah! That'll be the day. Your gran's got a sharper brain than most people in Kirriemuir."

"I know. That's why I wondered. She said something about footprints at Roseroot Pool."

Freya shrugged. "Footprints all look the same. I don't see how they could know if they were Donald's." She tossed a pebble into the river. "Will your father go on the wolf hunt?"

"I think so. I bet Arnor will."

Freya flashed a smile. "He can't wait. He still hopes he might find another one like the Summer Wolf. There are meant to be black wolves over by Dundee, but I've not heard of them round here, though Lachlan says he's heard stories." She rolled her eyes.

"Come on. It should be safe to go back now." Freya hopped down from the parapet.

Arnor had already packed the order on to the cart for Jess when they arrived, and she set off soon afterwards. This time, lost in her own thoughts, Jess forgot to think of eyes that might be watching from the shadows under the birch trees as she neared home.

Bathed in summer sun, Westgarth Farm was a welcoming sight: the farmhouse with its thick stone walls, and deep eaves to help the snow slide off and to shelter the woodpiles in winter. Around the farm buildings were the fields and little orchard and pastures that fed the family and provided their income, and beyond that the forest and the hills began – the summits of Glas Maol and Cairn Bannoch lost in cloud even on a fine day like this.

"I'm back," Jess called as she drove into the farmyard. Ashe came running from the stable on the off-chance that there was a surprise for him, and found himself lugging a sack of flour into the larder instead. Martha and Jess finished unloading then sent Ashe to unharness the horse.

While her mother put things away, Jess went to talk to Ellen.

"Gran?"

"Yes, child?"

"Yesterday, when you were talking about Donald drowning, you were going to say something else when Mother came in."

Ellen looked up from her knitting, with an innocent look.

"Was I, dear? I don't remember. Perhaps you imagined it."

Jess knew she hadn't. She looked hard at her grandmother, but the old woman returned her gaze calmly.

"At my age I'm bound to forget things sometimes," she said, and went back to her knitting.

Mist hung above the sea of grass, the sun no more than a suggestion of light beyond it. The land breathed quietly, waking.

There was a sound, a mutter that grew to a drumming: hooves. A half-grown horse emerged from the mist, black coat streaked with sweat, running desperately. It pounded across the grass without slackening pace. Behind it, gaining with every second, ran three black wolves, yellow fangs bared, bloodlust in their eyes.

As the grass gave way to trees the horse had to slow a little and the wolves closed the gap still further.

The path between the trunks was blocked by huge briar bushes. The horse swerved and turned, but there was no way through. It stopped at last, at bay, flanks heaving, trembling with exhaustion.

The wolves walked forward slowly. There was no need to hurry. The horse would not escape them now.

The horse's shape wavered like a disturbed reflection, and suddenly it was no longer there. Instead, there was a girl; brown haired, blue eyed.

The wolves paused for a few seconds.

Then they sprang.

Autumn

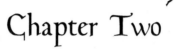

Chapter Two

He should have done it when he had the chance, but she'd sensed he was there, and then… and then he had had to fight the wolf that had somehow followed him through the gateway. She had fled by then, terrified, and she hadn't been back to the pool since. He would have to find another way.

His feelings for her were as strong as ever. She belonged with him, she just didn't know it.

As for his family… once he had taken her, there was nothing they could do.

Summer wore away. The hay was safely in, the barley harvested and the apples ripening. The blaeberry season was over and the brambles were almost ready for picking.

No one outside Donald's own family spoke of him any more.

Jess turned fifteen. Her parents gave her a jacket lined with fur for the winter and her grandmother knitted her some gloves. Freya gave her a string of blue beads and Ashe gave her a frog, hoping she would scream, but yelped himself later when he found she'd tucked it up in his bed.

The day of the harvest ceilidh came: a major social occasion in Kirriemuir and the surrounding farms.

Jess grumbled her way through the preparations.

"I should have made you a new dress," said her mother, frowning at her.

"There's nothing wrong with this one." Jess looked down at it. "It still fits." *Unfortunately*, she thought, but she wasn't about to say it.

"I know, but you wore it last year."

"Well, you and I are probably the only people at the ceilidh who're going to remember that," Jess said, a bit more sharply than she'd intended.

It was true. Jess would spend the evening with Freya, which meant no one would really notice her, *whatever* she was wearing.

Not that she minded. At least, that was what she told herself. Lately she seemed to have trouble knowing how she felt about lots of things.

Boys, for instance.

It used to be easy. They tried to pull your hair and you either ignored them or tripped them up so that they fell into a cowpat.

Lately though, it had got much more complicated. They went about in packs, like dogs. They stood and stared, and whispered to each other and sniggered. Occasionally one would sidle up and mumble something incomprehensible. Jess knew she ought to smile and encourage them to try human speech, but she was usually so disconcerted when it happened that her tongue would say something that sent them off with a scarlet face before her brain could stop it.

Freya didn't seem to have any such difficulties. She smiled and tossed her hair and turned her blue eyes on them until they blushed and stammered. Some of them were allowed to put an arm around her waist, but the one who once dared to try and kiss her got a slap that left her handprint clear on his cheek. After that, no one else tried.

No one had tried even once to put an arm around Jess's waist. She didn't know whether she was relieved or aggrieved.

Back in her room, she brushed her hair, tried it up, tried it down, and gave up altogether.

"Ready," she called as she came back into the main room to find Ashe complaining about being left at home with his grandmother.

"Next year," Ian was saying to him. "Maybe. If you stop moaning now."

Ashe thought about it and quietened.

"You look lovely, lass," said Ellen.

"I just look the same as always, really, except that the dress is clean," said Jess prosaically.

"I know." Her grandmother smiled. "Here. Put this on." She held out a flat wooden box and opened it. Inside lay a fine gold chain, set with small garnets.

"Oh no, Gran. I'd better not…"

Jess recognised it as the necklace her grandfather had given her grandmother as a wedding gift.

"Nonsense. I meant to give it to you on your birthday, but I forgot. I'm too old to wear jewellery any more and I always meant it to go to you." Ellen fastened it round Jess's neck. "There. Now you look ready to celebrate the harvest."

"Thank you." Pink with pleasure, Jess hugged her grandmother.

"Off you go then, all of you. I want to hear all about it tomorrow."

"Jess!" Freya called from halfway up the hall, her bright blue dress standing out clearly from the duller clothes of the people around her.

She came over, her eyes instantly drawn to Jess's new necklace.

"That's lovely," she said. "Was it a birthday present?"

Jess nodded. "From Gran."

"It's beautiful," Freya said, then spoiled the moment by adding, "But you should have had a new dress to go with it."

With an exasperated sigh, Jess followed her over to get something to eat.

"Anyway, never mind about the dress, no one else will notice. I've got a surprise for you," Freya continued.

"What?"

"Turn round and you'll see."

Jess turned and found that someone was standing right behind her. Someone so tall that she was staring at his chest. She looked up.

"Magnus!" She hugged him, then took a step back to look into his blue eyes. "My goodness, I'll get a crick in my neck. You've grown a whole foot since the last time I saw you. When did you get here?"

"This afternoon," Magnus replied, laughing. "And Freya hasn't stopped talking since."

Freya gave his dark blond hair a yank.

"Ow!"

"Behave yourself, cousin. Just because you're a city boy now doesn't mean you're allowed to be rude about your country relations."

"I bet she's been talking to you about clothes," said Jess with an evil smile.

"Yes. And boys."

Freya was scarlet. "Oh stop it." She drew herself up and tried to look dignified. "I was hoping you were both mature enough by now to have stopped ganging up on me, but obviously you're not."

Magnus howled with laughter. "Why would we stop? It's much too entertaining watching you rise to it every single time."

Freya tossed her head and flounced off.

"Oh dear," said Jess remorsefully, watching her back recede.

"She'll forget to be angry in about two minutes," said Magnus, looking around at the crowd of people gathered in the hall. "I miss this place, you know."

Magnus was a year older than Freya and Jess and, until two years ago, had lived just outside Kirriemuir. The three of them had been good friends growing up, but Jess had lost touch with Magnus a bit since he moved with his parents to Dundee.

The fiddlers struck up and Magnus dragged Jess off to dance a reel, despite her protests. After a minute Freya whirled past them with one of her admirers, hair flying and eyes shining, her good humour evidently restored.

Later in the evening, Jess, Freya and Magnus sat on the parapet of the bridge, letting the fresh air cool their sweaty skin. It was stiflingly hot in the hall now; when the people of Kirriemuir got together to enjoy themselves, they did it wholeheartedly.

"I heard about Donald," Magnus said. "I can't believe they didn't find any trace of him at all. It's like that other boy last year."

"Aidan," said Freya.

Magnus nodded. "What do you think happened?"

"Jess's grandmother said something about him drowning in Roseroot Pool, but that can't be right or they'd have found... him," Freya said.

"She didn't say drowned. I'm not really sure *what* she meant," Jess pointed out.

"Most people seem to think a rogue wolf must have taken him," said Freya. "There have been a few around since midsummer – there was another hunt about a month ago and they killed four – but there were no tracks or blood when he went missing… No one knows anything, really."

"Have you decided yet if you want to stay in Dundee?" Jess asked Magnus, wanting to change the subject.

There was enough light to see him shrug.

"I don't know. My parents like it there and I suppose I can get a job in the same sawmill as my father eventually. He earns good money. And he certainly smells better than I do when I come home from work at the tannery."

He jumped down from the parapet on to the road. "Come on, let's go back in. It must be time for another dance."

In the end, Magnus stayed for almost a fortnight, and seemed to Jess to spend nearly as much time helping around the farm at Westgarth as he did with Freya and Arnor; an extra pair of hands was never unwelcome.

"That lad's taken a fancy to you, you know," said Ellen after Magnus had gone back to Dundee.

"*Magnus?*" Jess turned to look at her gran, soapy water dripping from her hands. "No, he hasn't. We've known each other forever. He's a friend, that's all. Goodness, I hardly even think of him as a boy. He's just… himself."

"You must admit he's spent a lot of time here, the last two weeks."

"Well… yes. But that's because he misses farm life in Dundee. No, you're definitely wrong, Gran," Jess said firmly, and turned back to the sink.

Behind her, Ellen smiled.

Freya arrived at Westgarth to spend the weekend. She seemed to have brought a great many clothes with her for two days, Jess thought as she watched, mesmerised.

"Did I misunderstand how long you're staying? Not that I

wouldn't be happy to have you here right through the winter, but we'll need to get a bigger cupboard, or make Ashe keep his clothes in the barn." She thought for a second. "Actually, they smell as though that's where he keeps them already."

Freya gave Jess a hard look.

"Just because you're happy to live in three dresses all year round – last year's dresses at that – doesn't mean I have to. You're going to have to grow up sometime, Jess."

Jess sat down on the window seat with a thump, mouth open in astonishment.

"What on earth do you mean?"

"You want life to stay exactly the same as it is now: you here, me helping my father in the shop, spending time like this. But it won't. You need to start thinking about the future. Looking for someone. The farm will go to Ashe one day. You'll need to find somewhere else to be home."

"Ashe is only ten. It's not exactly urgent," Jess said, laughing. "What brought this on?"

"You scare off all the boys in town. You ought to be a bit more… patient with them."

"But I don't *like* any of them. Why would I want to encourage them? And anyway, what am I meant to do – flutter my eyelashes and pretend to be an idiot?"

Freya rounded on her.

"Is that what you think I do?"

"No! I didn't mean that." She got up and took Freya's hands in hers. "Of course I don't think that. It's just all that *I* can think of to do."

After an awkward few seconds, Freya turned back to her unpacking and, to Jess's relief, the subject was dropped.

Next morning, the girls went into the woods to look for mushrooms and late berries. It was surprisingly warm, and once they'd filled a basket with mushrooms they sat on a fallen tree trunk in a little pool of sunlight. Jess unpacked the bottle of water and slabs of apple cake she'd brought.

"Have you heard from Magnus since he went home?" she asked.

Freya shook her head. "He was never one for writing letters. I'm going to stay with them next month though. Father wants to go and see the cloth merchant in Dundee, so I thought I'd go with him. You could come too," she added, as though it was nothing more than an afterthought. "Magnus would like that."

Jess gave her a suspicious look. "You sound like my gran."

Freya's brow creased. "What do you mean?"

"Nothing. Never mind. I'll think about it – if you don't think I'd just be in the way?"

"Of course you wouldn't."

Jess brushed crumbs from her skirt and jumped down from the tree trunk. "I'm bored with mushrooms. Let's see if there are any brambles left."

The first two patches they reached had already been stripped.

"Let's try that big patch at Roseroot Pool," Freya suggested.

Jess felt a chill run through her limbs. "No," she said abruptly. She hadn't been to the pool since that odd day in the summer, and found she didn't want to go back, even now. "I mean, they're probably all gone too."

"They can't *all* be gone," said Freya. "Let's at least have a look." She looked at Jess curiously. "Or has what Ellen said about the pool got you spooked?"

"Of course not," said Jess. "Come on then."

Don't be ridiculous, she told herself. *You've been messing around there all your life. Nothing's changed.*

She followed Freya.

The brambles formed an impenetrable wall, higher than the girls' heads. They put down the basket of mushrooms when they saw that there were still plenty of berries, and their hands were soon scratched and stained purple.

Jess leaned forwards to grab a particularly large berry and found she was stuck, her hair tangled round a shoot. She tried unsuccessfully to free herself.

"Oh, blast the thing! Freya, come and help me." There was no answer. "Freya?"

"Shh! I'm listening."

"To what? No – never mind. I'm stuck here. Come and help me."

Unable to turn her head, Jess listened to Freya pushing through the undergrowth towards her, and then laughing.

"How on earth did you get so tangled up?"

"I don't know. Get me loose," Jess wailed.

"Hold still then."

A couple of minutes later, Jess was free and the girls decided they'd had enough of brambles for the day. They had a respectable basketful anyway.

Jess bent to pick up the mushrooms.

"What were you listening to, before?" she asked.

"I thought I heard a horse on the other side of the bramble patch. I wondered who was coming."

"No one, or we'd have seen them by now."

"I know. That's odd, isn't it?"

"Let's go round that way and have a look."

They gathered their things and strolled round the edge of the brambles until they could see Roseroot Pool itself.

Jess gazed across the water.

"No one," she said. "They might have stopped to say hello, whoever they were. They'll have known we were there, the amount of noise we were making."

Freya gripped her arm suddenly.

"No. Look." She pointed back towards the brambles.

There was a black horse at the edge of the bramble patch, close to the pool. A pure black horse, with a long tail and a flowing mane. It had neither saddle nor bridle, and watched them warily from blue eyes, the like of which they had never seen in any horse.

They stared at it, mesmerised. The horse tossed its head and they saw that its long mane was snarled on the bramble thorns, as Jess's hair had been.

"The poor thing," breathed Freya. "It's stuck."

She started towards it.

"Careful, Freya," said Jess. For some reason, her heart was beating fast. She was frightened though there was nothing to be frightened of. She handled horses every day. Still she hung back, and tried to catch Freya's hand to stop her.

"What's wrong, Jess?" Freya turned to look at her briefly. "We can't leave the poor thing trapped like that." She shook off Jess's hand and walked forward, talking softly to the horse to calm it as she approached. It tossed its head again and pawed at the ground.

There was something… Something nagged at Jess's mind; a memory that refused to make itself clear.

"Hush now," Freya was saying to the horse. "We'll soon get you free. Be still." She reached out a hand to begin untangling the horse's mane.

Although only a few feet away, Jess couldn't understand what she was seeing.

"Be still," said Freya, and reached out to free the horse… and was suddenly, impossibly, on its back.

Freya stared at Jess, uncomprehending.

"What are you playing at, Freya? Get down," Jess yelled, inexplicable panic overtaking her.

"I can't," said Freya. "I can't!" she shouted, eyes wide with fear, hands knotted in the horse's mane, no longer held by the snarling thorns.

Jess lunged towards the horse, but it danced sideways out of her reach, making for the pool.

"Freya, get down!" she screamed.

"I can't, I can't," Freya shrieked. "Help me, Jess!"

The horse reached the edge of the pool. It didn't stop, but trotted purposefully forward, water splashing silver under its hooves.

Freya twisted desperately, looking back at Jess as she was carried away, the water rising from hoof to hock to wither as the horse took her further from the edge.

"Freya!" Jess screamed.

The horse paused and turned to look at her, then leapt forward again towards the centre of the pool and plunged below the surface of the water, taking Freya with it.

Without thinking, Jess floundered into the water after her friend. She swam to where the horse had disappeared, took a breath and dived below the surface. The water was cloudy and greenish, but Jess could see enough to know that there was no trace of horse or girl. She surfaced and dived again and again until she was half drowned, until at last she admitted defeat and dragged herself out of the pool.

Freya was gone.

Chapter Three

As he watched her with the other girl he thought about the moment when he'd decided that he had to have her for himself.

It had been about a year ago, just after the first boy was taken. She'd looked round once as he watched her, as though she sensed his presence. The wind blew a strand of brown hair across her mouth and she stroked it away with her fingertips.

It was as though he'd never seen her properly before. He stared at her as though he was staring at the sun, unable to look away although he knew he would be blinded.

It was then he knew he had to find a way to take her.

And now he had her.

Ashe was the first to spot Jess stumbling drenched towards the farm.

"You went without me," he shouted angrily. "You went without me. You should have waited."

As she got closer and he saw more clearly the state she was in he said uncertainly, "Why are you wet? Where's Freya?"

Jess didn't answer. She'd run as much of the way as she could, and she was saving her breath for someone who could help. She ploughed on past Ashe towards the kitchen door.

He ran to reach it first, yelling as he did so.

"Mother! Mother, come here. Quick, it's Jess."

Martha appeared in the doorway, floury to the elbows, and stared at the half drowned apparition that was her daughter. She hurried towards Jess.

"Jess, what happened?" Her eyes searched the rest of the yard. "Where's Freya?"

"Roseroot Pool," Jess gasped, and saw her mother's eyes widen in shock. "There was a horse… It took her under the water." She collapsed into her mother's arms as Martha, struggling to keep her voice calm, spoke to Ashe.

"Fetch your father. Hurry."

Ashe looked at her face, and at Jess, and ran.

Martha led Jess into the kitchen, sat her down and went to fetch a blanket. By the time she came back, Ian was striding towards the door. She wrapped the blanket round her shivering daughter.

"Tell your father what happened."

Jess gathered her shaky breath.

"We were picking brambles at the end of Roseroot Pool. There was a horse with its mane caught on the thorns. Freya went to free it. I don't know what happened then… she was on its back and she said she couldn't get off and then it took her down into the water. I went after her. I dived under, I kept diving, but I couldn't find her. I couldn't find her." Her voice cracked and she covered her mouth with a hand.

Above her head, her parents exchanged a look of alarm.

"I'll send someone to town to tell Arnor, and the rest of us will go straight to the pool. Take care of Jess." He bent to kiss his daughter's wet head. "You did everything you could, Jess."

He was shouting instructions to the two farmhands before he was properly out of the house.

"I want to go with them," said Jess, rousing suddenly. "I can show them where to look."

"No," said Martha firmly. "No, Jess. Leave this to your

37

father. There's nothing more you can do. Come on, let's get you dry and warm."

Despite Jess's protests her mother led her upstairs and changed her wet clothes for a nightgown, towelled her hair dry and made her get into bed. She couldn't stop shivering, and Martha brought a hot bottle for her feet, and an extra quilt.

"They'll find her," said her mother, but Jess knew she was wrong.

When she woke, at first she couldn't remember why she was in bed in the middle of the day. Her grandmother smiled at her from the chair near the window.

And she remembered.

Jess sat bolt upright with a gasp.

"Freya! I have to go and help them look. How long have I been asleep?" She was already halfway out of bed.

Ellen rose and, coming over to the bed, gently pushed Jess back down.

"But…"

"There are plenty of people out there already. You'll only distract them – they'll worry about you if you go into the woods. You're to stay in the house." Her tone of voice suggested that there was no point in arguing.

"Can I at least get up?"

"Of course. You're not ill." Her grandmother gave her a searching look. "How clearly do you remember what happened?"

Jess shuddered. "I'll never forget."

She told Ellen her story. The old woman listened intently without interrupting.

"Freya's dead, isn't she?" Jess said finally.

"We don't know that," said Ellen. She sighed. "Up you get. The men will be hungry when they get back. I'm sure your

38

mother could do with some help." She kissed Jess on the brow and went out of the room.

As she dressed, Jess paused often to look out of the window for any sign that the searchers were returning, but there was nothing. She went downstairs, following the sound of voices to the kitchen.

"It's happening again," Ellen's voice said. "Why will no one listen?"

"Leave it be, Ellen," said Martha in a strained voice. "Ian and the others are searching. There's nothing else to be done. You swore you would never mention all this… rubbish about horses in front of Jess and Ashe. Now Jess is spouting the same nonsense."

"I didn't speak of it to her," Ellen sounded angry. "I made a promise to you and I've kept it."

"What are you talking about?" Jess said, coming unseen into the room.

Guilty silence enveloped the kitchen.

"Never mind," said Martha, forcing a smile. "It's nothing. How are you feeling?"

"I'm fine. But I want to know what you were saying."

"It was nothing that concerns you." Martha came across to where her daughter stood. "Jess, Arnor will want to talk to you. We've told him what we know, but he'll want to hear it again from you."

Jess nodded. "Is he here now?"

Martha shook her head. "He's out searching with the others. Oh, Jess, you can imagine the state he's in. Freya was all he had."

"You're talking as though you already know she's dead."

"I'm sorry. I don't mean to. We don't know that." Martha pointed to a number of jars and bowls on the table. "Come on, it's better if we keep busy. The men will all need to be fed when they get back. Can you make some dumplings to go in the stew?"

Jess nodded and rolled up her sleeves, glad of the distraction.

It was dark before the men came back. They'd searched the pond and the surrounding woods as best they could, but all they had found were the girls' abandoned baskets of brambles and mushrooms, now sitting sadly in a corner of the kitchen.

Arnor stared blankly at them, as though they might hold some clue to what had happened to Freya, dismissing offers of food and drink with a shake of his head.

After a while, Ian led him to the sitting room, signalling Jess to follow them.

"Arnor wants you to tell him what happened."

She nodded and swallowed, her mouth suddenly dry, then began. When she got to the end of her story she waited for the inevitable questions.

"But why would Freya get on a horse?"

"I don't know. I didn't see her do it; she was just suddenly on its back. And she kept saying that she couldn't get down."

"And you saw... you saw her go under the water?"

Jess nodded mutely, close to tears now.

"I'm sorry. I tried and tried, but…"

Arnor looked at her properly for the first time, a look so bleak that she could hardly bear it.

"It's not your fault, Jess. I know you tried to help her. Whatever has happened, it's not your fault."

Released from that terrible, grief-filled room a few minutes later, Jess went up to her bedroom, closed the door with shaking hands and sat on the bed staring out into the darkness.

"It's the shock," said Ian when she'd gone. "She doesn't know what she's saying. I'm sorry you had to listen to that. Her mind must have pushed away what really happened, and put this tale in its place."

Arnor nodded absently.

Freya was picking brambles, dropping them into a bucket behind her. Jess wanted to stop her, but she was stuck in the thorns. They even pinned her lips together so she couldn't open her mouth to warn Freya.

As the brambles fell into the bucket they changed, becoming part of something infinitely dark that was forming inside it, growing and pushing its way out until it was a horse, black as soot, black as midnight. It stood behind Freya, water dripping from its mane, until she turned and smiled at it and put her arms round its glossy, arched neck. And then she fell, impossibly, upwards on to its back. The horse reared and Jess saw that it had no shoes, and managed to open her mouth and scream.

And she woke.

She was trapped by the twisted covers of her own bed, sweating with fear. She unravelled herself from them as best she could and fumbled to light a candle to chase the shadows back into their corners.

Jess kept seeing the horse in her mind's eye: the real horse, not the one from the dream. But the dream was right, the horse hadn't been shod. It had nagged at her memory at the time and now she knew why – the hoof prints she'd seen at the edge of the pool after Donald had disappeared hadn't had shoes either.

There shouldn't be any wild horses in these woods. But hadn't she had a glimpse of one – maybe the same one – that day back in the summer?

Why would it carry Freya – and maybe Donald too – into the pool? Horses didn't behave like that. They threw people; they didn't carry them off and dive underwater with them.

Jess remade her ravaged bed, then got back in and pulled the covers up to her ears. She lay thinking. She knew what she had seen, but it didn't make sense.

Was she sure that the horse had gone into the pool with Freya on its back? *Yes.* That it had dived under the water and taken Freya with it? *Yes.* Was she sure that it hadn't emerged again with Freya when she was in the pool diving to look for her friend? *Yes. No. Yes.* She'd have seen or heard it happen. There would have been a trail. The searchers would have followed it. Freya would have been found.

So they'd never emerged. That meant that they had drowned. But why hadn't they been found? The men had searched for hours. Weren't bodies meant to float?

It didn't make sense. That was the only thing she was sure about.

The search went on all the next day, but was no more successful. Jess brooded in her room, unwilling to talk to anyone if she didn't have to, pretending to sew when her mother came in to check on her.

Late in the afternoon, she escaped to milk the cows, glad of their reassuring warmth and bulk and smell. She leaned into them, listening to the milk hissing into the pails.

She carried the milk to the dairy and found her grandmother waiting.

"Are you sure about the horse?" Ellen said without preamble.

"Yes, of course," replied Jess, puzzled.

"They were talking this morning as if Freya just fell into the pool and drowned."

Jess stared at Ellen in disbelief.

"Do they think I've lost my mind? Or that I made all this up? Is that what *you* think?"

"No." Ellen looked her in the eye. "I believe every word you

42

said. But don't be surprised if no one else mentions the horse again. It's easier for them that way."

"What do you mean?" Jess started to ask, but her mother came in just then and Ellen gave a quick shake of her head that said, clear as words, *not now.*

Jess tried several times that night to talk to her mother and father about what had really happened to Freya, but somehow they always turned the conversation in another direction or found something they had to do that couldn't wait.

Finally, Jess's patience snapped.

"Why won't you listen?" she shouted. "Don't you want to know what happened?"

Ian shot a glance at Martha.

"We do know what happened. Freya drowned. Stop upsetting yourself with this tale. I don't want to hear any more of it."

No one searched the next day. Ian went back to town with Arnor so that he wouldn't have to go into the shop or house alone yet. Life on the farm returned, outwardly at least, to something like normal, though Jess and Ashe were forbidden to leave the farmyard alone for the time being.

Which made no sense, Jess noted as she swept the kitchen floor, *if Freya, as people said, had simply drowned.*

Ellen appeared in the doorway, a cloud of white wool in her arms.

"You don't mind if I borrow Jess to help me pin out this shawl, do you?"

"No, of course not," said Martha, busy making bread at the big, scrubbed table.

Jess followed her grandmother upstairs and they began to pin the gauzy shawl out. She was sure that wasn't the only reason she was there, and waited impatiently for her grandmother to speak.

"The horse was black, you said?" Ellen said suddenly.

Jess nodded.

"What about its eyes?" Ellen said, watching for her reaction.

Jess gave a start. She hadn't said anything about its eyes, she was sure.

"They were blue," she said quietly.

Ellen closed her own eyes for a moment, then opened them as she spoke again.

"You deserve the truth," she said. "Even if those other fools choose not to see what's in front of them. Sit down, lass, and I'll tell you what really happened to your friend."

Jess sank down on the window seat as her grandmother settled herself in the chair.

Ellen tried to decide where to begin. *At the beginning of course, you old fool,* she chided herself silently. *How else will it make sense?*

"When I was young – a year or two younger than you are now – a boy and a girl disappeared near the same pool, a few months apart," she began.

"The boy – he was Ashe's age – disappeared first. There was a search of course, but no sign of him was ever found. There were no tracks to follow; the weather had been too dry. There had been a gang of children playing hide and seek in the woods and it had been Euan's turn to hide, so it was a long time before they realised he was missing. One of the other children said they'd seen a blue-eyed black horse near the pool a little while before, but none of the adults listened to her. They never found out what happened to Euan. A girl – I can't remember her name after all these years – went missing about nine months later. Same place, and this time there were footprints and hoof prints – unshod hoof prints – mixed up at the pool's edge.

44

One old woman in Kirriemuir remembered what had been said about the horse after Euan disappeared, and started to whisper about the *Kelpies*. The Kelpies were a legend: a race of beings who lived in another world that could only be reached through water. It was said they could appear in our world in the guise of a human or of a dark horse: a pure black, blue-eyed horse. It was said that sometimes they would steal a child away to live in their world.

But nothing like that had happened in living memory. The occasional child went missing of course, but there were enough dangers in the real world to explain that without having to invent ridiculous ones about horse-people stealing children. A legend was exactly what the Kelpies were. There was only the word of a frightened girl to link the tale to the disappearances. Who knew what nonsense she'd been fed, what stories she believed? Maybe she'd made up the horse to hide the fact that she was involved in the boy's death."

Jess felt the hair on the back of her neck prickle as she heard the note of bitterness in Ellen's voice and realised just what her grandmother was telling her.

"It was you, wasn't it?" she whispered. "You were that frightened girl."

Ellen looked at her with something like defiance. "Yes. I was." She picked an imaginary thread from her skirt. "And now it's happening again, and still no one will listen. Back then I was too young and now, it seems, I'm too old. But I don't want you spending half your life wondering if you dreamed what happened, or if you're going out of your mind."

"Is that what it was like for you?" Jess hesitated. "I'm sorry. I never knew."

Ellen got to her feet and crossed to look out of the window.

"There's no reason why you should, child. I soon learned that talking about it only caused trouble."

"You said that the Kelpies steal children to live in their world." Jess paused, half afraid of the answer she might get. "Does that mean Freya might still be alive?"

"If what that old woman told me was true. Mind, I never heard any stories of someone Freya's age being taken, just little children. I don't know why it's different this time." Ellen turned to look at her granddaughter again.

For a few seconds she hesitated, then plunged on again before she lost her nerve. "She told me something else as well, though she told me too late. She said that according to the legends, a child stolen by the Kelpies could be rescued if it was done quickly enough."

Jess leapt to her feet.

"How? Tell me how."

"Remember – I have no idea if this is anything more than a tale. The story went that a stolen child could only be rescued between the stealing and the dark of the moon that month."

Jess thought. "That's five days away."

Ellen nodded. "Someone had to make a halter for the dark horse and lie in wait for it. If the horse appeared they had to let themselves be taken by it and fasten the halter round the horse's neck before it took them both under the water to the land of the Kelpies. The halter would give the rescuer power to command that Kelpie, and to demand the return of the stolen child. Supposedly."

"But you don't know if anyone's ever really done it?"

Ellen shook her head.

"So it just needs someone to wait at Roseroot Pool with a halter from the stable and—"

"No," Ellen interjected. "I was coming to that. Not a normal halter. You have to make one – a strange one. There was a rhyme… Let me think…"

She closed her eyes and, after a few seconds, began to chant.

Hair of the taken,
Hair of the seeker,
Hair of the Kelpie.

Braided with birch,
Braided with bramble,
Braided with blood.

Hold fast the briar,
Hold fast the falcon,
Hold fast the flame.

Silence lay thick in the room as Jess tried to make sense of what she had just heard.

"Birch and bramble and blood and hair? How can you make a halter out of that? And what does the bit about holding fast mean?"

Ellen shook her head again, making a helpless gesture. "I've told you all I know. Now, if you don't think I'm raving, then for pity's sake find a way to convince Arnor so that he can try to save his daughter, for he'll not listen to me."

Jess's heart quailed at the thought of facing Arnor's grief again.

"I spoke to Arnor myself, but he looked at me as though I was mad," Ellen went on. "I've tried to persuade your father to talk to him, but he stormed out of the room without even listening to me. My story is the family's shame, you see. Your grandfather's family wanted to stop him from wedding me, and when your father was a lad he was always getting in fights with boys who said I was unhinged at best and a murderess at worst. He's determined not to believe such things happen." She gave an exasperated sigh. "He would never forgive me if he knew I had told you all this. No one really understands but the two of us. No one but us has seen the dark horse. No one but us believes in it. You're the only person who has any hope of making Arnor see the truth. You're the only one who can give Freya a chance."

"I know," said Jess miserably. "I'll go and talk to him tomorrow."

Jess lay sleepless that night, trying to work out what to believe. Things like this only happened in stories, not in the real world. But she'd seen Freya being taken; she knew it must be true. And now Ellen had given her an explanation that made sense – to the two of them at least.

She tried to imagine a conversation with Arnor that ended in him believing in the dark horse and agreeing to make the halter, but her imagination failed her. He had convinced himself that Freya had drowned, even though Jess had told him what had really happened. She couldn't think of anything more she could say or do that would make him change his mind.

But it didn't matter how impossible it seemed; she would have to find a way.

Chapter Four

This time he hadn't hesitated. This time he'd taken his chance. He'd taken her. He burst from the pool, elated. And then he saw what he'd really done.

It was a disaster. All the risks he had taken to get her, and he had failed. He had taken the wrong girl. He'd risked everything for this, ignored his family's warnings.

But it hadn't changed how he felt. She burned in his mind.

He wouldn't give up.

Next morning, her heart feeling like a stone she had somehow swallowed, Jess set off for Kirriemuir.

A despicable corner of her mind had been secretly hoping that her parents would forbid her to go, but on the contrary, they seemed to think that her pretext of returning Freya's clothes, which had still been in Jess's cupboard, was a good idea.

"It'll be some sort of comfort to Arnor to have Freya's things," said Martha, suspiciously bright-eyed. "Even if it is a very small one."

"So you don't mind me going on my own?" Jess said, just to be sure.

"It's the woods that are dangerous, not the road," said Ian. "The pool anyway," he corrected himself.

Seated in the corner, Ellen said nothing.

In her room, Jess took Freya's jacket from its peg, laid her carefully folded clothes on the bed, smoothed a wrinkle from a dress, and to her own surprise, burst into tears.

Martha found her five minutes later, sitting on the bed with red eyes and a swollen nose, damply clutching Freya's tear-spotted jacket.

"She's gone," said Jess thickly.

"Oh, Jess." Her mother sat down and put an arm round Jess's shoulders. They sat like that for a little while, then Martha said, "You don't have to go today, you know. Or maybe your father or I should do it."

"No," said Jess, suddenly filled with resolve. "I'm all right. I need to do this. I'll be fine."

"Sure?"

Jess nodded. "Sure." She wiped her eyes on her sleeve and started to pack the clothes in Freya's bag. Martha took one last look at her and left her alone.

Half an hour later, Jess rode out of the farmyard, Freya's bag strapped behind the saddle. She gave her mother a curdled smile as she waved goodbye. She couldn't remember ever dreading anything as much as she dreaded seeing Arnor today.

Her mind usually wandered on the way into town, but today it refused to go anywhere except through the door into Arnor's store.

They seemed to reach Kirriemuir very quickly. Jess kept her head down, ignoring the curious glances she drew, as she rode past the smithy and up to the shop. The wolf's head looked down at her with a sad expression she could have sworn hadn't been there before.

She climbed down from the saddle and tied the reins to the rail, then unfastened Freya's bag with clumsy fingers and walked slowly into the shop.

It was terribly quiet inside, in a way that somehow suggested not many people had been in that morning. Lachlan stood behind a counter, staring into space, but there was no sign of Arnor. Lachlan looked round at the sound of Jess's footsteps and his face brightened visibly when she got close enough for him to recognise her.

"Jess, lass! It's good to see you. How are you?" He went on without giving her time to answer. "Och, this is a terrible thing." He shook his head and sighed. "People are staying away. It's as quiet as the…" His voice trailed away as he realised what he'd been about to say and closed his mouth on it.

There was an awkward silence.

"I'm fine, Lachlan," Jess said. "I wanted… Is Arnor…?"

Lachlan gestured towards the rear of the shop.

"He's in the back room. On you go."

Jess tried to convince herself that her knees weren't trembling as she walked the long, long way to the back room. She knocked and went in before she lost her nerve and ran for it instead.

Arnor sat in a chair near the one small window, clutching something in his arms. Jess realised as she stared that it was the bolt of vivid blue cloth Freya had chosen for the ceilidh dress.

It was a moment before he looked up, and a longer one before he seemed to realise who she was.

"Jess?" he said uncertainly.

"I brought…" she said, but her voice didn't make any sound. She licked her lips and tried again.

"I brought Freya's clothes." To her relief, it worked this time. "I thought you'd want them back."

Jess walked towards him and was shocked by his appearance as she drew closer. He seemed to have shrunk inside his clothes. He looked diminished, in every possible sense.

She held the bag out to him. Slowly, he put the cloth down on a table next to him and took the bag. He took out Freya's jacket and looked at it, frowning, as though it was a puzzle he had to solve.

"It's her jacket," he said finally, as though it was something he had just discovered.

"Yes."

How could she do this? What on earth was she going to say?

She could just go. No one would ever know. She would tell Ellen she had tried. But that would mean betraying Freya. She couldn't turn her back on this chance that she might be saved.

"I don't think Freya's dead," she blurted out before she could think of all the reasons not to say it, and saw Arnor's hands tighten on the jacket, his eyes go wide with shock.

"What? What are you talking about? You were with her. You saw her fall into the pool and drown. You tried to save her."

Anger kept her going then.

"No! That's not what happened. I told you before. I keep trying to tell my parents. There was a horse… I think Freya was taken by the Kelp…"

"Why do you keep saying this? That old woman's been filling your head with her mad stories."

"It's true! And if you'll believe me, maybe there's a chance to save Freya."

He surged to his feet so violently that the chair crashed over behind him.

"You were her friend. Why have you come here to torment me like this? Get out!" he roared.

"But…"

"Get out!"

As Jess ran through the shop, Lachlan stepped out from behind the counter and tried to stop her.

"Wait, Jess! I need to talk to you," he called. "About the horse." But she was already gone.

Jess fumbled to untie the reins, afraid that Arnor would come after her, but there was silence behind her now. She hauled herself shakily into the saddle and kicked the horse into a reluctant trot.

When she got home, Jess took as long as possible to unsaddle the horse and stable it before she went inside, but she couldn't put it off forever.

Her main worry was that Arnor would come storming out to the farm and tell her parents what she'd done. He'd been so angry; more than ever he'd resembled a bear, but not a friendly one any more.

Then there was Ellen. Jess couldn't help feeling she had let her grandmother down, even though she had felt she had little chance of persuading Arnor even before she set out.

But of course, worst of all, there was Freya, trapped – if Ellen wasn't mad – in the Kelpies' world, with time running out.

Martha and Ellen were both in the kitchen. Her grandmother gave Jess an enquiring look as she came in. Jess shook her head slightly and watched Ellen's face droop in disappointment.

"How was he?" Martha asked.

"He's like someone else. Lachlan says hardly anyone's been into the shop. Arnor was just sitting holding a roll of cloth."

"What did he do when you gave him the clothes?"

"I think it upset him more." It was a half truth of sorts.

Martha gave her daughter a swift hug.

"It was brave of you to go and see him. I'm not surprised he was upset, but I'm sure he'd want Freya's things back."

Jess found an excuse to go to her room soon after that, and it was no surprise when she heard her gran's step on the stairs. Ellen came in and sat down on the bed, looking, at that moment, older than Jess had ever seen her.

"I'm sorry Jess. Maybe I was wrong to say anything to you at all."

"No!"

"It would be easier for everyone now – you as well – if you forgot about the horse and thought of me as a daft old woman."

"No," said Jess firmly. "I know what really happened, and so do you. It's everyone else who's wrong."

"Sometimes, knowing you're right isn't a great deal of comfort."

Jess couldn't wait for the rest of that miserable day to be over, so that she could escape for the night and try to find some peace in sleep. She'd been wound tight as a spring every time she heard a step in the yard, in case it was Arnor, coming to confront her parents about her behaviour.

She shut the bedroom door behind her with relief. He couldn't possibly mean to come today at any rate. She closed the shutters and changed quickly. It was a cold night, and she wanted nothing more than to disappear under the covers until morning.

As she reached for her comb there was a knock on the door that made her jump.

"Yes?" she called.

"It's only me," Ian's voice replied.

"Come in."

Ian opened the door.

"Are you sure you're all right?" he said. "I know how hard this must be for you anyway, and seeing Arnor today…"

Jess conjured half a smile from somewhere.

"I'm all right. Just tired."

Ian nodded. "Goodnight then," he said awkwardly.

"Goodnight."

As he closed the door again Jess turned back to the comb, but it wasn't on the chest of drawers. She must have knocked it down the back. She got down on her hands and knees and reached under the chest. At first, all she found was dust, then a mummified apple core. Finally her hand closed around the comb and she got up.

It was Freya's, a few bright hairs still caught in it. Jess hadn't known it was there.

She scrabbled around until she found her own comb, and then knelt there, staring at them both, hairs caught in both sets of teeth.

Hair of the taken,
Hair of the seeker.

No.

Hair of the taken,
Hair of the seeker.

The dark of the moon.
No one will listen. No one but us believes.
There was still a chance for Freya.
No, I can't.
You have to.

Martha put a plate of porridge down in front of Ashe as Jess appeared in the kitchen doorway.

"Dearie me," she said, looking at the dark circles under her daughter's eyes. "You don't look as if you got much sleep last night."

"No," said Jess ruefully as she sat down.

"I suppose you were thinking about Arnor and Freya."

"Mmnn," said Jess. It wasn't an out-and-out lie, after all.

Her mother handed her a bowl of porridge.

"Thank you." Jess reached for the milk and a spoonful of raspberry jam. Ashe stared at her as she ate it.

"Why are you gawping at me? Stop it."

"You look strange. Even worse than usual."

Jess couldn't be bothered to rise to the bait this morning, but to her delight Martha cuffed Ashe round the ear.

"Leave your sister be. She's had a terrible time. In fact, I think you should do her chores today, so that she can try to get some sleep."

Ashe opened and shut his mouth, speechless with dismay.

Jess doubted that she had slept at all, but not for the reasons her mother thought. She had tossed and turned under the bedclothes all night, trying to decide what to do. She knew what she *ought* to do, but she was frightened one minute and convinced the next that she and Ellen were simply mad.

It they were, there was nothing to be frightened of. But if they weren't…

What if she made this halter?

What if the dark horse appeared and carried her under the water? What if she too was trapped there?

Jess shivered. She had to try, there was no way round it. How could she live with herself, knowing there was a chance she could have saved Freya and she hadn't even tried?

She called it a decision before she had time to change her mind.

The first task then, was to make the halter. And there too was the first problem.

Hair of the taken
Hair of the seeker
Hair of the Kelpie.

It didn't seem likely that the horse would have left a comb lying around, so how was she to get its hair? All she could think of was to wait with the rest of the halter made up and when the dark horse appeared (*if* the dark horse appeared) try to pull a hair from its mane or tail and quickly tie it into the halter.

As a plan, it didn't have much to recommend it, but it was all she had. At least bramble and birch were easy to come by. And blood, though she didn't much like the idea of that.

The house would soon be quiet. Her mother thought Jess was trying to sleep, so wouldn't disturb her. It should be easy to sneak out to collect some twigs. They would have to be as thin as possible so they would bend enough to braid.

There were birch trees at the edge of the forest, and she wouldn't have to go far for the brambles either. Of course, the best ones were by the pool itself, but...

She gasped as she realised.

The horse's mane had been caught. Was it possible that some hairs might still be tangled among the thorns?

That settled any remaining doubts she had. If there *were* some hairs there, she was meant to do this.

Jess found a satchel and her knife and shoved her way into her jacket and boots with a new sense of determination. A quick look out of the window to make sure she wouldn't meet anyone coming in, then she crept down the stairs, trusting that Ellen would be safely ensconced by the stove, knitting. Sure enough, the regular click of needles was reassuringly audible.

Jess let herself stealthily out the rarely used front door and took a looping detour that kept her out of sight until she could get into the woods.

Her heart was beating fast as she went in under the trees. She hadn't been out here since Freya had been taken, and every sound seemed louder than it should, and full of potential threat. She kept thinking of the wolves her father had hunted during the summer, just a few miles from here.

She slowed as she neared the pool, alert for the sound of hooves, scanning the ground for prints, but there was nothing. Still, she waited in the trees for almost ten minutes before she could bring herself to approach the brambles where the horse had been. She'd thought, setting out, that she knew exactly where to look, but now she wasn't so sure.

Fifteen minutes later she was close to giving up. It seemed increasingly unlikely that any hairs would have stayed among the brambles until now. She didn't know whether she was devastated or relieved.

Jess took out her knife half-heartedly and cut a clutch of spindly bramble trailers, reaching in among the stems to get as much length as possible. The whirr of a duck's wings made her turn to see a Goldeneye scuffing to a halt on the water. The pool looked as though nothing out of the ordinary had ever happened.

With a sigh, Jess pushed the brambles into the bag and the knife back into its sheath and turned to go, watching where she placed her feet among the thorny stems. Half a dozen steps and she'd be clear of them.

Something caught her eye: there was a tiny scrap of colour at about shoulder height, only a few paces from where she was. Jess made her way to where it was, suddenly tense.

A fragment of red cloth, the size of a fingernail.

It must be from Freya's dress. If this was where Freya had been, Jess had been searching in the wrong place. She peered with new interest at the arching stems and only a few seconds later drew in her breath sharply and reached forward to unwind two long black hairs from a bramble spur.

She had it. *Hair of the Kelpie.*

She could scarcely believe it. Holding tight to the hairs with one hand, she reached into her bodice with the other and pulled out the kerchief she'd brought just in case. She wrapped the hairs up carefully and tucked the little bundle back into her bodice where there was no danger it could fall out. Appalled and elated in equal measure, she started for home.

Jess looked at the collection of objects spread on the bed before her: two combs, a tiny cloth bundle, half a dozen bramble stems and a selection of the longest, thinnest birch twigs she'd been able to find.

"Right then," she said to herself under her breath. "You've got all these things; it would be stupid not to use them."

She untangled two or three of Freya's long golden hairs and a few of her own from the combs, then unwrapped the two precious hairs from the horse's mane and tied them all together at one end with a piece of thread. She worked the hairs into a tiny braid and tied thread around the other end. Next she twisted the braid round a birch twig and tied it in place.

The rest was easy. Three stems of bramble, three of birch – including the one with the hairs – and soon she had a prickly braid. Was it long enough? She looked at it critically, decided it was. Any longer and it would just be unwieldy. She turned one end back on itself to form a loop, threaded the other end through and checked to see if it would run freely.

It didn't, of course, but considering it was covered in thorns, that was hardly surprising.

Now for the blood.

She'd pricked herself on thorns several times as she made the halter, but she wasn't convinced that the tiny droplets that had oozed from her fingers were enough, so she got the knife and made a little cut in one fingertip.

As Jess stood there watching the crimson blood drip on to the green stems and lie there like berries, her bedroom door opened and she looked up, startled.

"I'm sorry. I just came up to see if you were still slee…"

Ellen's voice froze, her gaze on the halter.

Chapter Five

"What are you doing?" Ellen said in a deadly whisper, coming in and pushing the door shut behind her.

"Just… I'm making a halter," Jess replied, unable to think of a convincing lie.

"You surely don't mean…" Ellen's face was so papery white that Jess feared she was about to faint. "You can't. You mustn't. Not you."

"Why not me? There's no one else. You know that." Jess wrapped her kerchief tightly round her bleeding finger.

Ellen sank heavily into the chair.

"When I told you all these things… It was for Arnor to do, not you."

"But I told you what happened when I went to see him."

"It doesn't matter. I would never forgive myself if you did this and something happened to you."

"Nothing's going to happen to me," Jess said with a confidence she was far from feeling.

"Your parents would never forgive me – and they'd be right," her grandmother went on. "The Kelpies have brought nothing but trouble to this family. Your father spent his childhood listening to people tell him his mother was mad, or that maybe she was a murderess. How will he feel if he finds you've gone off to do this?"

Ellen looked at Jess as she spoke.

"I found the Kelpie's hair," Jess said slowly. "What were

the chances of that, do you suppose? I *have* to do this. I'm *meant* to do this. The only way you'll stop me is by telling my parents everything and helping them keep me locked up. I don't suppose they'll be very happy to find you put this idea in my head though, do you?" Jess knew how despicable the words were as she said them, and what a terrible gamble she was taking that Ellen would remain silent.

She forced herself to look her grandmother in the eye, saw her lips tighten.

Ellen got to her feet. "Very well," she said, admitting defeat. "But at least have the decency to tell me when you mean to go, so that I know when to worry."

Jess nodded and watched her gran leave. She didn't feel as though she had won; she felt as though she had broken something fragile and irreplaceable.

"You haven't eaten anything, Jess."

Martha came across the kitchen, peered at her daughter's face and put a hand to her forehead. "Do you feel all right? You don't have a fever. You're very pale – are you cold? Did you sleep any better last night?"

Jess could almost feel the questions bouncing off her skin. She looked at her untouched porridge. There was no way she could force down even a mouthful, she was so nervous.

Now Ashe was staring at her too.

"I'm fine," she said to her mother. "I'm just not hungry."

"You have to eat something," Ashe said unexpectedly. "I bet you're just trying to get out of your chores again." He scowled at her.

"No, I'm not. I'll go and start them now to prove it."

Jess got up, her chair scraping on the flags as she pushed it back, glad to have an excuse to get away from her mother's scrutiny.

"I'm going to the dairy to skim the cream. I'll just say good morning to Gran first."

Martha nodded absently, her mind somewhere else.

Jess ran back upstairs, collected her jacket and the old satchel with the halter in it. She hesitated for a second before she knocked on Ellen's door, then went in.

Her gran looked at her.

"There's nothing I can say that will change your mind, is there?"

Jess shook her head.

"How long will you wait at the pool?"

"All day if I have to. But not past dark. I'll be home in time for supper."

"And if you're not?"

"I will be," Jess said firmly. "I'll see you later," she said with a queasy smile, and left before she had time to think better of it.

After that, it was easy. Jess waited until there was no one else in the farmyard, then slipped out and headed for the woods.

It seemed oddly quiet as the trees closed in around her. *Watchful*, you might say.

Stop it! she thought. She tried hard to keep her mind on everyday things until she was close to the pool, then stood for several minutes, listening for any hint that there was a horse nearby.

When nothing revealed itself, she began to walk towards the pool again, more slowly this time. Twenty paces, stop and listen again, nothing. Move on.

She wanted to find a spot from which she could watch the pool unseen. Surely the horse would come out of the water when it appeared? She paused again, scanning the trees and bramble thicket and the pool itself, in case the horse was already there somewhere, and when she saw nothing, she turned her attention to finding a good place to keep watch.

It only took her a few minutes to find three spindly pine trees growing so close together that their trunks almost touched, with a tangle of autumn-crisped ferns in front of them. With the solidity of the trunks at her back and the ferns screening her, she still had a good view of the pond. Jess made herself as comfortable as possible, and settled down to wait.

It was difficult not to daydream when you'd been sitting against a tree for... however long she'd been here. It felt like months, but the light told her it couldn't yet be much past noon. Jess had let her mind stray to Magnus for a while. Not that there was much to think about if she considered it properly: a couple of dances, some smiles, a few visits to Westgarth. Not a word, much less an arm round her waist, or a kiss. It was probably all imagination; it was her gran's fault really, she'd put the idea in Jess's head.

Jess got stiffly to her feet, more than ready for a break. In fact, as she eased her cramped legs and shifted the satchel strap on her shoulder, she wondered if she should just go home. The whole thing seemed faintly ridiculous now; she was nearly ready to believe it was no more than an old wives' tale.

And then...

There was no sound. No splash of water or crack of twig, no sign at all. And yet, Jess knew, though her back was to the pool, that the horse was there.

As she turned, she tried to convince herself that it was her imagination at work, but she already knew somewhere deep in her heart that it wasn't.

The horse stood at the edge of the pool, watching her.

Jess froze, poised for flight, balanced on the edge of fate, as the horse studied her with those too-blue eyes, and she studied it in turn.

She could run. She could probably lose the water horse where the trees crowded together. She could run.

But she didn't. She stood quite still, her heart beating painfully hard, as the horse's gaze settled on her face.

Jess moved forward slowly, almost without thought, one hand sliding into the satchel to check the halter. A few paces from the water horse she stopped, and time ran slow as they stared at each other.

The horse shook its head gently and moved slowly towards her. Almost against her will, Jess stretched out a hand and the horse nuzzled her palm. She felt its warm breath, the impossible softness of its muzzle.

Jess slid her hand up over its cheek and down to the strong neck. Her mind was a blank. Why was she here? There had been some reason, something important, but she couldn't remember what it had been. It didn't matter now anyway.

Her body leaned in towards the horse's flank of its own volition, and then she was no longer on the ground at all, but on the horse's broad back.

Jess took a gasping breath and came out of whatever trance she had been in. Terrified now, she tried to slide down from the horse's back, but her legs were clamped to its flanks and she couldn't budge them, however she tried.

"No!" she yelled, panic stricken. "Let me down. Stop!" But the horse was turning now, towards the water.

Her arms were still her own to move. Shouting all the time, Jess hit the horse on the neck as hard as she could, tried to reach forward to its head, but couldn't.

Water rose around the black hooves as the horse picked its way with an odd delicacy into the pond.

Jess flailed wildly, trying to pull herself free, not thinking at all now, blind with panic. Her right hand closed on something.

Thorns bit into her flesh. She gasped with pain, and with the pain came clarity.

The halter.

That was what she had to do. It came back to her as water touched her legs, began to climb up her skirts.

Desperately she pulled the halter from the satchel, kept tight hold of one end with her right hand as she let the other end dangle and reached under the horse's neck to catch it with her left.

The water had risen to her thighs now. The Kelpie was almost in the centre of the pond. Jess scrabbled frantically, caught the trailing end of the halter and brought both ends up. She felt the horse tense beneath her and prepare to dive. Jess somehow fumbled the free end through the loop and pulled as hard as she could as the horse's muscles bunched beneath her and it leapt forward.

In mid-leap the horse seemed to stiffen as it became aware of the thing round its neck, but its plunge into the pool continued.

Jess screamed once, felt blood running through her fingers as the thorns gouged deep.

Water closed over them. She held her breath, hands clamped on the halter, hauling on it so hard that it must surely break.

The water boiled around them. They were tossed over and over, insubstantial and powerless as bubbles.

Jess couldn't hold her breath any longer. She was going to drown. She was going to die.

Chapter Six

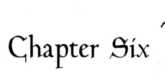

Jess opened her eyes to utter darkness. *I'm dead*, she thought. *I'm drowned and dead, floating in Roseroot Pool. What happens now? Can I feel? Can I move? What do I do?*

She moved a hand experimentally and felt what seemed to be grass under her fingers. As she lay looking up, the darkness resolved itself into different shades, and she found she was looking at a night sky through a lacing of branches, black on black; no moon or stars in the land of the dead.

It was cold, being dead. The cold had crept through her flesh and into her bones, slowing her blood.

My heart's still beating, even though I'm dead, she thought. *And I still need to breathe. And I'm cold.*

She sat up, hoping that the land of the dead wasn't going to be dark all the time. As if in answer to the thought, a light flickered and caught through the trees, a little way off to her right. It looked for all the world as though someone had just lit a fire.

Jess got to her feet, a bit unsteadily, and walked between massive trunks towards the light. There was a man crouched by the fire with his back to her, breathing on twigs and fragments of tinder to encourage the flames, adding bits and pieces to feed it. He didn't seem to have heard her approaching, so she stopped and simply watched him.

In the shivering firelight, she couldn't see much: dark clothes, longish dark hair. He half turned to reach for a branch as a resinous twig caught and spat flame, and she had a glimpse of his face in profile.

He was young. She hadn't expected that. The flame died and he was lost in shadow again, still now, and listening. He knew she was there.

Jess stepped forward into the light and heard him catch his breath, then let it out slowly.

He was staring at her, his expression unreadable.

"Hello," she said, for want of something better.

He didn't answer, but his hand went to his neck, pulling at something.

Shivering, Jess moved closer to the fire, still looking at him. Above his tunic, his fingers tugged at something twined green and gold, black and brown, barbed with thorns, tight about his neck.

She felt as if all her blood had drained away through the soles of her boots.

"I'm not dead," she said in wonder.

He stared at her, perplexed.

"No."

"It worked." She was talking to herself as much as him. "It worked."

Suddenly fearful, she looked around.

"This is the Kelpie world?"

He started to nod, then stopped suddenly, hand going to his throat. "Yes. To you it is."

"And you…" She pointed at his neck. "That… You… You were the horse?"

"Was… am…"

Jess's mouth went dry as just what she had done hit her properly.

It worked. I'm in the Kelpie world. Oh no. What do I do now?

"Are there more of you?" she asked. Ellen had said the

68

halter gave power over *one* Kelpie; this forest could be full of them, preparing to overpower her and free the horse-boy.

"Of course. But not here. Not just now."

"How do I know you're telling the truth?" She took a couple of steps towards the fire.

The boy pulled again at the thing round his neck. Why did he keep staring at her?

"Don't you know what you've done to me with this? I have to do what you tell me. I can't lie to you. How did you know how to make this if you don't understand what it does?"

When she didn't answer, he put another branch on the fire.

Jess sidled towards the flames and sat down, out of reach.

"I've come for my friend. You have to give her back to me," she said, amazed at her own daring.

Again his fingers went to his throat, and now she was close enough to see him wince in pain. He went back to feeding the flames. There wasn't enough light to see the colour of his eyes. Were they the same blue as the horse's?

"What's your name?" Jess asked impulsively.

"Finn," said the boy.

"I'm… "

"Jess," he finished for her.

She caught her breath. "How do you know my name? Did Freya talk about me?"

Finn shook his head.

He remembered the first time he'd seen her, when his mother had given in to his nagging at last and taken him to the Upper World to show him his father's people.

"Your father used to live in the Upper World," his mother had said. She had carried on speaking to him, but he'd not heard another word, staring transfixed at the small, brown-haired girl who stood hands on hips in the middle of the farmyard, scolding her tiny, mud-covered brother.

"Jess?" A woman's voice had come from the house.

"Coming." And Jess had pulled her brother to his feet and marched him off, still scolding.

"How do you know my name?" she demanded again, but Finn raised a hand to quiet her, looking round, listening now to something she couldn't hear.

"What? What is it?"

He ignored her, getting to his feet in one smooth movement, a burning branch in one hand.

"Stay close to the fire and keep quiet," he said softly. As he spoke, he was moving slowly away.

"What is it? Where are you going?" she hissed. "Stop!"

To her surprise, Finn stopped abruptly. He looked angrily at Jess.

"Let me go," he said in a venomous whisper. "Unless you want to get yourself killed. We're not the only creatures in this forest."

Jess gulped. She didn't know what to do. He could be trying to trick her, but...

"All right, you can go. But you have to come back. Alone."

He gave her an exasperated look and slid into the darkness between the trees. Jess watched the flame bob up and down, then disappear.

Silence surrounded her. She shivered, but not with cold this time. She got to her feet. What else was in the forest? If there was danger nearby, she wanted to be ready to run.

Jess moved slowly round the fire, straining her senses for any hint that someone – or something – was nearby, watching her.

Trees stretched away beyond the firelight. Here and there between the trunks grew huge briars with dark red flowers. Even in the firelight Jess could see the thorns. As she looked at a bush, she thought she saw a flicker of movement among the twisting branches: an eye, a suggestion of teeth.

She took a step back towards the fire, peering into the darkness. There! The gleam of long, curved claws made her gasp, before she realised they weren't claws, but thorns. Fool. She was seeing things that weren't there at all.

How long had the Kelpie boy been gone? If this was some sort of trick, it had succeeded. And if it wasn't... There was no point in running. She had no idea where to run *to*.

Come on, Jess, she told herself as she circled the flames warily. *This is no time for imagination. Things are strange enough as it is.*

She gave a squeak of terror as a figure appeared, seemingly from nowhere, on the other side of the fire.

It was Finn, now without the burning branch.

"Don't creep up like that," she said, trying to mask her fear with anger.

She was still here. He had half-expected her to have disappeared, like one of his mother's illusions. Only the bite of the metal at his throat convinced him this wasn't a dream. He'd imagined her in his world so often, but never like this. Not with power over him.

"I can't help it if I'm quiet," he said. "You can sit down again, it's all right."

Jess folded her shaking legs under her.

"What was it?" she regretted asking as soon as she said the words.

"A wolf. But it's all right; it can't get through to your world and it won't hurt you with me here, not one on its own."

His answer didn't quite make sense, but she told herself it didn't matter.

"I want Freya back. Where is she?" A terrible thought occurred. "Is she all right?"

71

"Yes."

"Then take me to her."

"It's not safe to go too far from the fire while it's dark. There are wolves, remember? And they're a lot fiercer than the ones in your world. You'll have to wait until daybreak." A sudden gust of wind stirred his hair and sent sparks flying as he spoke.

Jess reached to push a toppling log back into the fire while she thought about that.

"All right, we'll wait until morning," she agreed.

There was another gust of wind and, as though a curtain had been pulled, the sky was suddenly burning with stars as the clouds above the forest frayed into rags.

Jess looked up, open-mouthed. If she had needed any proof that she was no longer in her own world, here it was; stars flared coldly above her in numbers that she had never imagined. She searched in vain for a familiar constellation, but there was none.

She felt Finn's eyes on her, and brought her gaze back to his face.

"It's not the same sky," she said.

"It's not the same world." He glanced up. "We have more stars, but you have the moon."

"There's no moon here?"

Finn shook his head.

"But how… I don't understand." Jess was baffled.

"You don't have to," Finn said, and she turned to look at him properly as she heard the edge to his voice. "Why would you want to know about this world? You've come for your friend, that's all. Isn't that right? You're not interested in us."

"I'm… You're right. I've come for my friend. That's all I want," Jess said, but it wasn't true any more.

"Go to sleep," said Finn, in a voice that was far from friendly.

"You'll get your friend in the morning." His fingers were at his throat again, trying to ease the thing round his neck.

Jess didn't know what else to do, so she curled up in the lee of the fire and pretended to sleep, Finn's face caught behind her eyelids, half seen and undecipherable.

Finn watched as she fell properly asleep.

He felt he knew her, even though he'd never spoken to her. He'd spent so much time watching her that he sometimes felt he knew what she was about to do before she did.

The snatched glimpses weren't enough. He'd wanted her here, with him.

And now she *was* here, in his world. But she was only here because of her friend. That wasn't what was meant to happen. And when his family found out she was here... What had he done?

Jess slept fitfully. Fragments of dreams chased her to morning and she opened her eyes to find that the fire had died to a bed of grey ash, and the Kelpie boy was watching her.

She blinked several times, for the air between them seemed to shimmer and shift, then she sat up, pushing hair out of her face, aware, to her consternation, that she had flushed to her fingertips. Finn continued to watch her.

"Did no one ever tell you it's rude to stare?" she asked.

He frowned. "Why? How else are you supposed to learn what something really looks like?"

"It's... you're..." Jess was determined not to be lost for words. "You're not supposed to make it obvious that you're that interested in anyone. Anything."

He mulled it over.

"That makes no sense."

She blinked a few times, trying to force everything to stay still.

Embarrassingly, she found herself drawn to stare at him in turn. It was the first time she'd had enough light to see him properly.

The hair that came almost to his shoulders was black, his face fine-boned and sharply angled. His eyes were the blue of the iris flowers round Roseroot Pool, the blue of the horse's eyes, extraordinarily vivid. He was, Jess found herself thinking, very good looking.

"Now *you're* staring," he said, to her horror.

"I'm not," she blurted untruthfully. "I mean… Look, you were a horse, now you're a person. Of course I'm staring."

To cover her discomfort, she got to her feet.

"Take me to Freya. I came here to get her back. "Tell me what I'll have to do to get her out of here." Jess felt the colour sliding away from her face as the reality of her situation hit her again.

"Sit down again, and I'll tell you."

She came round the bed of ashes and sat down, closer to him than she had been before, close enough now to see the thing round his neck. It was no longer the halter she had made. In Finn's world it had become a torque of coloured metals, twisted together and bristling with tiny spines. Jess could see the red weal it had raised around his neck.

"Why did you take her?" she asked before he had a chance to speak. "You took the boys as well, didn't you? Why did you take them?"

"I took your friend. The boys were taken by other Kelpies." He gave her a searching look. "Do you care? Does it matter to you so long as you get your friend back?"

"Of course it matters," Jess said angrily. "Why do you take them? I'm trying to understand. Tell me."

He sighed, running his hands through his hair.

"You call us Kelpies in the Upper World, but we call ourselves

74

the Nykur. Long ago, this land used to be full of Nykur. The herds were everywhere on the plains. The horses made a sound like thunder as they galloped, there were so many of us. In those days, we hardly ever took human form here, only when we visited your world, so that we could speak to you.

But now the Nykur are a failing race. We are long lived, but we don't have many children – fewer still as the years pass. Some of them are sickly, some are taken by wolves when they are foals. There aren't many of us left now. And so we take children from your world to bolster our numbers, to breed fresh blood into our families. They forget your world, and live among us instead. We spend more time in human shape now that most of us have people from the Upper World in our families. Children of mixed Nykur and human blood survive childhood more often than pure-bloods do. Half-bloods like me are hardier than they are. We are the only ones who risk going between the worlds regularly now."

"One of your parents is human?"

"My father. My mother, Gudrun, is pure blood Nykur."

"And your father doesn't try to stop other human children being taken?"

"No. He is Nykur now. He has forgotten there was a time when he lived in the Upper World. He understands the need. He knows they will be happy here."

Jess was suddenly conscious that she should be concentrating on getting Freya back, not on this. She decided to ignore the other questions crowding into her head.

"So how do I get Freya back?"

He looked at her in silence for a few heartbeats. When he spoke, his voice was level, almost expressionless.

"She is with my family. I'll take you to where they are. She won't recognise you; she has already forgotten the Upper World."

Jess broke in. "But she will remember once she's home, won't she?"

"Perhaps. She's not been here long. But I don't know."

"Will I forget where I really belong if I stay here too long?" she asked, fearful.

"No. That only happens when we take people to keep. It's part of the spell when we take them between the worlds. It won't happen to you.

"I'll bring Freya to you. You must take her by the hand and walk towards the stream – I'll show you. You mustn't stop, and you mustn't let go, whatever happens. If you can get her away without my mother realising, then all you have to do is pull Freya into the water with you, and you'll both come out at the pool in *your* forest."

"Don't I have to get her back here for that?"

"No. The river that runs past my home is linked to the pool in the forest here." He paused.

"If my mother discovers what's happening, she will try to stop you. She is not bound by this." He touched the torque around his neck. "She will spin illusions so that you think Freya is something else. You must grasp tight to whatever you find yourself holding, and get her into the water."

Jess remembered the words that had made no sense, and their meaning was now suddenly clear.

Hold fast the briar,
Hold fast the falcon,
Hold fast the flame.

"All right," she said. "How soon can we go?"

"Now. It's light enough to be safe for you. It will take about an hour to get there." He rose and kicked apart the remains of the fire. "This way." He set off without looking to see if she was behind him.

It was just light enough to see where she was going, though

they weren't following any sort of path as far as Jess could tell. The undergrowth made the going difficult, and Finn stopped to wait for her when she fell behind.

As the light grew, she looked around her at the Kelpie – the Nykur – world. The light itself was disconcerting, making the air and the forest beyond it quiver unless she was looking at it directly; almost as though it wasn't solid, but a reflection in wind-ruffled water.

The trees were no sort she had ever seen, their trunks soaring high above her to open in a canopy of green and silver leaves that moved in the wind. The enormous briar bushes that grew among them were barbed with huge curved thorns. No wonder she had mistaken them for claws in the darkness. They were laden with blood-crimson flowers that had a strange musky scent, not like a flower scent at all. When Jess strayed close to one, Finn pulled her quickly away from it.

"Careful. They bite," he said, cryptically.

She found out what he meant a few minutes later, when she drew close to another one without thinking. She gasped in pain as a branch whipped against her, and thorns tore at her like teeth.

She stepped back quickly, sucking blood from her wrist.

"It moved. I swear it aimed at me," she exclaimed.

"I told you not to get too close," Finn said.

There was no sign or sound of birds, but the whine and buzz of insects filled the air and there were tracks through the grass where animals must move among the trees.

"It doesn't look like autumn here," Jess said, catching up with Finn again.

"It isn't. Time runs differently for us."

She thought a little before she spoke again.

"What will happen to you once I take Freya back?" she asked, prepared to be rebuffed.

77

"This will disappear once you go back to your world." He gestured at the torque.

"But will there be trouble for you, because you helped me?"

"The others will know I had no choice because of this, but they'll be angry that I was stupid enough to let myself be trapped, especially by you."

"I'm sorry."

He looked at her then, to see if she was mocking him, and found that she wasn't. *Was there a chance that she felt something for him?* he wondered.

"What about the boys?" She suddenly remembered. "Where are they? Can I rescue them too?"

"Other families have them. You can't take them back: they've been here too long and they wouldn't remember anything about your world. This is their home now. They don't know any other."

They had stopped walking during the last exchange. Now Finn said,

"Come on, Jess. We need to go."

That was it. That was what she had forgotten from last night.

"Stop!" she commanded.

He slammed to a halt, glaring at her.

"My name. How do you know my name? You didn't tell me last night."

"We need to go," he said, but he was helpless until her words released him.

"How do you know my name?" Jess repeated. She relented a little. "You can walk while you tell me."

"I watch you. I watch your family," he said unwillingly. "I've watched you for years. I've seen you sometimes look round as though you knew I was there."

"I *did* know," said Jess slowly. "All those times I've had the feeling I was being watched it must have been you." She slapped an insect away. "But why did you watch us?"

She wasn't sure she wanted him to answer.

"At first it was because… we're kin."

"We're *what*?"

"My father is your grandmother's cousin."

She gaped at him in disbelief.

"What? What's his name?"

"Euan."

"Your *father*? But he must be almost the same age as my grandmother."

"I told you, time runs differently here. I've seen your grandmother. My father is much younger here." Finn said soberly. "But it's best you don't see him. He'll try to stop you, the same as everyone else."

Ten minutes passed in silence, and the trees began to thin. Finn put a hand on Jess's arm to stop her, the first time he had touched her in human form. He snatched his hand away as though he'd been burned.

"When we get to the edge of the trees you'll see my family's home. Wait in the trees and I'll bring Freya to you. My mother will sense something happening as soon as you touch her, so be ready."

As they walked on, Jess could hear the sound of falling water. She was listening so intently that she walked straight into Finn's back.

He took a sharp breath, turned and realised the contact had been accidental. "There it is," he said after a few seconds, and she looked round his shoulder to see his home.

Now that it was fully light, she saw the Nykur world properly for the first time, and drew a breath in wonder.

To right and left, a rippling plain of grasses stretched to the limits of her vision, lush green shading away to blue in

79

the distance. In front of her lay a boggy meadow, covered in tussocky grass and rushes and starred with tall yellow flowers that she didn't recognise, but whose scent reached her, even here. A river flowed through it, silver water bounding from pool to pool. Behind the meadow was a procession of crags stacked like steps, water launching itself from the topmost one to tumble down to the river in a series of waterfalls, rainbows dancing above them where the air sparkled with water droplets.

Jess blinked again and again, astonished by the clarity with which she could see things. Not just see; she could hear the breeze pushing against the grass stems, smell the scents of flowers and water, even of stone. She was suddenly aware that under the bark of the tree she was leaning against, sap moved like slow blood.

"What's happening?" she asked Finn uncertainly.

"Nothing," he said. "You're just seeing my world properly now that it's light."

"But it's all so… sharp. So bright." She couldn't express it properly. It was as though, back in her own world, she had spent years seeing everything through a cloudy, muffling veil. Here, the veil was gone. "So beautiful," she murmured.

She turned her attention to Finn's home. At first, astonished, she thought the house was afloat in the air. As she looked more closely, however, she realised that it sat on a series of wooden piles that held it clear of the water. Built of wood, it almost looked as though it had grown from its surroundings, not been built at all.

Instead of a single structure there was a series of circular buildings, linked by little bridges and covered walkways. On the side that faced them, large windows stood open to the morning sun, but Jess could see no sign of any occupants.

"Wait here," said Finn quietly.

"No – stop," Jess hissed.

With a resigned sigh, Finn turned back.

"Promise me you'll bring her. Promise me you won't give me away."

He closed his eyes briefly.

"Don't you understand what this does to me?" He fingered the torque. "I have no choice. If you tell me to do something, I have to do it. I can't give you away. So, can I go now?"

"There's one more thing." Jess hesitated. "I'm sorry I've had to hurt you to get Freya back. I didn't know it would do that to you." She gestured to the angry weal under the torque.

Finn watched her face.

"But you would have done it, wouldn't you, even if you had known?" he asked quietly.

She nodded.

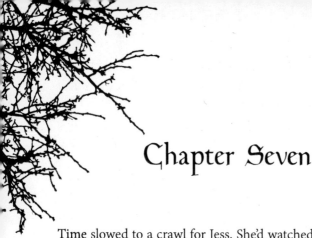

Chapter Seven

Time slowed to a crawl for Jess. She'd watched Finn make his **way** across the meadow without looking back, and disappear into the complex of little buildings. Since then, nothing. Not a glimpse, not a sound. She'd expected him to reappear with Freya more or less immediately. What was he doing?

Despite what he had said, she pictured him with his family, showing them the torque, the others working out a way to trick her.

She imagined how he must have watched her family and the farm, thought of all the times she'd felt there was someone near her in the woods. It was a disturbing idea, but it had never felt like a threatening presence at the time. Was he horse or boy as he watched? She found herself wishing she had spotted him, and that they could have become friends. She felt herself drawn to him in some way she couldn't articulate.

Where were they? Why was this taking so long? Something must be wrong. Five minutes more and then…

Wait.

Two figures emerged from the building at last. Finn and Freya, hand in hand, smiling and talking, looking as though they had known each other all their lives, as if they had nothing better to do than to stroll beside the river.

The noise of hooves distracted Jess. She glanced towards

the sound, and saw a horse galloping towards Finn's house. Had he found a way to summon other Nykur to help him? Was this a member of his family?

This horse was smaller than Finn, more delicate, but just as black, just as glossy. As Jess watched, the horse neared the floating house and…

…and was gone. Jess blinked, thinking this was some trick of the shifting light, but there was no horse any more. Instead there was a girl, a girl with black hair falling in curls and waves around her face.

It was one thing to have in your mind the *idea* of a horse that changed into a person, but to see it happen… Jess felt overwhelmed by Finn's world. What had made her think she could come here and rescue Freya from these people? She held her breath, waiting to see what the girl would do, and let it out in relief when she ran lightly up the steps into the house.

As soon as she was gone, Jess hurried out from the shelter of the trees, retaining just enough sense not to shout Freya's name. She watched as Finn's expression changed to dismay and Freya's to bafflement, saw Finn silently mouth *Get back* at her, and stopped dead.

They were close enough now for Jess to hear Freya's voice as she turned to Finn and said in puzzlement,

"Who's that, Finn?"

Although Finn had warned Jess that Freya wouldn't remember home, Jess had thought she would know *her*, but Freya looked at her as though she were a stranger.

Jess arranged her face into something that looked like a smile as Finn replied.

"This is Jess. She's a friend."

Jess could hear the tension in his voice, saw Freya glance at him as she picked it up too, and then look round at the house

83

from which they had come, Finn pulling her towards Jess all the time.

"Wait," said Freya. "Rowan just got back. Didn't you hear her? Surely she'll want to see Jess too?"

"She can see Jess later," Finn said, ploughing grimly on.

Freya stopped and tried to pull her arm loose.

"Stop, Finn. Let's call her. She'll want to come with us."

Before Finn could do anything, Freya had turned to the house.

"Rowan!" she shouted at the top of her voice. "Hurry up. Someone's come to see us."

There was no point in trying to stay hidden now. Jess saw figures appear outside Finn's house, staring across the meadow towards them: the girl she had glimpsed changing from horse shape, and a man and woman who must be Finn's parents.

Panic propelled her forward.

"Freya, it's me, Jess! Come on."

She grabbed Freya's free hand and together with Finn, began to pull her towards the river.

"What are you doing? Let me go!" Freya struggled to pull her hands free.

"Come on Freya. I'm taking you home," Jess gasped desperately.

"What do you mean? This is my home. Get away from me."

Freya twisted in Jess's grip, shouting back now to the other members of Finn's family who were hurrying towards them.

"Help! Help me!"

Jess heard the woman shout. "Finn! Stop her!"

Finn dropped Freya's hand and fell to his knees, his hands at his throat, caught between the imperatives of the torque and his mother's command. As Jess looked, the torque seemed to tighten.

Dredging up reserves of strength she had never dreamed she possessed, Jess began to haul Freya towards the water again.

"Let her go."

The woman's voice was impossible to ignore. Jess's steps faltered, and she looked round.

Finn's family stood poised, watching her: the black-haired girl, so like Finn that she must be his sister, a man who looked no more than forty, but must be Euan, and Finn's mother Gudrun, with a strong, handsome face, and golden brown hair falling past her shoulders.

"Let her go," Gudrun said again.

Jess shook her head, pulling Freya inexorably onwards.

The woman held up her hand and Freya disappeared.

Jess gave a scream as Freya's hand was replaced by the slimy, muscular body of a huge eel, writhing and twisting round her arms. She gritted her teeth and ploughed on towards the riverbank, her grip tighter than ever round the squirming thing.

Remember... this isn't real, she told herself.

Just as she felt she had a secure hold of it, the eel was gone. Jess stumbled as the weight of its body disappeared, and opened her hands. At once a white and gold butterfly fluttered from her open palm.

"No... no!" Jess stopped herself from clutching at it, watched it flutter onto one of the yellow flowers, trying to ignore the sound of running feet coming closer.

She crept nearer to the flower, reached out both hands and gently cupped them round the butterfly, then ran for the river.

The butterfly burst from her hands, changed into a peregrine falcon, hooked beak and slashing talons and angry yellow eyes. Jess gave a scream and gripped the bird as tightly as she could. She had it by both legs, safe from the talons at least, but it beat its wings, screeching angrily and stabbing at her with that wicked beak.

"I'm not letting go," Jess yelled, as she concentrated on reaching the river.

Nearly there, she told herself, then yelped in pain as the falcon changed and she found herself with an armful of briars, the blood-red flowers matched by the blood dripping from her hands, where the great thorns bit deep into her flesh.

"I'm taking her!" Jess screamed, turning to face the Nykur as she reached the riverbank at last.

Finn was still on his knees, face twisted in pain, fighting to breathe as the thorned metal bit into his neck harder and harder. Rowan knelt beside him, desperately trying to pull the torque from his neck.

Finn's parents were only a few steps away now.

"I'm taking her home," Jess called out, edging down to the water.

Gudrun held up her hand again.

"No," she said, and the briars burst into flame.

Jess screamed as flames engulfed her arm. She could smell her flesh burning. She fought the reflex that urged her to hurl the burning briars away from her.

Hold fast the flame.

She couldn't hold on. The pain was too much. With a despairing cry, Jess threw herself into the river.

She'd failed. Lungs straining, Jess kicked herself upwards. She'd let go. Freya was lost forever.

She could see a light above her now. Was it the sun of the Nykur world or her own?

She should have held on tighter. Her head broke the surface and she gasped in a lungful of air.

Trees. Brambles. A pool, not a river. Roseroot Pool.

She was home.

The water swirled beside her and another head broke the surface. Jess floundered away, fearing a vengeful Nykur, a great dark horse, but it was a human head, blonde hair darkened by water.

Freya. It was Freya.

Freya looked around her, treading water.

"Jess?" she said uncertainly.

"You know who I am!"

"Of course I know who you are. What are we doing in the pond?"

Too overwhelmed to say any more, Jess splashed her way to shore beside Freya. They pulled themselves out of the water and collapsed, breathless.

Jess rolled over to look at her friend, reached out a hand to touch her, to make sure she was real.

"It's you," she said through her soaking hair.

She focused on her own hands in wonder. "I'm not burned. Or scratched. Look – not a mark."

Freya stared at her as though she was insane.

"What are you raving about? Look at my dress – the dye's running. It'll be ruined. I can't remember how we got into the pond. Did you push me in? Jess? Jess? Why are you laughing?"

Jess managed to get herself under enough control to speak.

"You don't remember anything, do you?" she asked Freya, who was trying to wring the water out of her skirt.

"What on earth do you mean? We were picking brambles, and then I must have slipped, or you pushed me in, or something."

"Freya – you've been missing for five days."

Freya stopped what she was doing and stared hard at Jess.

"You must have hit your head. You're not making sense. Come on, we'd better get you home." Freya got to her feet and stretched a hand down to her half-hysterical friend. "Honestly, Jess, I wonder about you sometimes. It's a good job I'm here to look after you."

Arms round each other, the girls began to squelch their way back to Westgarth. Nothing that Jess could say to Freya as they walked would convince her that she'd been missing. Even the mention of the horse drew nothing from her but an incredulous stare. By the time they got within sight of the farmyard Jess was starting to wonder if it was Freya who was right, and not her at all.

How long had she been gone? It looked like late afternoon, but what day was it? She'd spent a night in the Nykur world. Finn had said that time ran differently there, but *how* differently? What if years had passed? She felt a prickle of fear.

The farmyard was empty. For a few seconds Jess imagined it abandoned, the buildings empty but for spiders and mice and dust, but then she heard a cow lowing and a measure of her usual common sense returned.

They got all the way to the kitchen door without seeing anyone, and it was Freya who shouted into the house.

"Martha! We're back, but we're soaking. Can we come in anyway?"

Jess heard the crash of a dropped dish from inside and her mother appeared in the doorway. She gaped at the girls, her hand clamped white on the door frame.

"Freya?" she whispered. "Jess... what... where...?"

She gave up, ran towards them and enfolded them both in a huge hug, then stood back looking at them at arm's length as though to convince herself it was really them.

Jess turned to Freya, and saw the first shadow of doubt appear in her eyes.

"Are we late?" she said. "I'm sorry we're wet." Her voice trailed away as Martha continued to stare. "Martha, what is it?"

"Where have you been, Freya? What happened? Oh!" She put a hand to her mouth. "We must get word to your father."

"Ian!" she shouted, making both girls jump. "Come quickly. It's Freya – she's here."

Jess felt Freya clutch her arm.

"Jess, what's going on? I don't understand." She sounded frightened now.

It was a few hours later. Freya, wearing one of Jess's dresses, sat mutely wrapped in Arnor's arms, trying to take in what she had been told.

Jess had managed to establish that it was still the same day here as when she had left. It was turning out to be, by some way, the longest day of her life.

When the inevitable questioning started, she feigned confusion before settling on the patently ludicrous claim that she had found Freya wandering beside the pool, and then they had fallen in.

Everyone seemed outwardly to have decided to accept it as the truth, though surely it must be clear it was nonsense. Jess saw her parents exchanging whispered words once or twice, and glancing at her when they thought she wouldn't notice.

In her usual chair by the fire, Ellen somehow continued to look calm, though Jess could have sworn she could feel the anxiety to hear the true story fairly crackling out of her. There was no chance of talking to her alone just now, though.

It was decided that Arnor and Freya would stay overnight, and everyone went to bed early, overwrought and exhausted, Freya back in Jess's room.

Jess lay awake for a long time, aware of Freya lying equally sleepless in the other bed. Normally, they would have talked until they fell asleep, but now they lay silent. Neither of them knew what to say.

Jess was drifting off to sleep at last when she realised that the sound of Freya's breathing had been replaced by muffled weeping.

"Freya? What's wrong?" Jess whispered, sitting up.

There was no reply.

Jess lit the candle, got out of bed and went over to where Freya lay curled up as small as possible, and sat down beside her.

"What's wrong?" she asked again.

There was a choked sob.

"What happened to me, Jess? Why can't I remember? I don't understand what can have happened. You all thought I was *dead*. Where was I? We were picking brambles and your hair got tangled... Tangled hair – black hair. Why do I keep thinking about that? And then we were in the pond. And now everyone says there are five days locked away in the middle of that. Am I losing my mind?"

What to say? Should she try and explain to Freya what had really happened? It was clear she didn't remember any of it.

Jess tried to imagine explaining about Finn and the Nykur and the halter...

...and gave up. Freya wouldn't believe a word of it. She'd think Jess was making fun of her. Jess decided that unless Freya herself remembered something, she wasn't going to tell her anything. She put her arms round the other girl.

"Don't worry, Freya. You're safe and you're back with us. Nothing else really matters. It'll be all right, you'll see."

Why didn't Jess believe her own words?

They waved Arnor and Freya off after breakfast the next day, Jess promising to visit soon. Freya was still uncharacteristically quiet.

It wasn't how Jess had imagined it at all.

When she'd been plucking up the courage to take the halter and search for the dark horse, she'd imagined returning with Freya, elated, full of the tale of what had happened. She'd imagined everyone apologising for not having believed her before, praising her for her bravery in saving her friend.

But that wasn't how it was at all. Instead of elated, Jess mostly felt worried. She was worried about Freya, of course, but she found that she was worried about Finn too. She couldn't get that last glimpse of him out of her head. Finn fighting for breath, the thing she had put around his neck slowly choking him. What if he died? What if she had killed him?

She shouldn't care. She told herself she shouldn't care. He was a stranger who had kidnapped Freya. He'd spent years watching Jess and her family. He wasn't even human. It should have made her angry or frightened; she shouldn't care what happened to him.

But she did.

Once Arnor and Freya had disappeared around a curve of the road, Jess and her family went back into the farmhouse. Ian gave her shoulder a quick squeeze and went off towards the orchard and Martha pointed at a basket of washing.

"Hang that out, Jess, would you?"

And that was that. Back to normal. No one had asked her where she had been for so long yesterday, or why she'd gone to the pool. No one had asked her anything. It was as though they didn't want to hear whatever answers she might give. Alone with her mother preparing breakfast, Jess had tried to start a conversation so she could tell the truth, but Martha had firmly turned the talk to another subject.

"I'll help you," said Ellen, shaking the peg bag under Jess's nose and startling her out of her reverie.

Jess picked up the heavy basket and they walked slowly together to where the clothes line stood, too far from the farm buildings for anyone to hear what they said.

Jess put the basket down and pulled out a shirt.

"Well?" said Ellen, handing her a couple of pegs.

"Everything you told me was true. I waited for the horse and managed to put the halter on. I woke up in the Kelpie world and the horse was a boy and it was night. Time's different there." She paused for breath and bent for another shirt.

"A boy?"

"His name's Finn. And he's Euan's son. I saw Euan, I think."

"Euan? My cousin Euan?" Ellen's eyes were wide.

"Yes. That's what Finn said anyway. He – Euan, that is – looks much younger than you. Because the time's different, I suppose."

"And the horse boy is his *son*?"

"Yes." Jess shook her head. "Oh, I'm not telling this very well." She paused to gather her thoughts.

"Their world is so beautiful. It's as if everything's brand new and clean and clear. It was amazing." She paused, remembering.

"Finn told me the Nykur – that's what they call themselves, not Kelpies – take children to grow up and live with them because there aren't many Nykur left. The people they take forget our world and think they belong in the Nykur world. When I saw Freya there, she didn't recognise me at all, so that must be true."

Ellen held up a hand to stop her for a moment. "The lad said that they take *children* to live with them. But Freya isn't a child. Why was it different this time?" she mused. "And we've stolen someone back from them; what will they do about that?" She saw that Jess looked alarmed and stopped thinking aloud. "Pay no attention, Jess. I'm talking nonsense. Tell me what happened when you found Freya."

"That's what the rest of the verse was about:

Hold fast the briar,
Hold fast the falcon,
Hold fast the flame.

I took Freya's hand and tried to pull her to the river. That was hard enough; she didn't know me, she didn't want to go, and then Finn's mother did something, and Freya *changed*. She changed shape. Finn had warned me she would, or I couldn't have held on. An eel, a butterfly, a falcon, a briar, a flame. I managed to hold on to Freya, even when the flame burned me, and I jumped in the river, and we came up in Roseroot Pool. And Freya knew me, but she doesn't remember anything about the Nykur."

Ellen was staring into space.

"I still can't believe you've seen Euan," she marvelled. "I've spent most of my life wondering what happened to him, if he was alive or dead. You don't know what this means to me."

"And what you did…" Ellen stared hard at Jess, then hugged her so tightly that Jess could hardly breathe. "You were always

93

a brave girl, even when you were wee. You faced all that and saved Freya. Your whole family should be proud of you, not just me…" She released Jess and held her at arm's length for a moment.

They finished pegging out the washing in silence and started back to the house, lost in their own thoughts.

Chapter Eight

Two days later, Jess stood in the barn, absently turning the handle of the apple press while Ashe fed apples into it and a stream of juice flowed into the stone jar underneath: the beginnings of this year's cider.

"That looks like hard work," a voice said from behind her, making her jump. "Here, I'll take a turn."

A large pair of hands covered her own and she turned to see Magnus.

"What on earth are you doing here?"

"Thank you for the unrestrained welcome," he said with a crooked smile. "My family's in town. We got the news that Freya had… was…" He drew a breath. "Anyway, we thought we were coming to try and console Arnor, and it turns out we're here to help celebrate Freya's miraculous reappearance." He started to turn the handle, his hands still on Jess's.

"She says she doesn't remember what happened. That's stupid," said Ashe firmly. "You can't just not remember five whole days."

"Ashe!" Jess pulled her hands free. "You don't know anything about it."

"It's all right," said Magnus equably. "Come on Ashe, keep the apples coming."

He addressed himself to Jess.

"That's why I'm here. How did you find her? Neither Freya nor Arnor are very clear even about that."

"Oh… of course." Jess felt foolish. Of course he was here because of Freya.

"Wait – that came out wrong… I came to see you too."

Did he mean her or the whole family?

"Away you go, Ashe," Jess said, taking his place. "I'll do the apples now that Magnus is here to turn the handle. You can go off and do something disgusting."

Ashe ignored the insult and ran for it before she changed her mind.

"The jar's full," Magnus said.

He corked the full one and lugged it out of the way while she brought a replacement, conscious as she had never been before of Magnus's eyes on her.

He wasn't turning the handle.

"Come on," she said.

"Is Freya all right? She seems… different."

Jess sat down on an upturned bucket.

"She was fine when I… when I found her. But realising that there are five days she can't remember has upset her. You know how much Freya likes to be in control of things… Everyone thought she was dead. That would be hard for anyone to deal with."

"What do *you* think happened?"

Oh, it was tempting… so tempting.

Jess shrugged. "The only thing I can imagine is that she fell and bumped her head and wandered about until I came upon her."

"For five days?"

"Have you got a better explanation?"

Magnus shook his head. "You have to admit though, it doesn't make a lot of sense."

"No." Jess sighed, wondering how Magnus would react if

she tried to tell him the truth. He wouldn't believe a word of it; that was the one thing she was sure of. He was cut from the same cloth as her, and not given to flights of fancy.

"Come on," she said. "Turn the handle. The apples won't crush themselves."

And by unspoken agreement they turned the conversation to less baffling topics.

In the end, despite protesting that he should go, he stayed for supper, and by then it was dark of course, with a thin, cold rain falling, and he let himself be persuaded to stay the night, and it was clear that that was what he had always intended.

Somehow, Jess found herself sitting alone with Magnus at the end of the evening, watching the fire die down; everyone else seemed inexplicably to have melted away. She suddenly felt horribly self-conscious.

"When will you go back to Dundee?" she asked abruptly.

"Not tomorrow anyway. Maybe the day after. Mother's trying to persuade Arnor and Freya to come and stay with us. Time to sort themselves out, you know? Until the talk dies down." He cleared his throat. "I don't suppose you'd come too, would you?"

She turned to look at him more closely.

"Are you asking me so I can look after Freya, or do *you* want me to come?"

She couldn't believe she'd just said that.

To his credit, he held her gaze.

"Both," he said with a slow smile.

"All right then. I'll have to ask, of course." It wasn't exactly a sparkling reply, but most of her wits seemed to have deserted her and it was the best she could do.

It seemed to satisfy Magnus anyway. He gave a transparently happy smile, followed by a huge yawn.

"All this weeping, and people throwing their arms round each other – it's exhausting," he said.

Jess bit back a caustic response, imagining Freya's elbow digging into her ribs.

"I'm off to my bed," said Magnus, rising. "Goodnight. I'll try not to wake Ashe when I go in."

"I doubt you could. I used to think he'd died in the night sometimes when we used to share a room, though actually, he might have smelled better if he *had* been dead."

Jess half thought that Magnus might try to give her a kiss as he went past, but it didn't seem to occur to him. Left alone, she stared into the glowing embers, wondering again if she'd got things wrong.

"I miss Freya," said Rowan as she walked among the trees with Finn. "It was like having a sister. But you should never have taken her."

"I know that. I don't need you ranting at me as well as Mother," Finn said testily. "And you know it wasn't her I meant to take."

"It wouldn't have been any better if you'd taken Jess. You've got to take a Nykur wife, Finn. You know Mother's right. You can't have Jess. We can't have more human blood in the family."

Finn didn't answer for a moment. What was the point? No one – not even Rowan – understood that for him, there was no possible substitute for Jess. He'd loved her for years. They were meant to be together.

"You know how I feel," he said at last. His voice was still hoarse, and the blistered weal around his neck where the halter had burned him wouldn't heal properly. He hadn't realised Jess had the strength of mind to hurt him like that.

"But…" Rowan started to say, then stopped abruptly at the sound of a growl. They stood back to back, scanning the shadows between the trees.

"It came from nearer the pool," whispered Finn. "Come on."

Here in the wood it was easier to move quietly in human form. Finn and Rowan crept towards the sound of the wolves.

There were two, prowling the edge of the wood, looking at the pool as though trying to decide whether to enter it.

Rowan turned to Finn. "They shouldn't be able to get that close."

He nodded. "I know. I'll have to deal with them."

"I can help you. I know what to do."

"No! You've never faced down wolves without mother there."

"I'll have to do it sometime. I'll be just as safe with you."

"All right."

They stepped out from the wood to the open ground where the wolves could see them. The wolves stood their ground, lips drawn back, snarling.

Finn and Rowan locked minds with the wolves, told them they weren't flesh, told them they weren't wolves, tried to force them to change shape, to root themselves in the earth.

One of the wolves began to whine, backing away, and its shape began to waver.

"Push harder, Rowan," Finn urged. "We're almost there."

He forced his mind into that of the wolf, told it to change, forced it to abandon its shape. Where it had been, a new briar bush stood. For a moment, the leaves shivered; yellow eyes gleamed among the foliage, thorns flexed like claws. Then they were gone, and there was only a bush.

Finn and Rowan shifted their minds to the second wolf.

Unmoved, unchanged, the wolf stared back, and Finn felt a prickle of unease. He gathered all his concentration, all his will, and tried again. The wolf remained a wolf, tensed to attack.

"It's not working. Get back!" he yelled, just as the wolf launched itself at Rowan.

Finn slid into horse shape as the wolf sprang, and he threw himself between it and Rowan. Claws raked his shoulder as he reared back and struck once, twice, three times with his hoof before he connected with muscle and bone. He struck again and again, until he was certain the wolf was dead.

As he calmed and moved back to human shape he found that Rowan was beside him, arms round his neck.

"I'm sorry, Finn, I'm sorry. I should have been able to help you more."

"It's all right. It's all right." He was out of breath, unsteady on his feet. *He shouldn't feel like this. He should be able to deal with two wolves, even without Rowan.* He sat down, Rowan beside him, and tried to ignore his shaking hands. "That was a big wolf."

"They're all big," said Rowan ruefully. "Are you all right?" She looked at his shoulder. "It doesn't look too bad."

"I'm fine. Absolutely fine," he lied. *Why had it been so difficult? He should have overcome that wolf the first time he tried. What was wrong with him?*

"The enchantments are failing," he said. "Soon there won't be enough of us to guard the gateways any more."

"Maybe when the wolves can get to the Upper World they'll leave us alone here. Maybe it would be better if we just let them out."

"You know we can't do that. We made a promise."

"But look at what it costs us to keep it. One death already this year."

Finn got shakily to his feet. "Come on. Let's get away from here."

"Nearly there," said Arnor. "Look." He pointed. "You can see the smoke over the next hill."

Jess looked at the twists and blots of grey and yellow smoke that were the first signs that they were nearing Dundee.

"How much longer?" Freya asked, pulling her scarf further up over her ears.

"Half an hour at most and we'll be in town. It'll be warmer there, you'll see."

Jess rubbed her chilled fingers together. Even the gloves Ellen had knitted for her birthday hadn't managed to keep the cold out.

It was a week since Jess and Freya had appeared, soaked, at the kitchen door of Westgarth, and four days since Magnus and his family had left.

Jess had only seen Freya once since then, but now they were both to spend a week with Magnus and his parents in Dundee. The prospect of a stay in the city had cheered Freya up, but she still wasn't herself, nervy and unsure in situations that she would previously have handled with a cutting glance and a toss of her head.

Jess was aware that *she* wasn't herself either. It was incredible that her life should go back to normal after what had happened over the last couple of weeks, but that seemed to be what everyone expected of her: to act as though nothing had happened. Even Ellen had found excuses not to let her talk about the truth. Jess had lost track of the number of times she had wanted to shout at her family,

"Stop pretending everything's normal! You know it isn't."

It was a relief to get away from the farm.

The weather had suddenly turned cold. It was the sort of change that made people check that their larders were well stocked and their woodpiles high. Winter wasn't far away.

"When I get into that house, nothing's going to move me from the fireside," Freya said indistinctly through the scarf.

"I hope there's room for both of us," Jess said with feeling.

Arnor laughed. At least *he* sounded almost like his old self.

"If I know you, Freya, you'll be off out to see what you can find to spend my money on, things that no one in Kirriemuir will have."

Freya stuck her head out of the swathing scarf like a stoat emerging from a burrow.

"What rubbish," she said. "I never buy anything I don't need. It's *ages* since I had anything new to wear."

Arnor guffawed. "Ah, that's my lass," he said fondly, for it was exactly what the old Freya would have said.

"Besides," Freya went on, warming to her theme, "It's my duty as a friend to make sure Jess has some new clothes. Most of what she wears is so old that even the *boys* in Kirriemuir recognise the dresses."

Jess was so pleased to hear Freya behaving normally that she decided not to take offence, but she couldn't resist baiting her.

"Nonsense," she said briskly. "I doubt those halfwits would notice whether I had clothes on at all. Anyway, there's nothing wrong with my clothes. Some of them have *years* of wear left in them."

Freya gave a shriek, genuinely appalled.

"Honestly, there's no hope for you. No one but Magnus is ever going to look at you."

It wasn't cold any more. It was suddenly ridiculously, unseasonably hot. That was the reason her face was red, Jess told herself firmly. Nothing at all to do with what Freya had just said. She hunched deeper into her jacket to hide her burning cheeks.

Ten minutes later they reached the straggle of dwellings that marked the edge of Dundee and soon they were in the city itself.

Crooked streets tangled together, clogged with people and

horses and carts. Cramped buildings lined them, three, four, five stories high. They leaned forward alarmingly on their foundations, as if they were reaching towards their neighbours on the other side, leaving half of each street in their shadow.

There were shops and houses and inns and weaving sheds crammed in together, here and there a church with a bit more space round it.

Jess stared around her, amazed by the noise and the number of people. It was the first time in her life she'd been somewhere bigger than Kirriemuir.

She turned to speak to Freya, but stopped when she saw the lost look on her friend's face. After a couple of minutes, Jess touched her arm gently.

"Come back, Freya."

"I thought for a moment I could remember something about when I was missing…" Freya shook her head. "But it's gone again." She gave a wan smile as the cart turned a corner.

"Look." Arnor pointed. "St Mary's Watchtower. It used to be a church tower, but the rest of the church burned down."

"Watchtower?" echoed Jess. "Who are they watching for? The English won't come back now."

"Not who – *what*," Arnor said. "There's always a watch kept for fires. That's the biggest danger in a city like this. The buildings are so close together that a fire could go from one end to the other and destroy the whole place."

"Don't people worry about it all the time?" Jess asked, eyeing the tower with interest. There were spikes protruding from the walls, and for a moment she thought she saw heads impaled on them.

"Not really. I suppose people just get used to being extra careful about fire. I know it bothered Magnus's parents when they first moved here, but they never even mention it now."

"They talk about the wolves instead," said Freya darkly.

"Why?" asked Jess. "Surely they don't come into the town?"

"They never used to, but in the last few winters packs of them sometimes roam through the city. No one knows where they come from."

"No one's been able to track them," added Arnor. "They come out of the darkness, cause mayhem, then disappear. And they don't just take livestock, they'll attack people too; adults as well as children."

"That's not normal," said Jess. "I know there are stories from long ago about people being attacked by wolves, but nothing like that ever happens now. Not around Kirriemuir anyway."

"Mmnn… it's a mystery, right enough. Anyway, the tower keeps a watch for wolf packs too, so folk know to get inside. Looks like there's been a hunt here recently, too." Arnor pointed at the spikes as they drew level with the watchtower, and Jess saw what was impaled there: wolf heads, half-rotted.

A few minutes later, they turned into a quieter side street, then into a narrow lane where the houses pressed close together. Arnor drew the cart up in front of a blue-painted door.

"Here we are," he said, just as it opened, and Anna, Magnus's mother, came out on to the doorstep smiling.

She was a small, cheerful woman, with brown hair and a round face: utterly unlike the sister who had married Arnor and passed her beauty to Freya.

"Come in, come in," she called, throwing her arms wide. "You must be frozen through. Come and thaw out."

The girls climbed down with their bags, stiff with cold, and Arnor drove off to stable the horses.

Anna fussed round them as they walked into a wall of heat inside the house.

"Gavin and Magnus won't be back from work for a couple of hours, so you can have some peace and quiet to warm through and unpack before they come thumping in. It's good to see you, Jess. We're all so glad you could come with Freya. We don't see nearly enough of you any more. How are your parents? And Ashe? He always looks to me as though he'll turn out a handsome lad when he's a bit older."

If Anna paused for breath as she talked, Jess didn't spot it, and there was certainly no chance of finding a gap in her words to answer any of the questions she asked. Jess contented herself with smiling instead, as she unwound the layers of clothing that had kept her from freezing solid on the cart, and got out the present she had brought.

She and Freya followed the still-talking Anna into the room at the front of the house. There was a fireplace all right, large enough to satisfy Jess's most optimistic imaginings, and in it roared a fire so perfect that she thought perhaps she'd just stay in this room until spring.

Anna was still talking. *Maybe she breathes through her ears,* Jess thought.

"Oh Jess, that's very kind but there was no need, no need at all, it's a treat for us to see you. Smoked eel, oh lovely! One of my favourites, I do miss it, you can't catch them in the river here – did you know that?"

Arnor came in blowing on his fingers and Anna disappeared, still chatting, into the kitchen.

Arnor rolled his eyes and Freya giggled.

"One night of it's fine, but more than that… I wonder how Gavin copes?"

"Magnus said once that Gavin pretends to be deaf. He said it just rolls over you like the noise of a stream after a while, and you stop noticing," Freya said, with the air of an expert.

"… don't you think so, Arnor?" said Anna, coming in with a laden tray.

"Definitely," said Arnor.

Anna distributed scones and butter to everyone, and a nip of whisky to Arnor.

"To keep the cold from your bones," she said.

For some moments, everyone's mouths were full, and peace settled on the room. As soon as the girls had finished, they escaped to unpack, leaving Arnor to smile and nod in appropriate places.

Smells of cooking and occasional laughter drifted up from below.

Freya sniffed. "Venison?"

"Could be. Shall we go down?"

"Mmnn," said Freya, checking her appearance in the mirror and pinching colour into her cheeks. She held out a comb to Jess.

"You might want to comb your hair first."

Jess sighed as she took the comb, but when Freya stood aside from the mirror she had to admit her hair did look like something designed to trap birds. Grumbling, she hauled the comb through it under Freya's disapproving gaze.

"That's better," said Freya. "Now let's go and have another scone before Magnus comes home and finishes the lot."

Gavin came in not long afterwards, tall and dark and smelling pleasantly of cut wood.

"I see the hunt's been out," said Arnor.

"The wolves? Aye. That was a fortnight or so ago. I took Magnus along, but neither of us got one. There were a good few taken though, and the crown's paying a decent bounty."

"We saw the heads on St Mary's."

Gavin fidgeted in the room trying to make conversation with the girls for about ten minutes, then took Arnor off out with him.

"We'll be in the Black Bull," he said. "Tell Magnus in case he wants to join us."

"Just make sure you're back for supper and remember

Arnor doesn't want to be driving back to Kirriemuir tomorrow with a sore head," said Anna, kissing him goodbye.

They met Magnus on the doorstep.

"Hello Magnus," Freya called. "Stay and talk to us instead of going to the inn."

Jess got to her feet and Freya started towards him.

"No, no," He waved them away. "Don't come any closer. I'll see you once I've washed and changed."

They heard him clump along the hallway and out of the back door.

Anna came back in a few minutes later.

"He hates that job, you know. I'm not surprised, working with the blood and the skins and the smell all day. The sooner his father manages to get him a job at the sawmill the better. I mean, there's nothing wrong with the tannery exactly, everyone's got to start somewhere, but it's so *dirty* – you should see what they throw in the river, no wonder the eels have gone – and it's no place for a clever lad like Magnus. There's much better pay at the mill, and a chance to advance yourself; he could end up managing it one day. That's what Magnus needs, a job with prospects so that when he marries he'll be able to look after his family properly."

Smile frozen on her face, Jess saw Freya's eyes slide to her briefly, and then away again. She tried to think of something to say, for a pause had developed in Anna's monologue that she seemed to be expecting Jess to fill.

"It's a shame about the eels," she said weakly, and heard Freya sniggering beside her.

She was rescued by the return of Magnus himself, washed and changed, wet hair sticking everywhere and smelling strongly of soap.

Freya leapt to her feet to hug him, pulling his head down by his wet hair so that she could give him a kiss. Jess got to her feet more hesitantly, horribly self-conscious, wondering what to do.

Oh don't be ridiculous, girl. You've always given him a hug before. Why should it be different now?

With a determined smile, she gave him a slightly awkward hug and suddenly everything was all right again.

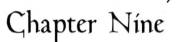

Chapter Nine

Finn finished checking the barrier at the pool and looked around to make sure everything was as it should be. Except that it wasn't, of course. He knew it wasn't. The wound on his neck was healing at last, but the real damage was hidden.

The halter had weakened him. He'd thought that what had happened the day that Rowan was here was a fluke, and so he'd challenged another wolf a couple of days ago, when he was on his own. He'd managed to subdue it, but it had taken all his strength to do it in human form, and left him exhausted. If another wolf had appeared then…

What if the halter had done him permanent damage? He couldn't guard the gateway any more, that much was certain.

He should tell his mother. Perhaps she'd know what to do. But he didn't want to tell her about this. She was already furious with him.

"How could you be so stupid as to go back up there so soon after you took Freya? I should have forbidden you to go to the Upper World long ago. Don't think I don't know how much time you've wasted up there, obsessed with that other girl when you should have been here, helping your own people. It ends now. You will not go there. Do not cross me, Finn. You are Nykur. The fact that your father came from the Upper World makes no difference. You are Nykur."

"I'm sorry," he had said. *"I never meant this to happen. I did the wrong thing, I know, but she was just there and I thought…*

Nothing went wrong when the boys were taken. I thought this would be the same. I never thought anyone would try to get her back."

"Thought? If only you would think. But you spend your life in a trance. Forget the girl. It is time you took a wife. "

"That's what I was trying to do! I want Jess as my wife."

His mother's face was implacable. "I forbid it. You must take a Nykur wife. I'll hear no more about this girl."

A sound shocked him back to the present, the whimper of an animal in pain. It didn't sound like any animal he recognised, though.

He stood still, listening. When the sound came again, he could tell where the animal must be: behind one of the great briar bushes. He moved towards it cautiously, giving the thorns a wide berth.

Nothing could have prepared him for what he saw as he came round the bush. It wasn't an animal: it was Rowan, in human shape. She was curled into a ball, her dark hair wet and tangled. Her skin was covered in scarlet weals and blisters.

Finn gasped in shock.

"Rowan! Rowan, what happened?"

She opened her eyes, saw him, and tried to speak, but her voice only emerged as a painful whisper.

He bent down to pick her up.

"Hush now. Don't worry. Mother will know what to do."

Magnus had a half day off. He and the girls had planned to climb the hill behind Dundee, but when the time came, Freya stayed behind, pleading a sudden headache.

Jess didn't believe a word of it, but Freya returned her

suspicious stare with a look of blank-faced innocence. She still didn't believe a word of it, but she had to admit she'd been outmanoeuvred.

She ploughed grumpily up the hill, answering Magnus's questions curtly and making no attempt to keep the conversation going until, three quarters of the way there, he caught her arm and swung her round to face him.

"You can go back, you know. You don't have to be here if you don't want to be."

He looked so worried that all her anger drained away on the spot.

"I'm sorry... I do want to be here. I just..." She shook her head, smiling. "Never mind. Come on – I'll race you to the top."

She couldn't compete with Magnus's long legs of course, and he laughed at her as she dropped, panting, to the ground at the top of the hill some minutes later.

"I hope you've got something to eat and drink in that bag," she gasped.

Still laughing, he unslung the canvas bag he'd had over his shoulder and passed it to her.

Jess looked inside.

"Water, that's a start. Apples." She sniffed at a slab of cake. "Fruit cake." She lifted out the final package. "And pie."

"Rabbit pie."

"My goodness, what a feast. Was the whole family meant to be coming? If you've remembered a knife as well I'm going to be really impressed."

With a flourish, Magnus produced a clasp knife from his pocket.

"Well, that settles it. I am genuinely impressed. And amazed. Actually, I think I'm mainly amazed. You never used to be this organised."

He sat down beside her.

"Well, I suppose my mother did most of it, really."

"But you remembered to bring it. And you remembered the knife. I'm still impressed."

They looked at each other for a long moment.

"Jess... I..."

"I'm starving," she broke in. "Go on – cut up that pie."

They didn't linger once they'd eaten. A cold wind had got up, and the clouds moving in towards Dundee promised rain.

Jess looked down at the town as Magnus repacked the remains of their meal.

"I like it better from up here," she said. "Where you can't tell how noisy and smelly it is."

"You wouldn't want to live here, then?" Magnus asked, coming up beside her.

Jess shook her head.

"Neither do I," he went on, to her surprise. "I was thinking of moving back to Kirriemuir."

Jess turned to look at him properly, pushing her hair out of her eyes as the wind tugged at it.

"Wouldn't you earn more money here? If you get a job in the sawmill?"

He shrugged. "Probably. But there's more to life than money. I've been trying to convince myself that I like Dundee, but every time I visit Kirriemuir it feels like coming home."

"Then you should come back," she heard herself say.

"How would you feel about having me around again?"

She opened her mouth to say something facetious in reply, but stopped when she looked into his eyes. After a few seconds, she gave him a proper answer.

"I'd like that very much."

"That's good," Magnus said, and then the rain arrived. He grabbed her hand and they ran for it.

"Keep still, Sorrel," said Jess, giving the cow she was milking a whack on the flank. "I know I left you for a week, but I'm back now. Anyway, it could have been much worse – you could have had Ashe milking you instead of Mother."

She and Freya had got back yesterday afternoon, and life at Westgarth had closed back around her already. She'd woken to a dusting of snow that morning, though it soon melted once the sun was properly up.

Last night at supper, when she was telling the family about her visit, she'd made the mistake of saying that Magnus might be moving back to Kirriemuir, and then had to endure falsely casual questions from her mother and pointed ones from Ashe. She thought of Magnus for a while, there in the warmth of the cow-smelling shed, trying not to let her imagination run away with her. At least it had a bit more to work on now: he had held her hand, and put an arm round her waist as they ran home through the rain from the top of the hill. He'd even kissed her – just once – just before they got to his house, and she hadn't felt the least bit like slapping his face in response. She found her heart beating faster at the memory. Heavens, Freya would say she was turning into a proper girl.

Now that she was home though, something else tugged at her mind. She tried to ignore it. She had been able to push it out of her head in Dundee, but now that she was back, she couldn't avoid thinking about him.

Finn.

His face haunted her. The events at Roseroot Pool might be over as far as the rest of the world was concerned, but Jess realised she would have no peace until she found out what had happened to Finn. She had to go back to Roseroot Pool and find him.

It took her another two days to find a free afternoon to go to the pool. Birch leaves crunched under her feet, still crisped with frost here in the shadows. Fallen larch needles lay in golden drifts; now only the pines kept theirs. Soon more wolves would come down from the high slopes where they hunted in the summer, and the livestock would need careful watching.

She remembered Finn talking about wolves in his world. He had said they were different from the wolves she knew.

Jess stepped out from the trees at the edge of the little meadow that bounded the pool on this side and walked to the margin. Something was terribly wrong. In the water drifted the bodies of fish, sickly silver, dull eyed in death.

What could have happened to the pool? She wondered briefly if it was some vengeance of the Nykur for her stealing back Freya, but that made no sense. The pool was their gateway to this world; why on earth would they damage it?

As she moved along the edge her foot crunched on something. She looked down at what seemed at first to be a lump of ice. It couldn't be, of course. She crouched to study it more closely.

Surely not?

Jess licked a finger and wiped it over the grey-white lump, licked it again and spat.

She knew what it was. It was a salt lick from the farm. What was it doing here? As she straightened, she began to notice more fragments here and there at the water's edge. A horrible suspicion began to take shape in her mind as she looked at the dead pool.

Scanning the ground, she moved along the margin of the pool, noticing lumps of salt, and one or two large boot prints where the ground was soft, and finally, shocking her to a halt, a little patch of coarse powder that looked just like the rat poison they used on the farm.

Exactly like it.

Her flesh crawled.

"Finn!" she yelled to the poisoned water. "Finn, where are you? I didn't do this, Finn, do you hear me? I didn't do this. I never meant you any harm. I'm sorry. I'm so sorry."

Her words fell to earth like dead birds. Nothing stirred. No one answered. Finn didn't answer.

Of course he didn't answer. How could he now? He must be trapped under the poisoned water.

Without stopping to think what she was doing, Jess began to wade out, still calling Finn's name. She pulled her feet free of the muddy bottom and swam out to the middle, then stopped, treading water.

What was she doing? What was she thinking? She'd swum here before. There was no way through to the Kelpie world without Finn. Even if there was, she was mad to consider going.

She took a deep breath and dived.

The water pulled her down immediately, spun her over and round until she had no idea which way was up. She whirled like a leaf caught in the current that shouldn't be there at all. And then the water simply spat her out, and she fell through air to land with a thump on dry ground.

What had she done? How had she done it?

She lay still for a minute, getting her breath back, before she sat up. She should be soaking, but she wasn't even damp. Around her breathed the Kelpie – the Nykur – world, shimmering as disconcertingly as it had the first time.

It didn't look like autumn here. The great trees still had their leaves, the huge briar bushes were still heavy with flowers. She could smell their odd musky scent from where she sat.

Slowly, Jess got to her feet and looked round, trying to find her bearings. The trees stretched away in all directions. She would have to be very careful not to get lost. She thought of calling Finn's name, but she didn't want to disturb the silence. She remembered what he'd said about wolves in the forest.

Jess looked around for a sharp stone, so that she could mark the tree trunks and find her way back. She picked up a short, thick branch as well. She wasn't sure it would be of much use against wolves, but it made her feel better.

From behind her came the sound of running water. She headed for it, scraping marks into the tree bark every twenty paces or so.

Her common sense was reasserting itself more every minute. What on earth had made her do this? She had never thought it would work, of course. But why had she even tried? These Kelpies were no friends to humans. They'd stolen Freya, and Jess had taken her back and hurt one of them in the process. What would they do if they found her here? This was the stupidest thing she'd done in her whole life.

No it wasn't. Finn's fate mattered to her. She had to find out what had happened to him. She didn't want to be haunted by a Kelpie for the rest of her days, like her gran had been.

Jess came to the edge of a stream. The rose bushes grew thick along its banks. She hadn't been here before, but surely this stream would take her back to Roseroot Pool.

And if it didn't? Would she wander the forest until she died?

"How did you get here?"

Jess gasped and jumped, heart racing. Finn stood among the trees, a look of utter disbelief on his face.

"I… I came through the pool."

"That's impossible." He walked slowly towards her.

So he was alive. Relief washed through her. But he looked drawn and tense.

"You couldn't have come through the pool," he said.

"But I did. I swam out and dived and I was here. I didn't think it would work: I've swum there before and nothing happened."

"It shouldn't be possible," said Finn. He was within arm's length now. Was he dangerous? Jess took a step back.

"Only Nykur can travel through the gateways alone. I would know if you had Nykur blood." His hand went to his neck and as he pulled at his tunic Jess saw the angry red mark that the halter had left.

"Could it be because of that?" She pointed. "When I trapped you, maybe it did something to me as well as you. It gave me power over you. Maybe it gave me some of your power as well."

She expected him to scoff at the idea, but he simply stared at her.

"Why are you here?" he asked abruptly.

"I…" What should she say? "I was afraid that I'd killed you with the halter. I only wanted Freya back, I didn't mean to hurt… anyone. I'm sorry. And then I saw what had happened to the pool…" She felt her skin glow with shame, as though she was the one who had poisoned the pool. "I wanted to know if you were all right."

He nodded. "I am. But my sister's sick. She went through the water and it burned her."

Jess was aghast. "I… I'm so sorry."

"You should go. If anyone else finds you here…"

Suddenly she felt danger all around her.

"Yes. Of course."

"The river here will take you back." She dropped the branch and the stone, and he walked with her to the bank in silence. *She cared,* Finn thought. *She'd come back because she cared about what she'd done to him.* He felt a surge of hope.

"You mustn't come back." He forced the words out, though they were the very opposite of what he wanted to tell her. "I don't know what my parents would do if they found you here."

Jess stepped down into the water.

"I'm sorry, Finn. I never meant this to happen." There was

so much more that she wanted to say, but she couldn't find the words.

He nodded. "Just go."

And so she did, and came to the surface again and saw brambles and dead fish. She was back in her own world. In the water her father had poisoned.

As she pulled herself out of the water and stood dripping, fury possessed Jess. She took one last, long look at the ruin of Roseroot Pool and turned for home.

When Jess reached the farmyard, she ran around the back of the barn and there he was, holding one end of the big pull saw, sharing a joke with the man on the other end.

He stopped as he saw Jess running towards him, her face white with anger.

"What's wrong? What's happened to you?" he demanded.

"What's *wrong*?" she repeated, incredulous. "You've poisoned Roseroot Pool. How could you?"

"What do you…"

"Don't pretend you don't know." She was almost screaming now. "Salt. Rat poison. How dare you? Do you know what you've done to them?"

So suddenly that she hardly saw the movement, her father raised his hand and slapped her hard across the cheek. Jess gasped and put her hand to her face, shocked into silence.

"You will never speak to me like that again," Ian said coldly. "Never. Do you understand? Get back to the house and stay there."

And he turned on his heel and went back to the saw as though she had ceased to exist.

There was a knock on the door. Jess ignored it, staring out of her bedroom window into the evening darkness.

She'd run straight up to her room after the dreadful

encounter with her father, and had stayed there, ignoring her mother's calls to supper and Ashe's none-too-subtle periods of listening at the door. If she touched her cheek, she imagined she could still feel the print of her father's hand on her skin. She didn't want to see him. She didn't want to see anyone.

Jess heard the sound of the door opening, and turned over on the bed so that her back was towards it and she was facing the window properly. She heard the creak of someone sitting down in the chair, but whoever it was didn't speak.

Silence stretched thin. Three minutes, four, five.

Curiosity got the better of her and she turned her head on the pillow.

It was her gran.

Jess sat up slowly.

"How long were you thinking of staying in here?" said Ellen, in a noticeably unsympathetic voice.

"I… I don't know," said Jess, taken aback.

"It's no use expecting your father to back down, you know that," Ellen continued briskly. "It wouldn't do any good even if he did. He can't undo what he's done."

"Did you know what he was going to do?"

"He didn't tell me, if that's what you mean. But I guessed."

"Why didn't you stop him?"

"And how could I have done that, even if I'd wanted to?"

It took a few seconds for that to sink in properly.

"You think what he did was *right*?"

"Life will be safer for the children here if the Kelpies have no way through to our world. Of course, what Ian did to the pond won't poison it forever, but it will keep them away for a while. They might decide it's not worth the risk at all any more."

Jess felt as though she'd been struck all over again.

"But… you've seen one of them. You know what they are,

that they have their own world. Euan is part of that world. Surely you care what happens to them?"

Ellen looked at Jess curiously.

"Do you think they care about us?"

"Yes, of course." Doubt surfaced in her mind. She had no real reason to think that. "That is… they *must*. Finn said he used to watch us on the farm. He was interested in us."

"That isn't the same as *caring*, my dear," her grandmother said quietly.

Jess stared down at her bed, confused. Ellen was right. Of course it wasn't the same. What had made her think it was?

"You've been through a very strange time," Ellen went on. "You've done something extraordinary. But you need to step back into your old life now for everybody's sake, especially your own. You need to let go, let the Kelpies drift out of your memory. It's what I did eventually. It's what you must do now." She got up stiffly and went out.

Jess lay on the bed thinking about what Ellen had said for a long time after her grandmother had left.

The hours she had spent in the Nykur world had been incredibly vivid. She couldn't imagine why Finn had ever spent time in this grubby, muffled place where she lived, when he had that pristine world of his own.

If she let go, let her memories of the world below the water fade as Ellen wanted, life would go back to normal much more easily.

But was that what *she* wanted?

She could keep her memory of Finn and the Nykur world fresh if she tried, but what was the point? She would probably never see him again. Why would he want anything more to do with her after all the trouble she had brought down on him?

Your life is here… now… Think about it sensibly, Jess. You can't live here properly with your mind full of phantoms. She's right. It's best if you let go.

And in her mind, she packed her memories of Finn and his world into a little box and pushed it into the dimmest corner of her brain, to lie there and gather dust until she could no longer find it.

Winter

Chapter Ten

The last leaves fell. Skeins of geese passed over the farm at dusk and dawn, going to and from their roosts. Darkness came early now and lingered late, and lamplight glowed from the farmhouse windows more often than not. Sometimes, deep in the night, wolves howled from the hillside, and folk from some of the higher farms talked about huge black wolves leading packs that raided right into the steadings.

On most mornings there was a skin of ice on the water trough in the yard, though it still melted during the day. The family slept cocooned in quilts, and stepped unwillingly out in the mornings on to cold floors, hopping from foot to foot while they dressed as quickly as possible.

Magnus came back to Kirriemuir with tales of black wolves being seen near Dundee. He started to work in the shop with Arnor, displacing the ancient Lachlan to some vague, unspecified job that seemed to involve a good deal of sitting and dozing. He came out to Westgarth regularly too; Ian always seemed to have something that he needed help with.

Magnus was staying in Arnor and Freya's spare room, but whenever Jess visited the house his belongings seemed to be spread everywhere, to Freya's exasperation.

"The next time he leaves muddy boots in the hall, they're going down the well," she said, as Jess stepped over them when she arrived one morning.

Jess sniffed. "Do I smell burning?"

Freya gave a wail and rushed for the kitchen.

"Biscuits," she said, pulling a tray out of the oven.

Jess gave them a calculating look.

"They're almost not quite burnt. I'm sure Magnus will eat them."

Freya rolled her eyes.

"It's about time he went out to Westgarth for a couple of days so that I can re-stock the kitchen. Your mother's had time to build up supplies again since his last visit."

Jess smiled.

"She seems to have got the idea now that she needs to cook twice as much if Magnus is going to be there. Ashe tries to compete, of course, but you'd have to scoop his legs out to give him any chance."

She picked up a biscuit, juggling it from hand to hand to cool.

"He said he was going to come out this weekend if Arnor could spare him."

"Oh, he will," said Freya in a voice that suggested Arnor would have little say in the matter. "I'll see to that."

Jess took an experimental bite of biscuit. "Hardly burnt at all. Just tastes a bit smoky. You could try it as a new flavour in the shop."

"You're as bad as Magnus," said Freya. "The two of you deserve each other."

Jess was slowly getting used to comments like this, and didn't go red at all unless they came when she wasn't expecting them.

Anyway, she and Magnus were practically performing a public service for Freya: keeping an eagle-eyed watch on their tentatively developing relationship took Freya's mind off the recent past. To most people she seemed back to normal now, and the speculation about her mysterious disappearance had died down. Sometimes, though, Jess caught her staring absently, suspended in the middle of some forgotten task, and knew the gap in her memory still gnawed at her.

Jess gazed out of the window, suspended halfway through drying the soup pot. Outside, fat white flakes settled unhurriedly, falling from a yellow-grey sky, but she wasn't really looking at them.

It was two days until Yule, and Magnus had set off for Dundee the previous morning. He'd be gone for a week or more, depending on the weather. It was hard to make definite travel plans at this time of year.

"Tsk!" said Ellen, shaking her head. "Miles away."

"She's thinking about Magnus," said Ashe in a high whining voice. "Oh Magnus..." He clasped his hands to his heart and rolled his eyes. "I can't sleep for thinking about you."

"Brat!" spat Jess, rousing as suddenly as a striking adder and flicking the corner of a wet towel at the back of his head with deadly accuracy.

She hadn't been thinking about Magnus. She'd been wondering if it was snowing in the Kelpie world. She'd tried, really tried, to forget about Finn and his world, but she couldn't do it. In truth, she didn't want to.

"It's time you two got out of the kitchen," said Ellen. "Get wrapped up and go and fetch in the holly so we can decorate the house. Get some ivy and mistletoe too."

"About time," Ashe said forcefully. "Coming, Jess?"

"As if you have to ask," she said, their altercation forgotten.

She fetched a couple of sickles from the tool shed while Ashe found an empty sack, and they set off into the still-falling snow.

There was a group of holly trees about half a mile along the road towards Kirriemuir. Jess had been checking them each time she passed, seeing the berries swell and colour. Holly was no good without berries.

"I think the snow's stopping," said Jess as they walked.

She was right. The steady drift of flakes slackened and then stopped as the sky grew a little brighter.

They reached the trees soon after and set to work. After ten minutes they had half a sackful.

"That's enough, Ashe."

"No, we need more than that."

"No we don't: look how much we've already got. There'll be no branches left for next winter if you carry on."

A twig cracked, somewhere off in the trees, and Jess turned sharply, her heart jolting.

"What's wrong with you?" Ashe asked, mystified.

"Didn't you hear that?"

"All I heard was a twig snapping. What's wrong?"

She looked round wildly.

"Hello?" she shouted.

"Have you gone off your head?" Ashe looked at her with frank incredulity. "It was a twig. There are trees all round us. Who are you expecting to be here? There won't be any wolves round here yet."

"Nothing. No one." She shrugged. "It just took me by surprise."

Ashe gave her another scathing look.

"Come on, let's get the mistletoe and ivy now."

The best place to look was the old doocot near the orchard. Roofless and birdless, its crumbling walls were swagged with long trailers of ivy. And inside the orchard there were three apple trees with mistletoe growing on them. Jess and Ashe walked towards them, spilling bits of ivy, arguing about who should climb up for the mistletoe, something they both wanted to do.

They stopped and looked up.

"Oh no," said Jess.

"That's useless," said Ashe.

The mistletoe was there all right, but there wasn't a single white berry left on it.

"There were plenty of berries the other day," said Ashe. "I checked."

They walked round the trees. Not a berry anywhere.

"I know where there's some more," Ashe said eagerly. "Maybe there'll be berries left there."

"Where?"

"Those two big ash trees up the hill." He pointed. "Look. You can just see the tops from here."

"I've never noticed."

"It's there. Not too high either. Come on."

"Just a minute, Ashe. We don't have time. Or at least, *you* don't. Remember Mother wants to cut your hair this afternoon. You take the ivy back and I'll go for the mistletoe."

"But I want to come too."

"I know, but you don't want to be in trouble at this time of year, do you…"

"Oh, all right."

Jess festooned Ashe with all the ivy he could carry, and sent him on his way back to the house, then set off for the path that led up the hill towards the ash trees.

She didn't come this way very often and it took her a little while to find the trees once she left the path, but when she did so, she could see the mistletoe, not too far up, just as Ashe had said, and still covered in berries.

Jess checked that the sickle was securely stuck through her belt, tucked her skirts up, and a minute later she was level with the mistletoe, deciding where to cut. She only needed a bunch to hang over the lintel so that anyone who passed into the house would have good luck.

She cut what she wanted and clambered awkwardly back down, dropping some of the mistletoe. Bending to pick it up, she saw a print near the base of the tree. Not one of her own footprints. Not a hoof print, shod or unshod. A paw print, large and very fresh. *Very* fresh. It hadn't been there when she started to climb, she was sure.

Jess straightened up cautiously, trying to quiet her breathing as she pulled the sickle from her belt. Her eyes darted around as she looked for any sign of the animal that had left the track – no, *tracks* – for now she could see a trail of them, leading out from the dense cover of the surrounding pine trees, and then back into the woods a bit further away.

There was no sound to alert her, but suddenly Jess *knew* that something was watching her. She turned very slowly and saw, no more than ten metres away from her, three great black wolves, crouched and intent.

Chapter Eleven

Jess and the wolves stared at each other unmoving for what seemed a very long time. For the first few seconds her mind was blank with panic.

She tightened her grip on the sickle and stayed absolutely still as she tried to think.

A thought hammered for attention. *They're huge. I've never been this close to wolves, but surely they're not this big?* She thought of the stories of black wolves she'd heard recently and had to remind herself that no one could remember an adult being attacked near here.

What are you going to do?

I suppose they might be frightened of me if I ran at them and shouted.

She looked at their steady yellow eyes.

On the other hand, they might not be.

Just at the moment, that seemed more likely.

If I stay still, maybe they'll go away. But how can I be sure they've really gone?

The wolves looked as though they could outlast her if it came to a waiting contest anyway.

That just left the tree.

If she could get back up there she'd be safe, and eventually someone would come looking for her. But to get up there she would have to move. And she would have to let go of the sickle. Could she get herself off the ground fast enough?

One of the wolves took a single, tentative step towards her. That decided Jess. The longer she waited, the less chance she would have.

Treading carefully, she began to move backwards, trying to remember exactly how she had climbed, but not daring to look round. As she did so, the lead wolf took another step and began to growl softly in the back of its throat, the ruff of coarse hair round its neck rising as it did so.

Jess kept moving, trying not to think of the moment when she would have to turn her back if she was going to climb.

All three wolves were on the move now. The growling was louder and their lips were drawn back from their long teeth.

Backing away, Jess stumbled on a root and almost fell. She saw the first wolf poised to leap at her.

And then another huge dark shape erupted from the trees on her right and hurled itself at the wolves without a second's hesitation.

Everything happened so quickly that it took Jess a few seconds to work out what she was seeing. She stared transfixed at the scene before her. Rearing and plunging in the clearing, trying to strike the wolves with its great hooves, was a black horse. It was gaunt and shabby-maned and she could see its ribs under its dull coat as it reared and plunged again. The wolves leapt at the horse and it spun madly, trying to avoid the snapping jaws and raking claws.

Jess took all of this in in a few numb seconds before she came to her senses and fled. She ran as fast as she could, jumping logs, heedless of the branches that whipped at her, imagining that any second she would feel a wolf's hot breath at her back, hear it gaining on her.

On she ran, breath sobbing. She burst out of the trees and kept going, somehow, until she reached the farmyard.

Gathering a single, ragged breath, she shouted, "Wolves!" and heard the sound of tools being dropped and running footsteps. Ian and the two farmhands ran towards her, looking round as though they expected the wolves to be there with her.

"Are you all right?" Ian yelled before he even reached her.

She nodded and suddenly realised that she was still clutching not only the sickle, but the mistletoe too.

"What happened?" her father asked as Martha, Ellen and Ashe appeared from the house.

"I was up the hill behind the orchard cutting mistletoe. There were three of them watching me – huge black ones." Jess stopped to gather more breath and for the first time wondered what else to say.

She needn't have worried. Ian didn't seem to need any more information.

"Get weapons," he said to the other men. "We'll go up there now." He turned back to Jess. "You're sure you're all right? They've never come down this early before."

Jess nodded, her mind in turmoil.

"Stay inside just now," Ian said to Martha, and turned to go after the men.

Martha ushered her family inside and latched the door behind them, then gently took the sickle and the mistletoe from Jess, who was still grimly clinging to them.

"Take your jacket off and come and sit down in the kitchen. You've had quite a fright," she said.

Jess followed her mother into the kitchen.

"They seemed much bigger than normal wolves, but maybe that's just because they were so close. And they were black," she said.

"Like Arnor's wolf?" Ashe suggested.

"Yes." Jess hadn't thought of that before. "Just like Arnor's wolf."

Ellen spooned honey into a cup of one of her herb teas.

"Sit, lass. This will settle your nerves," she said to Jess.

Jess sat obediently, and to her relief, everyone left her alone to collect herself, leaving Jess to think properly about what had happened under the trees.

The horse that had come to her rescue couldn't possibly just have been a normal horse. But it wasn't Finn either. The creature that had saved her had been a poor, broken-down-looking beast. Only the colour was the same. It couldn't be him. She thought fleetingly of the red weal left by the halter around his neck.

Another Nykur then? But why would any of the others help her? In fact, why would Finn even help her? She had brought them nothing but harm.

What was happening up on the hill now? She shivered, wondering what the men would find. Had the horse managed to escape? She felt sick suddenly, thinking of those slashing teeth and claws.

Should she tell her grandmother what had really happened? Jess thought about Ellen's reaction to the poisoning of Roseroot Pool and decided to stay silent.

The men came back about two hours later.

"Well?" asked Martha, as Ian kicked his boots off at the back door.

"The snow's all churned up where Jess was. There's a fair bit of blood; they must have caught something. No sign of it though. We followed their tracks back up the hill for a bit, then we lost the trail. It looked like they were heading back up to the tops."

What about hoof prints? Jess wanted to ask. *What about the horse?* She waited for her father to say something else, but he didn't. He looked at Jess keenly, as though trying to guess her thoughts. She returned his gaze, hoping she looked calmer than she felt.

"I don't know what's brought them right down this early in the winter," Ian said, "But from now on no one leaves the farmyard without letting me know."

That night, it began to snow in earnest. Great stacks of yellow-grey cloud pushed down from the north until the sky seemed impossibly full. Then the wind died and the snow began.

It was still falling when they got up next morning. A sickly light reflected from the clouds and the lying snow, which was now ankle deep. Tracks across the yard showed where Ian and the other men had already crossed and recrossed this morning.

It wasn't a day when anyone planned to be outside much anyway. The animals were always put in the barn together for Yuletide, even when the weather was mild and there were no wolves to worry about. It was a busy day, though: family tradition dictated that the house had to be cleaned from attic to cellar and the evening meal prepared before sunset.

Everyone helped, even Ian, once he had sent the farmhands off to their families for Yuletide. Jess and Ashe stood in the falling snow, shaking dust out of the rugs.

"I wonder how deep it's going to get? Ashe mused.

"I don't suppose it'll go on much longer. It's still too early in the winter for a big fall."

They went back in, passing under the precious bunch of mistletoe, now fastened securely to the lintel. In the house, holly was pinned over every window and chimney. Ivy twined round the handrail all the way up the stairs, and garlanded the Yule Log, waiting now in the big fireplace in the sitting room. It would be lit at sunset from a chip of wood from last year's log, carefully hoarded since then for this task.

Jess and Ashe put the rugs back. Ian was busy with the log,

splitting off a fragment for next year, and cutting slits in the bark for later.

He looked up.

"Have you written your wishes?"

"Not yet," said Ashe.

"I'll see if Mother wants any help first," said Jess.

He nodded and went back to what he'd been doing.

The whole house smelled of beeswax polish and cut wood and spices and, underlying it all, the fugitive chilly tang of snow. Everything seemed calm in the kitchen. On the table stood a blue-and-white plate piled high with a pyramid of ginger biscuits that made Jess's mouth water as she looked at them.

"Just one?" she said pleadingly, knowing it was hopeless.

"Not until sunset. It's only another hour or so; you'll manage." Martha was merciless.

"But I'm hungry."

"Then eat an apple. Or some bread."

"Not that hungry." She looked out of the window. "It's going to be hard to know when it *is* sunset, there's so much cloud. At least the snow's stopped though."

"Hurry up, Jess!" came Ian's voice up the stairs. "It's nearly sunset."

"All right. I'll be there in a minute."

She stared hard at the paper she was holding, then crossed out the wish she had started to write. Dipping her pen back in the ink pot, she wrote quickly, before she could change her mind and do the sensible thing.

I wish I could see Finn again.

As soon as the ink was dry she folded the paper up small, then hurried downstairs.

She was last to arrive. The rest of the family sat or stood round the unlit log, each holding a folded paper. A single beeswax candle burned on top of the fireplace.

Ashe went eagerly forward and poked his wish into one of the slits Ian had cut in the log earlier. Next came Jess, then Martha, Ian and finally Ellen.

"And oldest kindles the flame."

Ian handed the little piece of last year's log to Ellen, who held it in the candle flame until it caught. Once it was well alight she bent and touched it to the bed of kindling on which the log lay, moving across to set it alight in several places. Finally she set it, still burning, on top of the new Yule Log.

"May our Yule be merry and our winter short," she said, and Yule had begun.

Martha brought mulled ale and the biscuits from the kitchen while Ellen lit the oil lamps. The room glowed with firelight and lamplight.

"At last," sighed Jess, reaching for the first of many biscuits, and they settled down to watch until the wishes burned and the ashes flew away up the chimney, carrying their words into the sky.

It snowed for most of Yule day itself, though no one really cared, immersed in food and drink.

The light faded, the Yule Log diminished to nothing but embers, and still the snow fell. Yule was over.

As she closed her shutters, Jess wondered if the wolves had sensed this weather coming.

Where were they now, and where was the bedraggled horse?

Chapter Twelve

They woke next morning to a frozen wasteland. The snow had stopped at some point during the night, but a wind had sprung up to blow what had already fallen into drifts against the sides of buildings.

There was ice on the inside of Jess's window. She and Freya had half arranged to see each other tomorrow, but no one would be able to go anywhere with the snow this deep.

It took Ian over half an hour to dig a narrow path to the barn. Muffled in several layers of clothing, Jess and Ashe edged along it, the snow on either side well above their knees, to help with the animals.

They were all used to hard winters of course, and this was nothing out of the ordinary, but it was early for this much snowfall. If it went on all through the winter… As they worked, Ian started to calculate how much fodder they'd need to see them through. Just as well it had been a good summer for hay.

"Go on, you two. I'll finish up," he said, heaving a fork load of dirty straw onto the barrow.

Jess and Ashe pulled hats and gloves back on and went outside. The sky lowered, promising more snow soon. As Jess stood looking around, Ashe took his chance and shoved a handful of snow down her neck. Taken by surprise, she let out a scream, and whirled round for revenge, only to find that he had thrown himself off the path and was flailing his way through the unbroken snow, laughing like a madman.

"Just wait!" she shrieked after him. "You'll be sorry you started this."

With the advantage of longer legs and the fact that Ashe was having to clear a path for both of them, she was soon close enough to start snowballing him hard.

He roared in outrage and turned round to retaliate. They were so close that most of the snow found its mark and they were soon covered and almost helpless with laughter. Finally, one of Jess's snowballs caught Ashe on the side of the head. He lost his balance and toppled backwards into the unbroken snow, only his boots sticking out.

Jess went over and helped him lever himself out.

"That was good fun," he said, and Jess nodded, breathless.

"I doubt Mother'll agree when she sees how wet we are," she added ruefully, but Ashe wasn't listening.

He stared at the orchard, each tree swaddled in white.

"What's that?" he said, pointing.

Jess followed his finger to something dark lying in the snow between the trees. She couldn't make out what it was.

Ashe was already pushing his way closer. He got as far as the half-buried fence at the edge of the farmyard and stopped, Jess just behind him.

"It's someone," said Ashe in a quavery voice. "Someone's died in the orchard."

"Go and get Father. Run." Jess climbed over the fence and fought her way through the snow towards the still thing on the ground. Her heart gave a lurch of horror as she drew close enough to make out more of the motionless figure.

Let me be wrong. Please let me be wrong.

She heard her father coming up behind her and pushed forward even harder until she was close enough to be sure that she wasn't wrong.

It was Finn.

Jess came to a halt as though she'd run up against a wall.

"Let me go first, Jess," Ian said, catching her up, and ploughed on towards Finn.

Jess was almost too frightened to go any further, but she forced herself on. It was another five minutes before they reached him and in all that time he hadn't moved at all.

He lay half buried in the snow, curled on his side. Jess pulled off a glove and put out a hand to touch his face. His lips were blue, his skin like ice, utterly without colour.

Ian reached inside Finn's sodden tunic, feeling for any pulse in his throat. For ten long seconds he was silent, then Jess heard him catch his breath.

"He's not dead." He got to his feet, began scraping snow away so that he could get a proper hold of Finn.

"Go back to the house. Tell your mother. Help her get things ready. She'll know what needs to be done."

Shocked to a place beyond words, Jess turned and pushed her way as fast as possible back along the narrow alley they had carved through the snow.

Ashe stood by the fence, wide-eyed.

"Is he dead?"

"No." Jess didn't pause.

"Who is he?" Ashe called after her.

"I don't know," she lied.

Martha listened intently to Jess's half-coherent speech. "Your room," she said.

"What? Why?"

"It's warmest. Go and see to the stove. I'll get extra quilts."

By the time Ian tramped heavily into the kitchen carrying Finn, trailed by a silent Ashe, everything was ready.

"Take him up to Jess's room," Martha said.

Ian nodded, breathing too hard for speech, preparing for one last effort.

Jess was tucking the hot-water bottles into the bed when Martha pushed the door open for Ian.

"Put him on the floor until we get his clothes off."

Ian set his burden down as gently as he could and stood back to catch his breath and warm his frozen hands as the women fumbled with the buttons on the boy's jacket and tunic.

"He's not even dressed to be out in this. What was he thinking?" Martha wondered. "Oh my…"

They had pulled off his sodden jacket, aware that it and the tunic under it were torn and stained, and now they saw why. The boy's arms and shoulders were scored with the marks of claws and teeth.

Jess stared at him in horror.

"What's happened to the poor soul? Ian, should we clean these wounds?"

"Let's see if he's going to live first. Jess, go and get a towel."

"Don't you need me to help?"

"Not just now. Go and get it."

By the time she came back, Finn's clothes lay in an oozing heap on the floor, and he was in her bed, buried under layers of quilts, only his head visible. Jess stared at his white face. He was almost unrecognisable, his face gaunt and sunken-eyed. She thought of the broken-down look of the horse that had saved her from the wolves. That had been Finn, she knew it. He must have been ill before that. What could have happened to him to reduce him to this? Guiltily, she remembered the halter.

"Will he be all right?" she asked.

"We don't know yet," Martha replied gently. "He's so cold. All we can do is get him warm and hope that he's strong enough to survive." She looked down at the still figure and grimaced. "I"m afraid he doesn't look very strong."

"You're wrong," Jess said vehemently before she had time to think about it.

Martha looked at her curiously. "Let's hope so," she said.

"I'm going to change," said Ian, on his way out of the room.

Martha held out her hand for the towel and began to rub Finn's hair dry. "I'll sit with him just now. Go down and keep an eye on Ashe, would you? And help your grandmother with the cooking."

Not knowing what else to do, Jess went out, shutting the door behind her.

"Is he dead?" asked Ashe as soon as she went into the kitchen.

She fought down an overwhelming urge to slap him.

"No."

"Has he woken up yet?"

"No."

"Can I go and see him?"

"There's nothing to see. Go and ask Mother if you really want to. She's staying with him."

"Until he dies?"

Jess closed her eyes and counted very slowly to five.

"Until he wakes up."

To her relief, Ashe ran out of the room.

Jess managed to keep herself busy enough to be distracted for almost an hour, but that was as much as she could stand. Outside her room she took a deep breath and pinned on a smile before she opened the door.

"I'll sit with him just now. You go downstairs."

"All right." Martha got up. "He hasn't moved."

They both stared at the white face on the pillow.

Jess sat down, waited until she heard her mother's footsteps descending the stairs.

"Finn?" she whispered. "Finn, it's me, Jess. Wake up; please wake up."

There was no response.

Cautiously she touched his hair, then his cheek. His flesh chilled her fingers. He looked like a corpse.

Panicked by the thought that perhaps he had died without her noticing, she bent her head close to his mouth, her hair brushing his face as she listened for his breathing.

Yes; yes. He was breathing.

She sat down again, clasping her trembling fingers in her lap until they stopped shaking.

"What were you doing here?" she said to him, although she knew he couldn't hear her. "What's happened to you?"

She thought with a pang of her Yule wish.

For a few minutes she sat silently, watching him, then she lifted a corner of the heaped covers to look at the wounds of the wolf attack, trying not to imagine what it must have felt like for Finn as they tore at his flesh. Her eyes strayed to his neck and she caught her breath.

A thin scar, dark red, circled his throat. She bit her lip, fighting back tears. What had she done to him? Would it be her fault if he died? She tucked the covers firmly round him again.

"Please don't die, Finn. Please."

She had no idea how much time passed before she heard Ellen's slow footsteps on the stairs. She'd long since run out of tears, but she wiped her eyes anyway, convinced they would have left some trace.

"Any change?" Ellen asked as she came in.

Jess shook her head.

Ellen peered at Finn. "I don't know. I think his colour's better. Away you go and get something to eat."

Jess didn't want to leave, but she couldn't say that without having to think of some way to explain it, so she went without argument.

Downstairs, she noticed dully that the snow had begun again. She ate soup and bread mechanically while Ian showed Ashe how to mend the hinges on a cupboard door. Martha was kneading bread dough at the other end of the big table, catching up with the chores she'd set aside to tend to the half-frozen boy. Jess felt as though she was in a bubble outside which normal life was taking place, sweeping her along, completely separate, in its wake.

She finished eating.

"I'll go up and take over from Gran again."

"No. Just leave her. She's probably having a wee nap just now. Anyway, you've the dishes to do while I finish this."

Jess closed her mouth and got on with her task, hoping to be allowed back up once she had finished, but Martha seemed to have an endless list of things for her to do, and then it was time to fight her way across to the barn with Ian to see to the cows again. When she got back, Martha had taken over from Ellen and she was thwarted once more.

At a loss, she watched Ellen slicing cheese and vegetables for a pie and found herself rolling out pastry.

"I'll get the dish." Ellen went to the cupboard as the door opened and Martha came into the kitchen.

"He's awake," she said with a smile, and went to put on the kettle.

"Is he going to be all right?" Jess asked.

"Well, he's escaped freezing to death, but he's half starved, and injured. We'll have to see."

"Has he said anything?" Jess's heart thumped.

"The poor boy can barely understand what's happening. He hasn't said how he got here. But he did manage to tell me that he's called Finn."

There was a crash as the pie dish fell from Ellen's fingers and smashed on the floor.

They all stared at the fragments for a second.

"That was clumsy of me," said Ellen in a flat voice.

"Don't worry, Ellen. Jess, clear it up, would you?" Martha made tea and spooned in honey. "I'll take this up to him. Best if he just has to cope with one person for now."

She went out, leaving an ominous silence behind her in the kitchen.

Jess knelt and began picking up bits of shattered dish, bending so that her hair swung forwards to hide her face.

"Is it him?" Ellen said sharply.

"Yes."

"You've brought a Kelpie into this house?"

Jess looked up. "What should I have done? Left him to die in the snow?"

"Left him for his own people to find."

"You know he would have died if we hadn't found him when we did. It's my fault he's hurt. He saved my life."

"What are you talking about, girl? He wouldn't have done anything to help you if you hadn't forced him to it with the halter."

"No, no, not that. The wolves. They weren't just watching me. They were going to attack me. A horse came out of nowhere and fought them."

Ellen sat down, staring at Jess.

"Are you sure about this?"

Jess nodded.

"I knew it would just cause trouble if I told anyone what had really happened. I don't know what there was to see when father went up there. He never said anything." She picked up another couple of pieces of the dish. "The horse already looked ill – I didn't think it could be Finn at first." She got to her feet.

"Are you going to tell them?"

There was a long silence.

"He looks harmless enough for the moment... I don't know."

"Please, Gran. He couldn't do us any harm even if he wanted to, and I'm sure he doesn't mean to."

"I won't tell anyone today. I want to talk to him before I make my mind up to anything beyond that."

"Oh, thank you. Thank you." Jess put down the broken dish and hugged Ellen with relief.

"Come on. We'd better get this pie finished, or your mother will wonder what we've been doing."

Jess wiped her sweaty hands on her apron, tried to look calm, and pushed open the door to her room. Martha looked up and put a finger to her lips, and for a fleeting second, Jess thought her mother must be able to hear her heart hammering, before she realised that she was to be quiet because Finn was asleep.

Jess couldn't help staring at him. He was a more normal colour, but he still looked terrible, his face hollowed by hunger.

"I'll sit with him now," she said.

"All right. Let me know if he wakes up again."

When she was sure that Martha was safely downstairs, Jess leaned close to the bed.

"Finn," she whispered. "It's me, Jess. Wake up, Finn. I need to talk to you."

Nothing. Gently, she touched his cheek. At last, it was warm. He moved his head on the pillow a little at her touch, and she pulled her fingers away as though she'd been burned.

He opened his eyes.

Chapter Thirteen

At first, he didn't look at her. His gaze was on the ceiling, and she could see him struggling to remember where he was, and why.

"Finn," she said quietly.

He turned his head towards the sound, and she saw his eyes widen.

"Jess?"

He knew her. That was a start. She smiled at him. Before she could say anything, he spoke again, his words slurred and uncertain.

"I'm sorry. I should have stayed away. I didn't mean to cause trouble."

"You haven't. No one knows who you are." There was no reason to trouble him with the truth just now. "What happened to you? I don't mean the cold, or the wolves. Something else has happened to you."

He closed his eyes and turned his face away from her.

"I'm sorry. I didn't mean to…" *Come on, Jess,* she thought. *This isn't what he needs just now.*

"Are you warm enough?"

A smile. "Yes. I'd forgotten what it was like to be warm."

She bit back the questions she longed to ask, and concentrated instead on practical ones.

"Are you hungry? Thirsty?"

"Starving."

She looked at his hollowed face.

"You actually mean that. I'll go and get you something."

"No. Don't go yet. Sit for a bit longer first."

Jess nodded and sat back, wondering what it was safe to say, but after a couple of minutes he fell asleep anyway. She waited impatiently for him to wake again. How long would it take?

She heard footsteps on the stairs and Martha's head came round the door.

"Anything?"

"He did wake up, but only for a couple of minutes."

She came fully into the room and Jess saw that she was carrying a basin of water.

"Your father's coming up to help me clean his wounds."

"I can help."

"No, thank you." Ian stumped in with the medicine chest under one arm.

"Go and heat some soup," Martha said. "The poor soul needs some food."

Jess had no choice but to let herself be banished again.

Finn ran. He drifted between horse and human form. He didn't know if he was being hunted, or searching for something that kept sliding out of sight.

Wolves howled around him, but he couldn't see them, although he could feel them tearing at his flesh.

"Get out! See what you've done."

"Finn!"

Voices crowded into his head, shouting at him.

"Come back!"

"Get out!"

The wolves slashed at him again. He couldn't get free.

"No!"

He realised he'd spoken aloud and opened his eyes. Jess's mother was there again, the father with her this time.

"Jess?"

"She's downstairs," said her mother. "Lie still now. It looks as though a dog attacked you. We need to clean the bites."

"Wolves."

"What?"

"Not dogs. Wolves."

Jess's mother looked at him curiously, and he wondered if it had been a mistake to tell her.

"Anyway, we need to clean them up, or they'll make you ill. More ill." She started to wash the bites. "Your family must be worried about you. Where are you from? We'll get word to them as soon as we can."

"I don't have any family." He closed his eyes so he wouldn't have to think any more. It was too difficult.

He slept and woke and slept again. Sometimes the mother was there, sometimes Jess. He ate some soup, slept again.

"Wake up, lad. I want to talk to you."

Something poked him in the chest. He ignored it.

"Come on. You've slept for long enough." Poke. "Wake up and talk to me."

It seemed he didn't have a choice. He fought his eyes open and recoiled slightly. There was a face very close to him, bright-eyed and wrinkled with age. It retreated a bit as its owner sat down again.

"That's better. Are you thirsty? Here." She gave him a drink of water. "I'm Jess's grandmother. I know who you are. Why are you here?"

Surely she knew how they'd found him?

"They brought me here. I was in the orchard."

"Yes, I know that." Impatient. "What were you doing

out there in that weather? Why weren't you with your own people?"

I know who you are. Why aren't you with your own people? The words sank in slowly.

"Ah, now you understand me. I can see from your face. Why aren't you in your own world?"

Finn shut his eyes, hoping that he'd fall asleep and she'd be gone when he woke again.

Poke.

It was no good.

"I can't go back."

"Because the pool was poisoned? You're trapped here?"

He nodded. Let her think that. It was easier.

"And what do you mean to do to us? To Jess?"

She had his attention properly now. He opened his eyes.

"Nothing. Nothing, I swear. I don't mean you any harm. I didn't mean to come here." His voice was agitated now. "I don't want to cause trouble."

The old woman looked keenly at him. After a moment she spoke again.

"I believe you." She put a hand on his brow. "You've got a fever. I'll go and make you something for it." She got up. "Do I have your word that you'll leave here as soon as you're well enough, and do us no harm?"

"Yes. Yes, of course," he said, though in his heart, Finn knew how desperately difficult it would be to leave Jess.

"Very well. No one knows about you but Jess and I. We'll keep it like that."

"Well?" said Jess, looking up as Ellen came into the sitting room, where she sat darning socks very badly.

Ellen sat down.

"He swears he means us no harm and he'll leave as soon as

he's able. I'm inclined to believe him, but in any case he's too sick to be any sort of threat just now."

"How sick is he?"

"Oh, I dare say he'll be all right. He's young, and healthy despite what's happened to him recently."

"So you won't tell the others?"

"No. If he saved your life, I owe him that – so long as he keeps his part of the bargain. Now, I said I'd take him up some willow tea. He's feverish – not that that's surprising, rolling about in the snow for days with untended wolf bites. Will you take it? I can't be bothered to climb all those stairs again just now. Here – give me that darning. You're making a right mess of it."

Jess relinquished the sock with a grateful smile, and five minutes later she was stepping into her room with a cup of her grandmother's tea.

Finn had a heap of pillows under his head so that he could see out of the window to the snowy landscape beyond. He lay looking out now, and his expression as he did so made Jess stop, feeling that she was intruding on something private and painful.

"Tea," she said abruptly. He looked at her, half smiled and pulled himself up a bit so he could drink.

"I met your grandmother," he said dryly.

"She's decided you're not here to murder us all," Jess replied.

He took a drink and grimaced.

"That's horrible. What is it?"

"Willow tea. Gran says you've got a fever."

He made a face and took another swallow.

"How deep is the snow now?" he asked.

"Hip deep on me. There hasn't been any fresh stuff for over a day, but it's not moving either."

He started to say something, then changed his mind.

"Will there be snow in your world just now?" Jess filled the silence.

He shook his head.

"Things freeze – the whole river freezes sometimes – but it never snows. I remember seeing snow for the first time. I couldn't think what it could be. I watched you and your brother playing in it." He smiled, remembering. "You've no idea how much I wanted to come and join in. You both looked so happy."

He'd heard the screams and run towards the farmyard through the cold white that wasn't fog or rain, afraid that Jess was hurt or frightened, not stopping to think.

Then he'd seen the two of them throwing handfuls of the stuff at each other, flushed and elated, and realised as he ducked out of sight that the screams were screams of delight.

"I wish you *had* joined in," Jess said. "When was that?"

"Years ago," he said. "You must have been about nine or ten. I thought snow was beautiful back then, but I've seen enough of it now."

He took another swallow of tea and held the cup out to Jess. "Please – I can't drink any more of it. But don't tell your grandmother."

"I won't."

They lapsed into silence, and Finn went back to looking out of the window. Jess watched his expression change back to the melancholy one she'd seen when she came in.

"You'll be able to go home soon. Once you're well, and some of the snow's gone. Your family must be worried about you."

"I can't go back," he said flatly.

He kept his face turned away from her and she waited silently for him to speak again, afraid that if she pressed him, he would clam up altogether.

"I warned you," his mother had said. "I warned you that you would bring disaster down on all of us. Look at what you have done to your sister. All for a human girl. Go. Leave our world, since you think so little of it. Go through that poisoned water to the Upper World and stay there. Leave the Nykur world and never return. You are no longer Nykur."

Finn stood mute. He couldn't fully comprehend what he had just heard.

"Get out."

"But…"

His mother turned her back.

"Please. I didn't mean…"

She ignored him completely.

He backed away towards the door, too stunned to protest any more. In the bed, Rowan realised at last what was happening.

"Finn, stop! Come back."

"Hush," said her mother, sitting down beside her. "He has to go."

He ran then, Rowan's cries ringing in his ears.

There was no one to look after him when he burst out of the hideous water, burned and retching. He forced himself into horse shape so that he could get away from the pool and lay wincing among the mosses and trees high on a hillside while his skin healed.

He had no idea what to do, cast adrift like this. It was difficult to think, cold and hurt and hungry as he was. He wandered without purpose, managing to find enough food to keep himself alive, but not much more than that.

The farm pulled at him like a lodestone. He kept his distance as much as he could, but he couldn't bring himself to go elsewhere: every time he glimpsed her in the distance, his resolve to leave evaporated.

And then came the day when he'd smelled the wolves and knew they had broken through from his world and he'd had to fight them to save Jess; and then came the snow. He'd given up, decided to let himself slide away into a final sleep, but he'd needed one last look…

And he'd even got that wrong, for he woke again, trouble following him as usual.

Jess had sat waiting for Finn to answer. Now she couldn't bear his silence any longer.

"It's my fault, isn't it? For putting that thing round your neck."

He pushed himself up on the pillows, taking in her expression properly at last.

"No. No, Jess, it isn't that." He reached out and caught one of her hands. "I took Freya, and there was trouble about that. We weren't supposed to take anyone else. I disobeyed that. And then the pool was poisoned, and my sister was hurt… My family have disowned me. I can never go back to the Nykur world."

Saying the words aloud made it seem even more final. He let go of her hand and turned his face to the window so that she wouldn't see the tears in his eyes.

Jess had no idea what to say. Every word she knew was useless.

"I'm tired. Let me sleep," he managed to say.

She went without a word, and closed the door behind her.

Ellen limped upstairs, muttering to herself. The boy's fever was gone, but he was – there was no other word for it – *moping*. Ellen had no patience with mopers. When she pushed open the door he was lying in bed staring listlessly out of the window. Again. He didn't even turn his head to see who it was.

She flung back the quilts that covered him. That got his attention.

"Come on, horse boy. You can't lie there forever. Time to get up."

"I can't," he said dully.

"Rubbish. You just don't want to."

"There's no point."

"You made me a promise – remember? To leave when you were well enough. I want you to make some effort to keep it."

"But," and she poked him in the chest to emphasise the point, "I don't want you to just wander off to die in the snow somewhere."

"Why not?"

"Because Jess would never forgive herself. She thinks this is her fault."

"It's not. I've told her."

"I know that. But when you leave here, you leave with some purpose other than to pine away. You're not the first person to lose their family, you know. It happens every day."

"Not like this."

"No, not like this. Always different, and always terrible for the one who's left behind. You'll have to make yourself a new life. It's been done before."

"Why do you care what I do anyway?"

"I told you: I don't want to see Jess miserable, or blaming herself for something that's not her fault." Ellen paused.

"But there's another thing too. You know we're kin. Your father is my cousin. I was there when he was taken." There was no friendliness in her eyes or voice now. "Most people thought I was lying when I told them what had happened. Some of them thought I'd done away with poor Euan myself. The tales followed me for years. So, horse boy, I don't have much patience with your self-pity. We all make our own way in life, whatever it gives us to work with."

She went out of the room without another word, leaving Finn to consider his future.

Chapter Fourteen

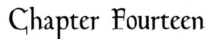

"Someone's coming!" Ashe came thudding down the stairs. "There's someone on a horse coming along the road."

He ran back upstairs, his mother close behind. She peered out of the window. He was right. Against the dead white of the snow, a small black blot stood out, moving where the road should be.

"Can you see who it is?" Ashe asked, craning his neck for a better view.

Martha shook her head. "No. They're too far away just now. Go and tell your father and Jess. Whoever it is, it'll be good to see someone else's face for a bit of variety."

Ashe dashed off, delighted to have some news to spread.

On the way back down the stairs, Martha paused and knocked on Jess's door, then went in.

Ellen sat in the chair. Finn was up and dressed, standing by the window. Martha was intrigued. Her mother-in-law had spent a lot of time in here talking to the boy in the last few days, though she answered in the vaguest of terms when Martha asked her what they spoke about.

Alhough Martha didn't want to throw Finn out, friendless, into the winter weather, she was pleased to see signs that he would soon be well enough to go. His presence had disturbed the atmosphere of the house in a way that she was hard put to explain. Neither Ian nor Ashe – of course – seemed aware of anything, and looked at her in bafflement when she asked them if they had noticed. Jess however, was fractious and preoccupied, quite unlike her usual self. As for Ellen, Martha didn't know what to make of her attitude to Finn: she radiated disapproval of him for reasons that were entirely obscure to Martha, and yet she spent hours talking to him.

They'd all been shut in together for far too long.

"There's someone on the road," she told Ellen and Finn. "It looks as though we've got a visitor."

By the time Ashe came back with his father and sister, Martha had recognised the rider.

"It's Magnus," she said as they came in. "He's riding a carthorse."

"Magnus?" said Jess blankly. "I'll… I'll just…"

"Go on," said her mother, shooing her up the stairs.

When had she last thought about Magnus? Jess pounded upstairs to Ashe's room, which she was temporarily sharing. She hauled off the filthy dress she'd been wearing to help with the animals, pulled on a clean one and tidied her hair. There; she was ready.

She sat down abruptly on the bed, feeling anything but ready. Her mind had been concentrated on Finn for days. It had never crossed her mind that he and Magnus might meet.

Fleetingly she thought of running out into the snow to hide until one of them – either of them – left.

"Stop being stupid," she said aloud. "As far as Magnus is concerned, Finn is just some boy you found in the snow."

And as far as Finn was concerned, who was Magnus? She'd never talked to him about Magnus, and regretted that more and more with each second that passed.

She risked a look in the mirror and was surprised to see that she didn't look like the unravelling lunatic she felt she was. There were still a few minutes to spare. She went into her own room and found Finn alone. He turned from the window and looked at her.

"You look…"

"Clean. I know – it's quite a change. We've a visitor coming, you see," Jess said. "You don't count any more. You've been here too long." She stopped and took a breath. "That came out wrong. I just meant… We haven't been making an effort to look our best for you."

"You look – you've always looked… fine."

Fine? What did that mean?

There was an unquiet silence.

"The visitor – Magnus – he's Freya's cousin. I've known him a long time – we all have. He's a… He's my…" She couldn't say the word.

"Oh. I see. I'm… I'll… Don't worry, I'll keep out of the way."

"No. I didn't mean that. Just…"

"I'll be careful what I say."

"Yes… yes, that's what I meant." But it wasn't. At all.

"I'd better go," she said. "But you don't have to hide up here. Magnus is an easy person to like. Come and meet him." It was probably best to get it over with, after all.

"I'll come down in a while. You should have some time with him first. All of you, I mean."

"All right. But you can't hide up here for too long. Ashe will tell Magnus all about you as soon as he gets through the door. You're the most exciting thing that's happened in ages. Happened to him."

They parted with uncertain smiles, and Jess ran down the stairs.

The family clustered round the open front door, watching the big horse almost burrowing its way through the snow towards them. Magnus jumped down to help it force its way through the last drift.

"You're all well?" he asked, breathing hard.

"We are that," Ian replied.

"And all the better for seeing you," added Martha. "Come inside. Ian will see to the horse."

Magnus let himself be led indoors. Jess hung back as Martha and Ellen fussed around him.

Ashe was jumping up and down in an effort to be noticed.

"You'll never guess," he said, very loudly. "We found someone dead in the snow. Well, not dead, just nearly dead and the wolves had tried to kill him, the wolves have come down already, and his name's Finn and he's upstairs. He's nearly better now. I can take you up to meet him." He stopped bouncing. "If you want."

Magnus opened his mouth and closed it again, unsure who he should respond to first.

Ellen caught Ashe's arm and steered him firmly towards the kitchen, Martha following.

"I'll get the kettle on. Hot drink," she said, disappearing along the passage.

Jess looked at Magnus.

"I wanted to see if you were all right. All of you, I mean," he said, beginning to peel off layers of clothing.

"We're fine. Yes." Jess came forward to help him.

"Good." Magnus stopped, halfway out of a jacket, and put his arms round her instead. "I mean, I knew you would be, but…" He stopped talking and kissed her instead, and for a moment she forgot to be worried about Finn.

"Magnus!" Martha called suddenly.

They jumped apart.

"Come and tell us what's been happening in Kirriemuir."

Magnus grinned at Jess. "Coming," he called. He took her hand and towed her along to the kitchen.

"Freya sends her love," he said to everyone as he entered.

"She's in bed with a cough or I don't know how I could have stopped her coming."

Martha put a steaming mug and a huge slab of fruit cake down in front of him. "Eat. Drink. Get warm. And then tell us everything."

"It sounds as if you've more to tell me than I have to tell you. Who's the mysterious not-dead person upstairs?"

"He's called Finn." Ashe wasn't having anyone else get the chance to pass on such important information. "He's staying in Jess's room."

"Which means I'm staying in Ashe's room," Jess added. "Which is lovely, of course. Peaceful."

Magnus gave her a conspiratorial smile.

"I hope you're staying the night?" Ian asked as he came in from stabling the horse.

"Please – if I won't be in the way," Magnus replied. "The horse will be tired. I'd have to turn straight round to be back before nightfall, and with what you've said about the wolves…"

There was a chorus of protest that he should even consider such a thing and the matter was settled. He'd only stay one night though: any longer and Freya would have Arnor out searching for him.

"Why don't you take Magnus up to meet Finn?" Ellen asked Jess with counterfeit innocence. "It'll give us a chance to cook enough extra food for him."

Magnus laughed, taking Ellen's jibe, as always, in good part.

Jess had been hoping that everyone had somehow forgotten about Finn. Despite what she had said to him earlier, this was not a meeting that she was looking forward to.

"I'll take him," Ashe volunteered selflessly.

"We'll both go with Magnus," she said quickly. "Off you go and tell Finn we're coming up."

Following more slowly, Jess gave Magnus a quick version of

Finn's official story. When they went into Jess's room Finn and Ashe were sitting on the window seat. Finn was whittling at something with Ashe's knife.

"Look." Ashe pointed, forgetting all about introductions. "He's made a horse. It's really good." He took it from Finn and held it up for Magnus's approval. "This is Magnus."

"I've heard a lot about you," said Finn, rising.

Who from? Jess wondered. It certainly wasn't her.

Magnus studied Finn curiously. "I like the horse."

Finn shrugged. "It's something to do to pass the time."

"You must all be bored to distraction stuck out here in the snow for so long," Magnus said.

"Well, it's certainly good to have a different face to look at," said Jess with feeling.

"But we've had Finn," Ashe said, as though she might have forgotten. "He's been a different face."

"Yes, I suppose he has," said Magnus, looking suddenly thoughtful.

"Jess!" Her father bellowed up the stairs.

"What?"

"Your mother needs a hand."

Not now.

"Can't it wait for a bit?" She didn't want these two talking without her there as a buffer.

"No. Come down please."

"I'll have to go. Magnus, are you coming?"

"I'll stay here for a bit with Finn and Ashe. I'm sure we'll find plenty to talk about."

She waited for Finn to help her by saying he was tired, but he didn't say anything. Seething inwardly, she forced a smile.

"Right. That's fine then."

She remembered just in time that it would look childish to slam the door.

"The snow in Dundee's nothing compared to here," said Magnus later on as they ate. "Not even up to your knees. But the folk are terrified that it will bring the wolves. A lot of people won't go out at all after dark."

"How bad *are* the wolves?" Ian asked.

"I've got nothing to go by but the stories – there hasn't been a real wolf winter since we moved there."

"What stories?" asked Finn.

"Great black wolves that come into the town and attack people – adults as well as children. No one knows where they come from – they just appear, create havoc, then disappear again."

Jess looked curiously at Finn, trying to read his expression. He had said little during the meal, and she had been aware of him quietly observing Magnus.

Later, Jess was making up a bed for Magnus in the sitting room. Normally he would have shared Ashe's room, but of course...

"You'll be glad to get your room back when he goes," Magnus observed, watching Jess shove a pillow into its cover. "It can't have been easy having a stranger stuck in the house with you. Mind you, he's been here so long he hardly counts as a stranger any more, does he?"

Was she imagining it, or was there an edge to his voice?

"Why does Ellen watch Finn all the time?" he continued.

Jess stopped what she was doing, taken aback. "Does she? I hadn't noticed that."

"It's as though she doesn't approve of him, or she's watching to see what he's going to do." Magnus shook his head. "Maybe she knows something about him that none of the rest of you do. His Dark Secret. I'm pretty sure Ellen would be able to uncover anyone's Dark Secret."

Jess gave a forced laugh. Magnus was straying in a direction she didn't like at all.

"And what about *your* Dark Secret?" she asked with false lightness. "Has she uncovered that?"

"Ages ago," said Magnus ruefully. "Long before you realised what it was."

"Idiot." Jess threw the pillow at him.

Magnus left next morning after what he called a fortifying breakfast.

"He's so fortified it's a wonder the horse's legs don't buckle," Martha observed as they waved him off.

Having their isolation broken had cheered everyone up, as had the discovery that the snow was beginning to melt. That would bring its own problems, but at least they'd be different problems.

Jess was alone in the barn when the door opened and Finn came in. He'd kept to his room when Magnus was leaving. Jess smiled at him and carried on with what she was doing. She wanted to know what he thought of Magnus, but she didn't want to ask him.

Finn watched her work in silence for a moment, then said abruptly, "I'm going to leave in two or three days."

Jess stopped.

"That's too soon. You're not ready – and the weather…"

"I'm better now, and the snow's melting. Magnus will tell people in Kirriemuir that I'm here. I have to go before things get complicated."

"You can't leave just like that. Where will you go? What will you do?"

Finn shrugged. "I'll find something. I'll find a place. Your grandmother…" He searched for words. "She made me see things differently. I'll be all right."

"You *can't* go. I… I'm…" Words stuck at the back of her throat.

They looked at each other for several seconds.

"I'll let you get on." Finn turned to leave.

After he'd gone, she stood for a long time staring at the closed door.

It wouldn't take him long to pack. He had no belongings, except what Jess's family had pressed on him: a couple of changes of clothing, two blankets, a knife and a tinderbox, some food and a little money. He'd tried to refuse the money when Ellen had given it to him, but she had insisted.

He could hardly bear to look at Jess, yet at the same time he wanted to look at her constantly. He might never see her again. It was *likely* that he would never see her again. He had to go far enough from here that whatever it was that seemed to bind him to her would be broken.

She mustn't know how he felt. That would be the final indignity. He imagined the look of horror on her face; or, worse still, pity.

His thoughts turned to his family. Rowan, surely, would be better by now. He wondered if his mother regretted banishing him. Probably not; he'd never known her change her mind about anything. And his father would never go against his mother's wishes.

That part of his life was finished. He had to forget that he had ever been Nykur. From now on, he could be only human, could only live in this grey, muffled, grubby world.

It would be like being only half alive.

Finn let two more days pass before he forced himself to leave. He had thought about simply going without telling anyone, but that seemed poor payment for their kindness. He told them as they sat at breakfast, then went to gather his things together, while Ian, Martha and Jess went to see to the animals.

He could hear some sort of commotion going on downstairs, but he ignored it, anxious now to be on his way, until Ashe's voice caught his attention.

"Magnus only left a couple of days ago. Why is he back so soon?"

Finn heard a girl's voice replying.

"Because I couldn't come before and I wanted to see Jess. Go and fetch her out of the smokehouse or wherever she is, please, Ashe. I'll wait upstairs for her."

"Won't Magnus fetch her?"

"He's seeing to the horse first. That's too long to wait. I haven't seen her in ages. Please?"

"All right."

Light footsteps ran up the stairs, and the door opened.

Finn froze, appalled. It was Freya.

The girl didn't see him at first; he was standing at the head of the bed by the pack he'd so recently strapped up. She came in, humming under her breath, and crossed to the window.

Jess had said Freya didn't remember anything about him or the Nykur world, but what if she was wrong? Could he sneak out past her and make a run for it?

At that moment, the girl turned round and gasped.

"What a fright! What are you doing, sneaking up like that?"

"I… I wasn't…" Finn stammered.

Freya put a hand to her mouth.

"Oh no – I forgot. You've had Jess's room, haven't you? I'm Freya, Jess's friend." She eyed the pack by his hand. "I see I've only just come in time to meet you."

The question of whether she remembered him seemed to be settled.

"Where are you heading? We came in the cart; we could take you as far as Kirriemuir if that's the way you're going. Of course, you'd have to wait until later." She stopped and smiled.

"I'm talking too much. I haven't spoken to anyone but Magnus and my father for days. There – I'll be quiet now and you can say something."

She waited.

He was very good looking, Freya thought. Too thin though; but then, he'd been ill.

She waited. Was he shy, or just stupid?

"Jess often talks about you. She'll be pleased to see you." His hand went to his neck, and she noticed a fine scar like a red silk thread encircling it. Something about it nagged at her memory.

"I'd better go," he was saying. He seemed nervous. He picked up the pack and started for the door.

"I'll come down with you," Freya said.

He touched the scar on his throat again. She wondered why he kept doing that.

In silence, they came out of Jess's room. Finn stood back to let Freya go down the stairs first. At the bottom, he turned to the right, intending to go straight out of the front door, desperate to be away from Freya.

"Surely you're going to say goodbye?"

He stopped reluctantly and turned to face her again.

"I already did that. I'm just going to go now. I don't want a fuss."

At that moment the back door was pushed violently open and Jess shot in, looking apprehensive. She glanced from Freya to Finn beyond her, read their expressions and relaxed a little.

Freya ran forward to hug her.

"You're just in time. Your guest is trying to sneak off without saying goodbye."

Jess looked helplessly at Finn over Freya's shoulder.

"I'm leaving now. I have to," he said.

Jess detached herself from Freya and went across to where Finn stood, trying to think of something she could say in front of Freya that would convey what she felt, whatever that was.

And Freya looked at the two of them standing there together as Finn touched the scar on his neck again.

And she remembered.

Chapter Fifteen

Freya remembered. Fragments, like pieces of a dream…

Finn clutching his throat as though it pained him… a dark haired girl smiling at her… water rushing around her, filling her mouth and nose, eyes and ears… a black horse in a bramble patch.

She shook her head, realised she had made some sort of sound. Finn and Jess stared at her.

Freya raised a finger and pointed shakily at Finn.

"I know you. I remember you. I… was with you."

She saw the colour leave his face.

"Freya?" Jess stepped forward. "What is it? What's wrong?"

"He was there. So were you. He took me somewhere."

Jess fought down panic.

"You've only just met him," she said desperately. "You should go, Finn. You need to be on your way."

Like an automaton, he picked up the pack again.

"No!" Freya's voice rose. "It was him." She was backing away now.

"Go, Finn," said Jess sharply.

"Freya, what is it?" Magnus had come in unnoticed, and was striding to Freya's side.

"It's him. When… when I was lost. I couldn't remember, but now I do. He was there. He took me somewhere."

Magnus's gaze followed Freya's pointing finger. He

stared at Finn as though he was seeing him for the first time.

"Magnus, she doesn't know what she's saying." Jess stepped in front of him. "Just go, Finn. I'll sort this out." She didn't dare turn to look at him. "It's a mistake, Magnus, that's all."

Magnus turned to Freya. "Are you sure it's him?"

She nodded, wild-eyed. "Of course I'm sure."

Magnus pushed Jess gently out of his path.

"Fetch your father," he said as he went past her.

"Magnus, wait."

He paid her no attention, but confronted Finn.

"Well? You heard what she said. Do you deny it?"

"Of course he denies it!" Jess yelled. "He hasn't done anything."

Finn said nothing.

For three or four seconds no one moved, then Magnus drew back his fist and felled Finn with a single blow.

Jess gasped and ran to where he lay.

"Freya," said Magnus, "go and get Ian. Now."

Freya looked blankly at him for a few seconds, then turned and ran.

Magnus glanced down at Jess as she tried to rouse the unconscious Finn.

"What's going on, Jess?" he asked.

She looked at him pleadingly.

"Let him go, Magnus, please. He hasn't done anything."

"How can you know that? Freya says he has. Why would you believe him instead of her?"

"What's happening down here?" A new voice, sharp: Ellen coming down from her room, disturbed by the shouting. She came far enough to take in the scene in the hallway and stopped.

"What's happened to the boy? Jess? Magnus? What's going on?"

Before either of them could answer, the back door crashed open and Ian burst in, Martha following, her arm round the whey-faced Freya.

"Did he try to get away? Does he deny it? What has he said?" Ian demanded.

"He hasn't said anything. He didn't get the chance," retorted Jess angrily.

"Why won't you believe what I'm saying, Jess?" Freya asked, coming forward.

"You… you said you couldn't remember anything about what had happened."

"I couldn't before, but once I saw him…"

"What do you remember now?"

Freya frowned, concentrating.

"Bits and pieces. Him." She pointed to Finn. "That mark on his neck. That's what made me remember. There was a girl with dark hair. She was kind to me. And there was a black horse somewhere."

Jess could almost feel Ellen's gaze burning into her skull. She avoided looking at her grandmother.

"But where were you, Freya?" she asked. "I found you in the forest, don't you remember?"

She watched Freya's uncertain face, hating herself for what she was doing to her friend.

Martha put her arm round Freya again.

"We can't decide anything like this," she said. "Ian, Magnus, carry Finn down to the cellar and lock him in. After that, Ian, you go to Kirriemuir and fetch Arnor."

"He's not there," said Magnus. "He set off for Forfar with Lachlan when we left to come here. They were going to stay the night with Lachlan's family."

"Even if I leave now, I won't get back from Forfar before nightfall," Ian said, frowning. "I'll have to stay the night there and come back with Arnor first thing tomorrow."

"Freya," Martha said, "Come and sit down with me and give yourself time to think properly. See if you can remember anything else."

"Jess, take a lamp down to the cellar," her father said.

Mind in a whirl, she did so. Ian and Magnus carried Finn down the steep stairs and laid him on the floor.

Jess watched her father lock the cellar door and put the key back on its hook, then say a distracted goodbye to Martha before setting off for Forfar.

What could she do? What could she do? She had never felt so helpless in her life.

She was staring blankly out of the back door towards the stables when an iron grip closed on her arm.

"We need to talk now," said Ellen. "Your father suspects what Finn really is. If Freya remembers any more, your parents are going to realise what they've been nursing in their own house."

"Maybe not," Jess said, more in hope than expectation. "Freya doesn't remember much. If she doesn't remember any more, maybe I can convince everyone she's wrong."

"Let's hope you're right. But what if the opposite happens, and she remembers *everything*? They will realise you knew what Finn was when they took him in."

Jess tried not to imagine her father's reaction if he found out. But that wasn't her biggest concern.

"Gran, what will they do to him if they find out everything?"

Ellen was silent.

"I have to get him out of here."

"Have some sense!" her grandmother snapped. "How could you possibly explain it to your family, to Freya, if you did that? And anyway, why would you risk so much for him?" She stared at Jess through narrowed eyes. "Has *he* enchanted *you* this time?"

"No. Don't be ridiculous," Jess said, trying to ignore the flush she could feel creeping up her throat. "But don't you think enough bad things have happened to him already?"

Ellen didn't answer.

"Surely you don't think he deserves to die?" Jess continued.

Ellen gave a weary sigh.

"Nothing will happen to the boy until Arnor gets here. Before he does, we need to know exactly what Freya remembers. Go and make some tea and take it in to them."

Jess took camomile tea into the sitting room where her mother and Freya sat side by side. Freya was absently chewing a thumbnail, evidently still trying to remember.

Jess gave her what she hoped was a reassuring smile.

"Have you remembered any more?" she asked, trying to look encouraging, while inwardly willing Freya's memory to fail her.

Freya shook her head.

"I don't know. It's all so confused. Just jumbled glimpses of things that don't go together and don't make sense."

The next few hours passed like one of those nightmares where time slows down and walking is like wading through treacle. A meal appeared at some point, and everyone gathered in the kitchen and ate, mostly in edgy silence. All the time Jess ached to know what was happening in the cellar.

When they had finished, Jess ladled soup into a bowl and put it on a tray to take down to Finn with some bread and cheese. Magnus got up to go with her.

"It's all right," she said. "I can manage."

"You're not going down there alone," Magnus said.

"Why not? He won't do anything to me."

"You don't know that. I'm coming with you."

Jess bit back a retort, realising she wouldn't change his mind.

Magnus unlocked the door and went down the stairs to the cellar with a lamp, a couple of steps in front of Jess with the tray.

Finn sat hunched against the wall on the opposite side of the cellar. He watched them come down the steps.

"I brought you some food," Jess said. It was so cold that she could see her breath hanging in the air.

"Thank you," he said.

In the lamplight, Jess could see the bruise on his jaw where Magnus had hit him, as she crossed to where he sat.

She put the tray down and stood there looking at him, desperate to speak to him privately, willing him to look at her properly so that he would see that, but he wouldn't look up.

"I'll bring you some blankets," she said.

"I'll wait here while you get them," Magnus said.

Jess was about to protest, then thought better of it, though she didn't want to leave the two of them alone together.

She went quickly up to her room. Keeping an ear open in case anyone came in unexpectedly, she scrawled a note.

I'll be back when everyone's asleep.
Don't worry – I'll get you out of here.

She folded it up small, and rolled it up in the middle of a couple of blankets.

"What have you done to her?" Magnus asked Finn in a voice he was carefully controlling.

"I didn't hurt her, I swear. Has she remembered anything yet?"

"I'm not talking about Freya. I'm talking about Jess."

Finn grew very still.

"What have you done to her that she would take your side against her best friend, against her family? I know you must have had a lot of time alone with her. She's got a good heart. Did you play on her sympathy, pretend to be more ill than you were? Is that how you've wormed your way into her heart? I've seen how she looks at you. How did you make her think she loves you?"

"I didn't... she doesn't!" said Finn, trying to salvage the situation for Jess. "You know I was about to leave. I don't mean her any harm. I don't mean any of you any harm."

"It's a bit late to be saying that, don't you think? We'll see what Arnor says, but I don't think you should be expecting to walk up these steps again."

When Jess got back to the cellar, neither Finn nor Magnus seemed to have moved. She put the blankets down beside Finn and went back upstairs without trying to talk to him again, Magnus close behind her. She managed not to look back as she heard the key turning and the click as Magnus put it back on its hook.

The rest of the evening passed in a blur and Jess was relieved to head up to bed with Freya. She said goodnight, then lay wide-eyed in the darkness waiting until it was safe to go to Finn.

Jess woke with a start, horrified to find that she had slept. She wanted to leap straight out of bed and run down to the cellar, but she forced herself to lie still.

The bar of moonlight that came through the crack in the

shutters had moved almost halfway across the room, so she must have slept for at least a couple of hours. From the sound of Freya's breathing, she was fast asleep.

Jess slid out of bed, reaching for a shawl to tie round her shoulders. Stepping around the creaky floorboards, she eased the door open and listened. Nothing. She crept down the stairs.

She went to the kitchen first, to light a candle. It would be pitch dark in the cellar; she wanted to be able to see Finn.

At the cellar door Jess stopped to listen again, but the house slept quietly around her. She took down the key. If anyone found her now, there could be no pretending. She went in and pulled the door closed behind her. The light from the candle didn't quite reach the bottom of the stairs.

"Finn?" she whispered loudly. "It's me."

There was some sort of movement from below, but no reply. Perhaps he was asleep. She went on down the stairs.

When she reached the bottom step she saw him sitting where he had been before, the blankets bundled round him.

"You shouldn't be down here," he said softly. "I don't want you to get in trouble."

"That doesn't matter. Come on." She held a hand out to him. "This is your chance to get away. If you're here when Arnor arrives, I don't know what will happen to you. You have to go now."

"But if they find you helped me to escape…"

"My gran asked me earlier if you'd enchanted me. If the worst comes to the worst, I'll say that you did. Now come on. It's freezing down here."

He took her hand and she helped him stiffly to his feet.

"Bring the blanket – it's freezing outside," she told him.

"There's no way I can thank you for this," said Finn.

"Just don't get caught," Jess replied.

They crept up the cellar stairs and through the kitchen to the back door. Unlocked as usual, it opened noiselessly.

Jess and Finn looked at each other.

"I don't know what to say," Jess murmured.

"Just say goodbye."

"Not like this."

They stared into each other's eyes.

"Please," Jess said. "Please wait for me at the pool. I'll get away somehow. Please. I might never see you again otherwise. Please."

"No. You mustn't. They'll know it was you who helped me."

"I don't care! You have to wait – I'll bring you some supplies. You need food, a knife, a tinderbox… it's too risky to get them just now, but I'll bring them tomorrow." She tried to pretend that it wasn't just an excuse.

"All right. I'll wait until noon."

"I'll be there. Now go!" she said, and watched him disappear into the darkness.

Jess swallowed her porridge the next morning as if it were ashes. She didn't suggest taking food down to Finn in the cellar, of course, and thankfully nor did anyone else.

As soon as possible, she sneaked upstairs for her jacket and a satchel and stuck her knife in a pocket. When she crept down again the kitchen was empty, and she grabbed some bread and cheese and a tinderbox, then went straight to the barn. She was in there for just long enough to reach down a threadbare old jacket of her father's that had hung there for months.

She peered cautiously round the barn door. Luck was on her side: no one was in sight. Without stopping to think, she went into the woods at a trot.

At first, Jess thought Finn hadn't waited after all. She reached Roseroot Pool and stood in the open, expecting him to step out from between the trees, but there was no sign of him. She looked around. The bramble thicket at the eastern end was bare of leaves now, a bleak, thorny tangle.

"Finn?" Jess called softly, and again, "Finn?"

After a few seconds she heard sounds of movement from the trees at the far side of the pond, and he was there suddenly, looking at her a little warily.

"I'll come round," he called, and she lost sight of him for a few seconds.

"I thought you would have seen sense and changed your mind by morning," he said with a tentative smile as he got close.

"Of course not!" she retorted, stung that he could think that of her. "I brought you this." She held the jacket out to him.

He put it on gratefully.

"And a knife; you'll need a knife wherever you're going." She handed it over with the rest of the things she'd brought him.

They stood silently then, until Finn said, "You should go now. You might get back before anyone realises you've gone."

Jess knew there was no hope of that, but she wasn't going to let her mind dwell on what would happen on her return.

"We should both go," she said, managing to return his smile. "So… I suppose we should say goodbye."

"Yes."

"Will I see you again?" She had tried not to ask, but in the end it was impossible.

Finn tried to think of something to say that wasn't simply *no*.

Jess took a step towards him.

"Good luck," she said. "Stay safe. Don't forget me, will you?"

"There's no chance of that," he said, and then his face changed and, without warning, he reached for her and pulled her into his arms. Jess gasped, taken by surprise, but didn't resist. Finn held her so tight that she could feel his heart beating, and for a second she thought he was going to kiss her. Then she saw his expression, fierce and watchful, focused somewhere behind her. She turned her head to see a blur of dark fur disappearing into the trees.

"What was that?" Jess asked, afraid that she already knew.

"A wolf." Finn was pulling her back from the pool as he spoke.

"Like the ones you saved me from before?" She looked around wildly.

He nodded. He was watching the pool intently, backing away from it, his hand on her arm.

Why was he watching the pool? Surely the danger was among the trees?

"Finn?"

He didn't answer, clutching her arm more tightly instead. Following his gaze, she saw the surface of the pool seething like a pot of boiling soup.

Finn swore under his breath and hauled her properly into the trees.

"What is it? What's happening?" she hissed in a terrified whisper.

He didn't answer, but there was no need. She could see for herself.

Three, four, five black heads broke the surface of the water, thickly furred, yellow-eyed. Five black wolves swam to the shallows and stalked out of the pool, shaking water from their coats. They stared towards the trees where Finn and Jess stood. Five muzzles rose, scenting the air.

"Run," said Finn.

Chapter Sixteen

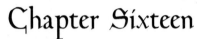

Jess ran. By her side, holding tightly to her hand, Finn kept pace with her easily. She had never run faster in her life, but she knew with awful certainty that it wasn't going to be fast enough. There were no climbable trees here to offer them refuge. The nearest point of safety was the farm itself.

Her breath was burning in her lungs, muscles labouring. The wolves couldn't have come after them straight away or surely they would already have caught up? Perhaps they hadn't followed them after all…

She heard a howl close behind her and abandoned that idea.

Finn was shouting something to her, pulling at her hand.

"Stop! You have to stop."

"You're mad!" she shrieked. "They'll tear us apart."

She saved the rest of her breath for running. Finn kept shouting.

"We're not fast enough like this. We have to stop so I can change. I can outrun them as a horse, even carrying you. Stop! It's our only chance."

She skidded to a halt among the slushy leaves.

He let go of her hand and closed his eyes.

Every muscle in Jess's body urged her to run. She ignored them and waited, watching Finn.

He was utterly still and then… And then he simply *flowed* into the form of the horse. However hard she tried afterwards, she couldn't think of any better way to explain it.

The dark horse stood beside her. As she reached out a hand to its mane, she saw the first of the wolves appear among the pines behind them.

She knotted her hand in Finn's mane, preparing to scramble up, and found that she was already astride his broad back. She felt the horse's muscles bunch beneath her and it sprang away as the first wolf leapt. Jess clung to Finn's mane, pressed as flat to his spine as was possible, aware of branches whipping past above her and the sound of the wolves behind them. She didn't dare turn round to see how close they were.

She was terrified, but at the same time exhilarated. Their wild careering progress was faster than anything she'd ever known, yet she didn't believe for a second that Finn would stumble, or take a path that would endanger her.

If he could just outrun the wolves...

Jess risked a look back and could no longer see the wolves. She expected Finn to slow down, but his pace didn't slacken. They'd reach the farm soon. He had to stop before that, or someone would see him. She began to shout at him to slow down, but he ignored her. Or maybe he didn't understand her when he was in horse form?

She could see the farm buildings now; the wolves were out of sight. She yelled at Finn over and over to stop, but he kept going. He jumped the fence into the farmyard and slid to a halt near the kitchen door, and suddenly Jess was stumbling as her feet hit the ground and a hand grabbed her arm to steady her; Finn, back in human form, panting for breath.

"Get inside," he gasped. "These are no ordinary wolves. Get inside."

"You've got to get away again. Go! Quickly!"

The barn door opened.

Magnus appeared, drawn out by the sound of hooves in the yard. He took in the scene in front of him and reached an inevitable, wrong conclusion.

"Let her go!" he yelled, and ran towards them.

Six wolves swerved around the edge of the stable and stopped.

And Ashe stepped out of the stable door.

Time seemed to slow.

Magnus had almost reached Jess and Finn when he heard Jess scream, "Ashe – get back inside!" and turned to follow her gaze.

The wolves looked at Ashe.

Finn closed his eyes, ignoring Magnus, ignoring Jess, and concentrated on changing…

…and the black horse shot across the yard to where Ashe stood petrified in front of the wolves.

One of the wolves sprang, crashed into the solid bone and muscle of the horse and was kicked aside.

Ashe reached an uncertain hand out to the horse; the world twisted round him, and he was on its back and moving through a rush of wind to the frozen figures of Jess and Magnus near the farmhouse door. Just as suddenly he was on the ground again and Finn was yelling urgently.

"Get inside!"

Magnus scooped Ashe off his feet and they all piled into the kitchen. Over Magnus's shoulder, Ashe saw the wolves racing towards them just before the door slammed shut.

Finn was still yelling.

"Close the shutters or they'll break in through the windows. Close the shutters."

"What just happened out there?" Magnus demanded, staring at Finn in utter disbelief, but such was the urgency in Finn's voice that he hurried to close the kitchen shutters. As he dropped the bar that secured them a wolf crashed against the door.

"The other rooms," Finn went on. "Close all the shutters and lock the doors."

As they spilled out of the kitchen they met Martha, Ellen and Freya hurrying down the stairs to see what the commotion was. Freya gave a cry when she saw Finn and shrank behind Martha.

"Where did you find Finn?" demanded Martha.

"Never mind that. There are wolves outside," said Magnus succinctly. "They're trying to get in."

They scattered to the other rooms to make the house secure then gathered in the kitchen. In the half-light coming around the barred shutters, all eyes turned to Finn, standing with his back against the wall like an animal at bay.

"What happened out there?" Magnus asked, his mind full of the impossible events he had just witnessed. "What did you do? What *are* you?"

He had eased his knife from its sheath as he spoke. Now he moved into the middle of the room, putting himself between Finn and the others.

"Why have you come back? What are you trying to do to us? What did you do to Freya?" he asked, his voice dangerously quiet.

"Put that knife away, Magnus." Her voice icy, Ellen stepped forward. "You'll not spill blood in this house today. No one will do anything they have cause to regret later. Martha, Jess – get some lamps lit so we can see what we're doing. Freya, child, come here to me." Ellen held out a hand. Visibly trembling, Freya walked to her and the old woman put an arm round her.

"He won't hurt you. He won't touch you. He won't even look at you if you don't want him to. You're safe. Do you believe me?"

Freya nodded mutely, comforted by the certainty in the old woman's voice.

As Martha and Jess lit lamps, Ellen went on, "Ashe, come over here too. You're safe. The wolves can't get in."

Ashe flung his arms round his grandmother's waist, tears running down his face.

"Where's the horse that saved me? Did the wolves get it?" he quavered.

Magnus looked at Ashe, then at Jess, then at Finn.

"No," he said slowly, as though he had to force the words out. "The horse is here. The horse is Finn."

Martha gave a gasp and put her hand to her mouth.

"Or am I mad, Jess?" Magnus went on. "Tell me you saw him change too."

The time for lying had passed.

"You're not mad," Jess said.

"Then *what are you*?" Magnus spoke to Finn again.

"The boy is a Kelpie," Ellen said in a weary voice, and moved to sit down, taking Freya and Ashe with her.

"*A Kelpie?*" Martha stared at Finn and watched as he nodded.

"Kelpie? What's that?" Magnus was still baffled.

A howl came from outside, and glass smashed in one of the windows as a wolf threw itself against it.

There was silence for a few seconds then Finn answered.

"The Kelpies are my people, though we call ourselves Nykur. We live in the world below the water. Sometimes we visit your world – the Upper World – and sometimes we take horse shape."

"And sometimes you take people from here?" Magnus's voice would have etched metal.

"Yes."

"And you took Freya." It wasn't a question.

"Yes."

"What did you do to her?" Magnus's hand went to his knife hilt again.

"Nothing. We didn't hurt her."

"Magnus, stop… don't," said Jess desperately.

"It's true." They all turned at the sound of Freya's voice. "I remember now. I remember. There was a horse. I was on its back and it took me under the water." She frowned, concentrating hard. "There was a house built over a river, and a family – Finn's family. There was a girl called Rowan; she was my friend."

Freya looked at Jess, wide-eyed. "And then Jess came, and took me back. Brought me back here."

"You were there. You saw them," she said directly to Jess.

Jess nodded wordlessly.

Magnus stared at Jess blankly.

"You went to the Kelpie world? To get Freya back?" Her mother's voice shook.

"Yes." Jess found her voice somewhere. "I had to. No one else would believe me when I told them what happened. I tried so hard to tell you, but you wouldn't listen."

"But how did you know about Kelpies? No one in this house has ever spoken about Kelpies in front of you. Have they?"

Before she could think of a convincing lie, Jess saw her mother realise the truth. Martha fixed Ellen with a gimlet stare.

"*You* told her about this? You put my daughter in danger?"

"Only so she could tell Arnor, persuade *him* to go. I never, ever thought she would go herself." The distress was plain in Ellen's voice.

"Don't blame Gran. It's not her fault," Jess burst out. "She tried to stop me going. But I couldn't leave Freya if there was a chance to bring her back."

An uneasy silence grew, broken by the sound of a wolf growling outside the door.

"What about these wolves?" Magnus asked, searching for something he could understand in this avalanche of impossible facts. "Why are they behaving like this?"

"They're not normal wolves. They won't give up this hunt until they've killed or *been* killed," Finn said.

"Where have they come from?"

Finn paused.

"They've broken through from my world. They shouldn't be able to. We have enchantments in place to hold them back. I don't know what's gone wrong."

"You've brought these things on us as well?" Magnus exclaimed angrily.

"No! The Nykur have been protecting you from wolves for years."

Magnus looked at him sceptically. "So we need to kill them?" he asked, concentrating on the most pressing problem.

"Yes."

"How?"

Finn looked nonplussed. "How do you normally kill wolves?"

"Bow, or better still, crossbow."

"Then these will be the same."

Martha hadn't spoken for some time, but she cut in now.

"What about Ian and Arnor? They're going to be riding straight into this."

Magnus and Finn glanced at each other. In the face of the immediate danger, some sort of unspoken truce seemed to have been declared.

"Are they armed?" asked Finn.

"They'll have knives, but nothing else," Martha said anxiously.

"Then either we need to kill these wolves ourselves or find a way to warn Ian and Arnor," said Magnus. "Let's have a look from upstairs, see what we're up against."

"Jess, where does your father keep his crossbow?" Magnus asked her.

"In the tool shed," said Jess, heart sinking. It was clearly not the answer Magnus had wanted to hear.

"What about a normal bow?"

"That's in the tool shed too."

Magnus swore. "Upstairs then. At least we can have a look."

Magnus, Finn and Jess ran up the stairs and into her room. Below, the snow that still remained in the farmyard was churned with wolf prints. They could see four of the wolves pacing near the house. From the barn came the sound of the cows bellowing, disturbed by the howling and the smell of wolf.

"Where are the other wolves?" Jess wondered. "There are only four out there."

"Perhaps they're at the front."

They moved through to Ian and Martha's room and found Freya there. She flinched away when Finn came near, then steadied herself.

"There are two down here."

"Well, at least we know where they all are."

"Finn," Freya said his name with obvious reluctance. "You need to change to horse shape and draw them off so that Magnus can get to the tool shed for the crossbow."

"No!" Jess exclaimed. "That's far too risky. There are six of them."

"No Jess, Freya's right," said Finn. He looked at Magnus, who nodded. "We don't have much time. If Ian and Arnor left Forfar at first light, they can't be far away."

"We need to get those two away from the front so that I

can get out there and change." Finn was thinking aloud now. "Then I'll go through the yard and hopefully, they'll all chase me."

Jess's heart was in her mouth. There was far too much that could go wrong with this. But Freya was right: they had to do something.

Minutes later Ellen, Martha, Freya and Ashe were ready to bombard the wolves at the front, Magnus was poised by the back door ready to dash for the tool shed, and Finn stood at the door, waiting for Martha's shout to tell him it was safe to go outside.

Jess stood with Finn, ready to lock the door behind him, heart hammering so hard she could hardly breathe.

"Please, please be careful," she said softly to Finn. She took a breath. "And don't come back. Get away while you have the chance."

"And leave you all like this?" He shook his head. "I'm coming back, Jess."

Martha shouted downstairs, "Are you ready?"

"Yes," they chorused.

There was a cacophony of noise as objects began to hit the ground near the front door. Judging by the way the growls outside changed to whimpers, some of them hit their marks on the way.

"Quick, Finn! They've gone round to the back," called Martha.

Jess unbolted the door.

"Good luck," she whispered, opening it.

"I'll be back in five minutes," Finn said, and kissed her as he stepped outside.

Jess slammed and locked the door and stood with her back to it, listening in terror until she heard the sound of hooves. She locked the kiss away at the bottom of her mind – there was no time to think about that now – and hurried to the back door where Magnus waited.

Upstairs in Jess's room, Martha watched as the black horse trotted across the yard. The wolves turned to it as one. The horse stopped for long enough to get their attention fully, then shot out of the yard.

Martha watched them bound after it. Were they far enough away yet?

"Magnus! Now!"

Jess hauled the back door open. Magnus pounded across the slushy yard and disappeared into the shed. He soon reappeared, laden with crossbow, bolts, bow and arrows. He half-fell in at the back door and Jess shoved it shut behind him. Magnus ran straight upstairs without pausing, Jess on his heels.

They looked out of Jess's window, but there was no sign of Finn or the wolves. Jess ran through to where the others were watching the front.

"Anything?"

Martha shook her head.

Jess went back to where Magnus waited, the crossbow primed and ready.

"He should have been back by now," Jess fretted.

Maybe it was all right. Maybe he had decided to escape, and was heading for freedom, the wolves far behind him.

She felt sick. She couldn't help imagining the wolves tearing at Finn, remembering the wounds he'd had when they found him in the snow. And that had only been three wolves…

"There!" Magnus pointed suddenly, and Jess's heart lurched with relief as she saw the black horse galloping towards the farmyard.

"Can you see the wolves? Is he far enough ahead?"

Magnus squinted. "I can only see one. I'm not sure how far behind it is."

"I'm going down to open the door."

"Don't open it until I tell you it's safe," Magnus said sharply.

"But we've got to let him in."

"Only if it's safe. Wait for me to tell you. Jess?"

But she'd gone.

Magnus swore and turned back to the window. The horse was nearly at the farmyard now. How long did it take Finn to change? He hadn't noticed before. He shouldered the crossbow.

Down in the kitchen, Jess stood at the back door, straining to hear through the heavy wood. She heard the sound of hooves and wrenched the door open without a second thought.

The horse had come to a halt outside the back door and stood motionless, flanks heaving. Magnus watched from upstairs and saw a single wolf tearing towards it from the edge of the farmyard. He heard Jess yelling, "Quick Finn, get inside," and realised to his horror that she'd opened the door.

All his attention on the wolf now, Magnus let the bolt fly.

Then the horse was gone and Finn was there, as the wolf leapt and dropped abruptly, tumbling across the ground, leaving a trail of blood.

Finn threw himself inside and they locked the door together, before Finn slid down it on to the floor, chest heaving with exertion.

"Are you all right? Are you hurt?" Jess was frantic with worry.

He shook his head, lacking breath in his lungs to speak.

Magnus clattered down the stairs and into the kitchen, starting to reload the crossbow as he went, Ashe close behind him.

"You're all right?" he said to Finn, who nodded. Ashe ran over to Finn and gave him a hug, then went to fetch him a drink.

"You opened the door," Magnus said accusingly to Jess. "You knew it wasn't safe. That wolf could have got in."

"But you killed it."

"I might have missed."

"I knew you wouldn't." Jess gave him a placatory smile.

"No, you didn't." Magnus wasn't going to be placated. "You should have waited until you knew it was safe."

"I wasn't going to leave it shut and listen to him dying outside," Jess said with finality. "And the wolf didn't get in. Now, what about the other five?"

Finn had got to his feet, still breathing hard. He came over to Magnus.

"Thank you," he said.

"I never thought you'd come back," Magnus replied, staring hard at him. "You could have escaped."

"I wouldn't abandon anyone to these creatures. None of my people would."

They held each other's gazes for a few seconds.

"The other wolves are back," Freya called, and they all headed back upstairs.

The wolves were unsettled now, prowling round the body, sniffing and pushing at it, snapping at each other jumpily.

Magnus aimed carefully and loosed a second bolt. He didn't get a clean kill this time. Instead, the bolt must have broken a front leg of the wolf it hit. It staggered and fell, whimpering and growling, trying and failing to get up again. Ears flat, the rest of the pack scattered.

Magnus passed Finn the bow.

"I can't shoot," he said as he took it.

"The crossbow then – here."

"No. I've never shot anything. I don't know how to."

"Are you serious?"

He nodded. "We have other ways to deal with wolves in the Nykur world."

Magnus muttered to himself as he hurried to reset the crossbow. A few seconds later he shouldered it, chose his target and fired. This time the bolt took a wolf in the throat, and it fell without a sound. It had been the furthest away, and the others didn't seem to notice what had happened to it.

"The only trouble with a crossbow," Magnus said through gritted teeth, "is how long the damn thing takes to load. It's giving them too long to think."

As he spoke, the two remaining wolves put back their heads and howled, making everyone's flesh crawl.

"Why are they howling like that?" asked Jess.

"They're angry. They want vengeance," said Finn.

The wolves began to move towards the house – too close for Magnus to see them properly. He swore, hanging out of the window as far as he dared. From below came the sound of smashing glass.

"What's happening?" Martha's voice was tight with fear.

"They're trying to break in through one of the windows downstairs." Finn was already heading out of the room.

"Finn – wait!" yelled Jess. Magnus hauled himself back inside and he and Jess ran after Finn.

Finn paused at the bottom of the stairs. Everything had gone quiet. They waited, holding their breath.

"Do you think they've gone?" Jess whispered.

Finn shook his head and started to say something, but the words were drowned by the sound of a wolf hurling itself against the shutters in the kitchen.

"Stay upstairs," Finn yelled to the others, edging into the kitchen ahead of Magnus and Jess and watching in horror as the shutters rattled under the impact of a wolf's body.

Magnus shouldered the crossbow as they stood there in the gloom. His face was grim. The shutters shook as the wolves threw themselves against them over and over.

"Jess, get out of here. Get upstairs and barricade yourself in somewhere with the others."

She shook her head, too frightened to speak. *If the wolves got inside, they were all dead,* she thought. *There was no barricade they could make that would stop them. They had to kill them somehow.*

She opened the drawer where the knives were kept and picked up the biggest one with a trembling hand. Finn reached across her for another one.

Magnus kept his eyes on the shutters, where one of the panels was starting to splinter under the onslaught.

"Any minute now," he muttered.

One, two more jarring impacts. On the third, the weak panel finally gave way completely and a head was thrust inside, yellow-eyed, snarling with bloodlust.

Magnus squeezed the trigger. At this distance, he could hardly miss. The bolt hit the wolf in the back of its open mouth with a dreadful sound of tearing flesh. With a choking gurgle, the wolf fell back from the shattered wood.

Magnus started to reload.

From outside came a howl as the one remaining wolf realised what had happened, then a terrible crash as it tried to break through the shutter.

Magnus reloaded the crossbow as quickly as he could.

The wolf struggled, growling, trying to make the hole in the wood big enough to get through. Jess watched, mesmerised with terror.

And then Finn darted past her and struck at the wolf's throat with the knife as hard as he could. Blood fountained out, but the wolf kept coming.

"Get back, Finn," yelled Magnus, taking aim.

Finn threw himself out of the way of the wolf's slashing teeth as Magnus fired. The bolt hit with such force that it toppled the wolf back out of the wreckage of the shutters.

There was silence.

No one moved, afraid that at any second another snarling muzzle would be forced through the window, but nothing happened.

The silence stretched on. Finn moved first, sidling up to what was left of the window. He risked a quick glance out, then a longer one, and turned back smiling grimly.

"We've done it. They're dead."

Chapter Seventeen

Ian and Arnor stared at the scene of slaughter before them,
then at the white faces looking out from the shattered kitchen
window.

"Is everyone safe?" Ian yelled as the back door opened and
Ashe and Martha tumbled out.

"Yes, yes, everyone's fine," Martha reassured him.

Arnor stared at the wolves, living and dead. Without a word
he dismounted and drew his knife, strode to the two that were
still alive, and cut their throats.

"Look at the size of them," Ian marvelled, joining him.

"I haven't seen a wolf like these for twenty years," said Arnor
slowly, staring fixedly at the bodies.

He turned and looked at the doorway where Jess, Magnus
and Finn stood, staring out at the bloody farmyard.

"Is that him?"

"That's him," Ian said, frowning. "I left him locked in the
cellar. I want to know who let him loose."

Jess saw Arnor staring at Finn, and all her fear for him came
flooding back. She drew Magnus aside.

"Magnus – don't let Arnor hurt Finn," she pleaded. "Make
him see sense. You know Finn didn't hurt Freya. She told you
so herself."

"But he took her. Arnor won't forgive that."

They backed into the kitchen as Ian approached.

"Who let him out?" He gestured towards Finn.

"It was me," said Jess quickly.

"He helped kill the wolves," Magnus added.

"Well, they're dead now. Get him back into the cellar."

Finn didn't try to resist as Magnus unlocked the cellar door and Ian shoved him inside. Then Ian went upstairs, leaving Jess and Magnus alone together for the first time that day.

"What's really going on, Jess?" he asked, without preamble.

"What do you mean?"

"Finn was gone this morning, then you disappeared too. Everyone but Ian and Arnor knows you let him out of the cellar last night. You wanted him to escape, didn't you?"

"Yes." She forced herself to meet his eyes. "I knew he hadn't harmed Freya. I was afraid Arnor and my father would kill him – I still am. And it will be even worse if they find out what he really is. He doesn't mean any of us any harm. He came back to help us when he could have escaped and left us to deal with the wolves. Please don't let them kill him. I've never asked you for anything before, but please, please help me now."

Before Magnus could answer, Arnor came in with his arm round Freya.

"I need to talk to my daughter," he said, ushering her into the sitting room and closing the door. Ellen and Ian came downstairs and everyone gathered in the kitchen.

"Is someone going to explain what's been going on?" demanded Ian, looking at the shattered window and bloodstained walls.

Martha spoke up quickly.

"The wolves came out of the wood and tried to get into the house. They wouldn't give up. We were afraid for you and Arnor, but Magnus managed to kill them – with Finn's help."

197

Jess stared at her mother, astonished. She was missing out half the story to protect Finn.

"How did you get to the shed to get the weapons?"

"We… eh… we managed to distract the wolves for long enough," Magnus said in a strained voice.

"That was risky." Ian shook his head. "You were lucky."

"It was Finn," said Ashe, into a horrified silence. "He changed into a horse, like when he saved me from the wolves. And the wolves chased him."

Ian turned from face to frozen face around him.

"A horse?" he said slowly.

No one answered. Even Ashe realised that he'd said something wrong.

"A horse?" he said again. "Are you serious? Martha? What's the boy talking about?"

Martha had no answer.

"Is this true? He is a Kelpie? Freya was taken by the Kelpies?" He stopped, hoping he had somehow misunderstood, but no one contradicted him.

"Mother," he said finally. "Is this true?"

"Yes," said Ellen. "You can't pretend any more that they don't exist. Not even to yourself."

At that moment, Arnor and Freya appeared in the doorway.

"Freya has told me what happened. She remembers it all now," he said, looking from Ian to Jess. "Jess, what can I say? You tried to tell me and I wouldn't believe you. Freya told me how you brought her back from the Kelpie world. How can I thank you? I owe you my daughter's life."

Ian gaped. "*Jess* went to their world and brought Freya back?"

"Yes," said Freya smiling.

Ian did not smile in return. He stared at his daughter.

"Tell me I'm wrong, Jess. Tell me you didn't let this

creature into our house knowing what it was. Tell me that when we found him in the snow, you didn't know he was a Kelpie."

Jess swallowed, searching for her voice.

"I knew who Finn was when we found him."

Ian stared at her as though she was a stranger. "You have betrayed everyone you know." He drew back his hand and Jess closed her eyes and waited for the blow that she knew would come.

Nothing happened. She opened her eyes.

Magnus had hold of Ian's arm. The two men glared at each other.

"You'll not touch her," Magnus said very quietly.

"She's my daughter, and you are in my house," Ian replied venomously.

"Ian! Stop this." Martha's voice was sharp. "There's enough trouble without starting more."

"I'll see to you later," Ian said to Jess, then turned his back on her.

"Arnor," he went on. "Let's get this over. You and I will deal with what's in the cellar."

"What do you mean?" asked Freya, and read the answer in Ian's face. "No – you can't!" she gasped.

There was uproar in the kitchen as the others realised what Ian meant. Jess and Ashe were shouting, but no one paid them any notice.

"Ian – no!" Martha said. "He's just a boy."

"He saved Jess and Ashe from the wolves," said Magnus. "He helped us."

Arnor said nothing at all and for a moment, neither did Ellen. Then she rose stiffly from the table and walked the length of the room to confront the stony-faced Ian. She spoke to him quietly at first, but he ignored her. Jess saw the anger kindle in Ellen's eyes just before she slapped Ian as hard as she could across the cheek.

The room was suddenly silent.

Ian stood with his hand to his cheek, mouth hanging foolishly open.

"You *will* listen to me," said Ellen, her expression daring him to utter a word. "I have three things to say to you. Arnor and Freya are the injured parties here, not you. That is the first thing. What Magnus said is true: the Kelpie boy has saved both your children – and probably you and Arnor – from these wolves today. That is the second thing." She took a deep breath. "And the boy is the son of my cousin Euan, who was taken by the Kelpies. He is our kin. Think very carefully, son, before you decide to become a kin killer. That is the third thing."

And with that she turned her back on him and went back to her chair.

Jess saw the moment when her father realised that his mother, too, must have known exactly who was in his house, but he said nothing to Ellen.

Eventually, Ian looked at Arnor.

"You are the injured party," he said stiffly. "What do *you* want done with him?"

"I want to talk to him alone," said Arnor, to everyone's surprise.

Jess and Freya sat side by side in awkward silence in the main room, waiting for Arnor to come back.

"What do you want to happen to Finn?" Jess forced herself to ask, dreading the answer.

Freya thought for a few seconds.

"I certainly don't want him killed. He did kidnap me, but no one in his world meant me any harm. I was never frightened when I was there; I thought it was where I belonged. It was only when I came back and I couldn't remember that it was frightening. Now that I *can* remember it doesn't seem nearly so bad. And he did save us all. I think that balances things out a bit, don't you?"

Jess's heart surged. Surely, if Freya didn't want Finn harmed, Arnor would listen to her?

"But what's going on between the two of you?"

Freya's words brought Jess's thoughts crashing back into the room.

"Going on? What do you mean? There's nothing going on."

"Jess," said Freya gently. "You hid who Finn was from your parents. You tried to persuade me I was wrong about him. And you helped him escape last night, didn't you?"

There was no point in pretending. Jess nodded.

"But there's nothing going on," she said quickly. "I just didn't want him to die. He's been banished from his world. I thought that was punishment enough for what he'd done."

Freya gave her a long look. "Magnus is worried too. Not that he'd admit it."

"Worried? About…"

"About what Finn means to you. And don't say *nothing*. We both know that's not true."

Jess didn't know what to say. She remembered, suddenly, the moment when Finn had kissed her. What *did* Finn mean to her?

"Magnus has nothing to worry about," she said flatly.

A shout came from the cellar. Glad of the distraction, Jess jumped up to unlock the door.

Arnor came out alone.

"Do I lock the door again?" Jess asked.

He nodded, went into the room where Freya sat and closed the door. Jess went into the kitchen, where Martha was putting something in the oven.

From the window, she saw that her father and Magnus had dragged the bodies of the wolves into the neighbouring field, and were building a pyre.

"Let's not bother telling your father about Finn disappearing during the night," Martha said suddenly. "It makes no difference now, and it will only make him more angry. I take it that it *was* you who let him out, and not Ashe?"

Jess nodded, shamefaced.

"I don't want this to end badly for the boy, but you mustn't get any more involved than you already are. No more secrets, Jess – all right?"

"All right," said Jess.

Footsteps came along the hall and Arnor came in.

"I need to talk to everyone," he said.

"These wolves," Arnor began. "They're not normal. I've seen one like them before: the one whose head is over the front door of the shop. They're from *his* world – the Kelpie boy."

He paused.

"The Kelpies have been stopping them getting into our world for years." Arnor shifted in his seat. "There was an agreement made between the people of Kirriemuir and some of the other towns and the Kelpies: they would keep the wolves from us and in return," he took a deep breath, "they would be allowed to take a certain number of our children to live in their world."

Ian erupted from his chair.

"The creature's tricked you. No one would ever agree to that."

"You promised to hear me out. It wasn't the boy who told me this."

"Then who was it?" Ian demanded.

"It was Lachlan."

"Lachlan?" Ian stared at Arnor, sure he must have misheard.

"Yes. Now sit down and listen, as you promised. Lachlan

showed me a document last night when he heard what was going on here. He overheard Jess when she came to the shop just after Freya disappeared to try and tell me what really happened, so he already knew the truth."

There was utter silence in the room now, except for Arnor's voice.

"This agreement was made in Lachlan's grandfather's lifetime. His grandfather was one of the men who negotiated it with the Kelpies. The wolf winters had been terrible. Too many livestock dead to count them sometimes, but that wasn't the worst of it. The wolves were man-eaters – like those ones burning outside. No one was safe. Children were taken; adults too. Everyone lived in fear.

"And so the negotiators agreed to let the Kelpies take a small number of children from time to time. In return the Kelpies would protect the Upper World from the black wolves. It made sense: the Kelpies would take fewer children than the wolves did, and they wouldn't be harmed, but it was a betrayal of their children that these men were agreeing to, and they knew it. They were so ashamed of what they were doing that they swore never to speak of it. The children would simply disappear and never be found. They told everyone in their home towns that the negotiations had failed.

"When he was on his deathbed, Lachlan's grandfather told his wife what had happened, and she wrote it down. But the family never told anyone else."

Arnor fell silent, watching the others try to comprehend what had been done in their names, without their knowledge, all this time; the betrayal of the children, year after year, generation after generation.

After a moment, he spoke again.

"The Kelpies have been living by that agreement ever since, assuming that we were as well. But we never knew what had been promised in our name. People forgot about the black wolves, thought they'd died out or moved on. Children disappeared, and there was no explanation. No one has spoken of the Kelpies for years, but it seems that all this time *they* were keeping their side of the bargain."

Ellen spoke up. "When my cousin Euan went missing, an old woman told me he'd likely been taken by the Kelpies. It was she who told me how a taken child could be brought back. She was Lachlan's grandmother."

"Arnor, are you sure that this is true?" Martha asked.

He nodded. "Why would Lachlan invent such a story? And what Ellen just said backs it up. I think it's time to let the boy out of the cellar and hear what he has to say."

A minute later Finn stood in the room, looking warily at the faces turned towards him, trying to gauge his likely fate.

"Tell them about the agreement," Arnor said.

Finn spoke, aware that his life might hang on what he said now.

"The wolves from our world used to break through to your world and kill livestock and people. We knew how to contain them in our world, but our race was failing. We needed new blood to survive. We made an agreement with men from Kirriemuir and Forfar and Cortachy. We would take one child from each settlement every few years to live with us. In return we would stop the wolves from breaking through. We've lived by that agreement since it was made."

"So the two boys who disappeared here – Aidan and Donald – were taken by you?"

"Not by me, but by other Nykur families. As far as the boys are concerned, my world is their home now."

"And my mother's cousin Euan, all these years ago…" Ian said in a cracked voice.

"My mother's family chose him for her. He's my father."

"And you chose Freya?"

Finn's head came up sharply.

"No. No, that was a mistake. I never meant to take her, I swear."

Ian opened his mouth to ask something else, but Ellen spoke before he had the chance.

"Why have the wolves broken through now?"

Finn shook his head. "They shouldn't be able to," he said, anxiety clear in his voice. "There are charms round the pool in my world that should stop them from getting through. My family should be checking them, making sure they work." He drew a deep breath. "Please, let me go back to my world and find out what's happened."

Chapter Eighteen

Jess kept as busy as she could, so there wouldn't be a chance for anyone to talk to her. She wanted to be alone in the dark with her thoughts, but there was the evening to endure first. Arnor, Magnus and Freya were to stay the night. The short winter day was already darkening and no one wanted to be on the road after nightfall.

Finn was gone.

To Ian's fury, Arnor and Freya had let him go.

Jess had forced herself to be still, to look calm when he left, though her mind was churning.

He was safe.

He was leaving.

It was Freya who went through to the back door with Finn. Jess heard her voice as she said something to him, but not the words.

He was gone.

At last, she climbed into bed with a sigh of relief. A few minutes later though, Freya joined her.

"Move over," she said as she finished braiding her hair. "It's too cold to sleep in the other bed, and I have to talk to you."

"It's not *that* cold," Jess protested, sliding over.

"I don't want to be overheard," Freya whispered as she climbed in beside her.

Jess rolled over to face her.

"Why not?" She found herself whispering in turn.

"I'm going out at dawn to meet Finn. He's going to take me to the Kelpie world."

Freya put her hand over Jess's mouth to stifle her squawk of horror.

"Are you out of your mind?" she hissed.

"Just the opposite. This is what I need to do to fill in the last blanks in my memory. It'll never be over for me until I can do that," Freya whispered.

"He'll never agree."

"He already has. I spoke to him before he left. Made him promise to take me and bring me back. It was easy. He still feels guilty about taking me before."

"What about Arnor?"

Freya made a dismissive gesture.

"Once I'm home safe he won't care. I've left him a note so he won't worry."

Jess didn't know whether to laugh or cry at that. Really, what she wanted to do was shake Freya until her teeth rattled.

"And what about poor Finn when your father – and my father – find out what he's done?"

"But it's *me* who's making him do it. He doesn't really have a choice. I made him feel he had no alternative but to do what I asked."

Jess had no trouble at all believing that.

"I could go and tell them now what you're planning, you know."

"I know, but you won't," said Freya with absolute conviction. "I want you to come too."

Jess sat bolt upright.

"You're insane," she hissed. "My father's already furious with me."

"Exactly. He can't be much more angry with you than he already is."

Oh can't he? thought Jess, but didn't say it.

"Don't pretend you don't want to see Finn again. At least this way you can say goodbye to him properly." Jess avoided looking at Freya's face, tried not to let the idea of seeing Finn again take root. "There'll be no harm done. We'll be back before you know it."

"I'll have to come and live with you if my father throws me out, you know."

Freya laughed under her breath.

"I'm not joking," Jess said as she lay down again.

"So you'll come?"

"How could I not?" Jess paused, trying to think this through properly. "What about wolves? What if there are more out there?"

"Finn's already at the pool. He would deal with any more that came through. But we'll take knives, just in case."

Jess knew it was ridiculous to accept that as reassurance, but she let her desire to see Finn override her common sense.

Of course she had to go. Freya was right. Jess couldn't let go of the chance to see Finn one last time, whatever the consequences.

Before dawn, they were up and dressing in silence. Jess decided to let Freya's note stand for both of them. Nothing that she could have said would have been likely to improve the situation when she returned anyway.

They tiptoed downstairs and into the kitchen, to collect the two biggest kitchen knives and a lantern. Although the moon was nearly full, they would need some extra light once they were in the woods.

They made their way in silence out of the farmyard, past the stinking, still smouldering remains of the wolf pyre, unaware of the shadow that detached itself from the barn and slipped after them.

Grey light lay across Roseroot Pool. Mist floated just above the water, tendrils curling and twining through the trees. It was absolutely silent once they stopped moving, waiting for Finn to show himself.

His voice suddenly came from the trees behind them.

"I only agreed to take Freya. What are you doing here, Jess?"

Freya turned and answered before Jess had a chance.

"I asked Jess to come. I didn't think you'd mind."

He said nothing for a moment, then shook his head.

"One, two, twenty – what's the difference?" he said with a shrug, but his eyes were fixed on Jess as though the rest of the world was invisible.

"In my world, you have to do as I say, Freya," he added.

"I promise. I only want to see where I was, then I swear we'll go."

"All right. We need to wade out near the middle, then hold on to my hands and don't let go."

Finn led the way, and Jess walked into the achingly cold water, Freya a step behind. Finn ploughed on without looking back until he was hip deep, then stopped and waited for the girls to catch up. Jess wondered if she could still get to Finn's world alone, was about to ask, when a figure hurtled out of the trees and into the pool, shouting. In the half light it took a few seconds to recognise Magnus.

"Get away from them! Leave them alone," he yelled.

Freya grabbed Finn's hand as Magnus plunged towards them.

"Never mind him, Finn. Just do it," she urged him.

Jess reached out and grasped Finn's other hand.

"Are you sure?" he said.

"Yes! Do it!" Freya yelled as Magnus lunged for her, and suddenly the water was over and around them and they were being spun around like leaves in a whirlpool. Jess held grimly to Finn's hand, trying to hold that last breath in her lungs, trying and trying…

Just as it ran out, the hurtling, spinning water was gone, and she landed with a thud on dry land. After a few seconds Jess opened her eyes to broad daylight, and her heart surged as she realised at once from the shimmering air that she was in the Nykur world again.

She sat up. Finn was already on one knee, looking in horror at Freya, who was sprawled in a heap on the ground, limbs tangled with Magnus's.

Jess gasped. "Oh no."

Magnus and Freya untangled themselves and sat up slowly, glaring. Finn was on his feet now, looking down at Magnus. Before he could say anything, Freya launched into a tirade.

"Magnus, you idiot, Finn hasn't kidnapped us. I made him promise to bring me here to fill in the gaps in my memory, and I persuaded Jess to come with me."

Magnus got to his feet.

"Is that true, Jess?"

"Of course it is. Do we look as though we're here against our will?"

"You shouldn't be here," Finn said coldly. "This is none of your business."

"Yes it is. But I'm not here to make trouble. I was too late to stop them going with you, but I can make sure they're safe."

"You think you can do that in my world?"

"I think so," said Magnus coolly.

"All right then, let's see," Finn said, as though he was issuing a challenge. "All of you wait here until I check it's safe." He walked away a little.

Magnus relaxed visibly and looked round, blinking and rubbing his eyes.

Jess took pity on him. "It's not your eyes. The light's strange. I remember from when I was here before. Things look as if they're quivering if you're not looking straight at them."

She hadn't expected this surge of joy as her senses reacted to the heightened intensity of Finn's world. She had forgotten how seductive it was.

"Do you remember that happening when you were here before, Freya?" she went on.

"No," Freya replied. "But I remember the roses." She was looking at a huge crimson briar.

Finn came back over.

"It's safe."

"I remember the roses from before," Freya said to him.

"They're not exactly roses," he replied.

The others turned to him.

"Remember how surprised you were when you found I didn't know how to shoot?" Finn said to Magnus, who nodded, puzzled. "This is one way we deal with the wolves here."

"You turn them into roses?" Jess thought she must have misunderstood.

"Not exactly. We can lay a spell of illusion round a door to your world. If wolves cross the boundary, the spell twists their minds and makes their bodies take the shape of roses. Really, though, they're still wolves; they've just forgotten. You should be able to see, if you look at one of them out of the corner of your eye."

Half convinced Finn was simply making fools of them, Jess tried looking sidelong at a rose bush. Nothing happened.

"No: not like that. Look at me." He moved into her line of vision. "But be aware of that bush that's right at the edge of your sight."

Jess did as he said, staring at him for once without having to look for an excuse. She gasped and looked round sharply. For the tiniest flicker of time, in the space between heartbeats, the briar bush had shivered into the form of a wolf, then back to a rose.

She heard Magnus and Freya exclaim as they too saw the bush's true form.

"That's impossible," Magnus exclaimed.

"In your world. That's why you need to know how to shoot."

Magnus strode towards the nearest bush.

"Careful!" warned Finn. "They can still bite."

Magnus paused.

"You said that to me when I was here before," Jess remembered. "And I could have sworn that one of the branches moved so the thorns could get me."

"It probably did," Finn replied. "They don't remember they are wolves, but they still enjoy tearing flesh."

The others looked at the bushes, grown suddenly sinister.

"But somehow, in spite of this, six wolves got into our world," Magnus reminded him.

"Yes," Finn said, suddenly distracted. "I need to find out why. Give me a minute to check something."

He moved away from them slowly, eyes flicking between the ground and the briars and the trees. Jess tried to work out what he was looking for, but to no avail.

She turned back to Magnus and Freya instead, just in time to see Magnus, unable to resist, stretch his hand out towards a rose. So quickly that there was barely time to register it had happened, a long, barbed twig had whipped out and raked down his arm.

He jumped back with a yell and glared at the bush, cursing.

"Magnus, you great fool," said Freya unsympathetically.

"It's torn my jacket," Magnus said in pained amazement.

"Well, it's a wolf. It could do worse than that," said Jess. "Let's see your arm."

Magnus took off his jacket and examined his bloody arm. The gouges in his flesh did look more like claw marks than thorn scrapes.

"You should wash it," said Jess, ever practical.

"Not here," said Magnus, pulling his jacket back on. "Why would I trust the water if the roses can do that?"

Jess looked back to where she had last seen Finn. For a moment she couldn't spot him, then she realised he was standing in the fork of a tree. There was something in his hands, but she couldn't make out what it was.

Leaving Magnus and Freya bickering, Jess made her way to the foot of Finn's tree, being careful to give the briars a wide berth.

She leaned against the trunk and peered up at him.

"What are you doing?"

"Mending the barrier."

She couldn't see any barrier.

"What do you mean?"

"Just a minute. I"ll show you when I come down." As he spoke he was edging out along a limb.

As Jess waited, she concentrated on the feel of the tree bark under her fingers, rippled like wet sand, warm with slow life. She watched Finn reach up to tie whatever he was carrying to the branch above, then swing himself down to drop neatly at her feet.

"Here." He held something out to her.

It was a little garland, less than a hand span wide, woven of what looked like hair, with faded rose petals worked into it. Jess looked at Finn, waiting for an explanation.

"This is the enchantment," he said, obviously expecting her to have understood already. "Wolf and rose, twined together."

When she still looked blank, he went on. "Wolf hair and rose petals worked together with my mother's power. This is what blocks the door to your world against the black wolves. I can mend these, but only my mother can make them. It was my job to look after the barrier when I… before. It seems no one else has thought to do it." He was trying to keep his voice light, but he couldn't disguise the worry in it. "I don't think any of it's been checked since I left. I suppose my mother was too busy looking after Rowan."

"Can I help?"

"You don't have the skill – but thank you." He scanned the trees in front of him for the next garland and, now that she knew what to look for, Jess saw it too.

"Are the others all right?" Finn asked.

"Yes. Magnus ignored your warning and got clawed though."

Finn couldn't suppress a smile. "I thought he would."

"I think they're coming." Jess saw that Freya and Magnus had started walking towards them.

Finn turned her to him with a hand on her arm.

"Listen," he said urgently. "I don't want them here for any longer than necessary. I know you'll have to go with them, but if I can make my peace with my family, maybe you could come back. I'd never make you stay, but…" He fell silent as the others came within earshot.

Jess was glad she didn't have to answer. She was already confused enough. Finn and his world shouldn't mean anything to her, but…

Finn worked his way round the remaining garlands, retying and repairing while the others watched.

He jumped down from the last tree.

"It's done. The barrier will work now. The wolves can't get through to your world any more."

"That's really all it takes?" Magnus queried, incredulous.

"Yes. No. It's not the wolf hair and the rose petals that are important – even you could weave those. It's the *power* that goes into the weaving that tricks the wolves into accepting the illusion. That, you cannot do, and nor can I."

Finn's reply silenced Magnus. He turned to Freya.

"Do you still need to go further?"

Freya nodded. "I want to see the house. Then I'll go, I promise. We all will."

Finn sighed. "All right."

As they set off among the great trees of the Nykur world, Magnus took in his surroundings warily.

"I don't hear any birds."

"There *are* no birds." Finn shot Jess a complicit smile. "No birds, and no moon."

"No moon? Surely that"s impossible?"

"Impossible in your world. Normal in this one."

"But where has the moon gone?" Magnus asked, fascinated in spite of himself.

"It hasn't *gone* anywhere. It just doesn't exist here. That's another reason the wolves try to get to your world: the moon draws them. The wolves strayed here from your world long ago, following Nykur through one of the doorways. They hid away in the forests at first, the few that had lost their way. Some of the power of this world seeped into them: they grew bigger and stronger, and much more ferocious. They were afraid of the Nykur, but not of anything else, and they hunted between the worlds, killing for pleasure. We kept them at bay in the forests here, so they hunted more and more in the Upper World, leading packs of your wolves." Finn paused.

"Eventually, we made the agreement and penned them here, though the moon and their kin still draw them back to their old home. Now, as we diminish, they grow stronger. They don't fear us any more. They hunt us, they kill our children too. As you in the Upper World hunt down your own wolves more and more, these ones feel it. They feel the fear and pain as those wolves die. The black wolves are going to your world for vengeance."

They followed Finn between the wavering trees for almost an hour before they left the wood and stepped into the meadow at the foot of the crags.

Jess noticed that the yellow flowers were still in bloom and breathed in their honeyed scent again. Was that because time passed differently here, or did they simply flower for a long time?

Freya stopped and pointed.

"That's your house," she said excitedly. "I can see it in my mind: all the rooms, and Rowan, and your parents."

"Yes," said Finn absently. Jess noticed that he looked pale. He turned to the others.

"Please, wait here. I'll come back for you – just me – but I need to do this alone."

He didn't wait for an answer, but turned and walked away through the tall grass and the yellow flowers.

Jess saw Magnus looking at things from the corner of his eye, checking that nothing else had something unexpected hidden in its shape. The wind ruffled the dry grass, moving it in endless waves across the blue-green plain; otherwise there was no sound but the fall of water.

Finn reached the house, paused for a second, then disappeared inside.

They watched the house quiver like a mirage above the water, searching for any sign of movement at the windows, any sound; but there was nothing.

Magnus reached out for Jess's hand.

"Wolves that are roses... no moon... This is no place for

us. Surely you've seen enough now, Freya?" He glanced at his cousin, who was staring at Finn's home, waiting to see who would emerge. "Why do they have houses anyway, if they're horses here?"

"Don't be an idiot, Magnus," snapped Freya. "They only use the house when they're being human. Remember, Finn's father's human, so they spend a lot of time as humans."

Five minutes passed, then Finn appeared from the nearest door, alone. He didn't even look towards the others as he sat down heavily on the top step outside the door.

"Something's wrong," Jess said and pulling away from Magnus, began to run.

"What is it?" she said urgently as she approached Finn, the others close behind.

"They're gone," he said simply. "Gone."

Chapter Nineteen

"They've gone," Finn said again. "I don't know where they are." His face was as bleak as Jess had ever seen it.

"Maybe they're just… out. Gone for a walk, gone to visit someone."

He shook his head. "No. I mean packed up and gone. The place is deserted. I don't know how long it is since they left, or where they've gone, or why."

"Can we go inside?" asked Freya. "Maybe there's some sort of clue that you haven't noticed."

Finn waved them in. Freya went at once, pulling Magnus with her, but Jess paused.

"Are you coming in?" she said to Finn.

"In a minute."

She went in without him, stepping over the threshold with some foreboding.

Immediately Jess was in a circular room and surrounded by wood, gleaming golden, polished by the smoothing of hands over many years. She looked out of a window over falling water. It made the house feel as if it were pulling upwards, away from the river, towards the sky.

Chairs and tables and chests stood here and there. The lid of one small chest was still open, but all it held now was the scent of lavender.

Jess wandered from room to room, never quite catching up

with Freya and Magnus. Some rooms were quite bare, others looked much like the familiar ones at Westgarth: bedrooms, sitting room, kitchen.

She opened cupboards in the kitchen, looking for any clues to how long the house had been empty, but even here there was nothing that helped. There were jars of meal and flour, but no fresh food left to rot.

Freya and Magnus came back past her, Freya lost in her restored memories. Magnus looked at Jess and shrugged as he went past, staying close to his cousin.

Jess moved on to another room: a narrow bed with a dark blue woven cover, a chest under the window. This window faced up-river and beyond it falling water formed an iridescent curtain. A shelf on one wall held carvings of birds and animals.

"This is my room," said Finn behind her, making her jump.

"Where's everything else?"

"There is nothing else. This is all I need," he said, going to look out of the window.

"All I needed," he corrected himself. "This *was* my room."

"No one's moved your things out," said Jess gently. "Surely they would have if they really didn't want to see you again?"

He shrugged.

"I don't know," he said, sitting down on the bed. There was the sound of paper rustling as he did so. Looking puzzled, he rose again and turned back the cover.

There was a single sheet of paper covered in writing in a firm, round hand. Finn stared at it.

"That's Rowan's writing."

He picked it up and sat down again. Jess resisted the temptation to try and glimpse it over his shoulder. Finn was silent, reading and re-reading Rowan's letter. She couldn't tell from his face whether it was good news or bad. Finally, he handed the paper to her.

"Are you sure?" she asked.

He nodded, so she started to read.

Dear, dear Finn,

Please come back and read this. I've watched for you every day. I tried to go back through the door to look for you up there, but Mother and Father wouldn't let me, even though they want you back as much as I do. They don't say so, but I know they do.

We've gone to the ruined gateway at Dundee. There are dozens of wolves massing there to attack the town. We have all gone to try to lure them back through to our world so we can destroy them. This is our best chance to save ourselves and the town.

I wish you were here. I'm afraid that even all of us together may not be enough to do this.

Please come back. I want everything to be the way it was.

Rowan

"They want you back," said Jess, forcing herself to ignore the information about the wolves for now. "Why aren't you more happy about that?"

"Rowan could be wrong," he said. "My mother isn't a woman who usually changes her mind."

"But she's your *mother*. Surely that's the point? She was angry, but now that you've been gone for – for however long it is here, she's realised she was wrong to tell you to go."

"Maybe." Finn got up. "But whatever happens, I have to go after them to the gateway. If everyone has been called there to help they'll need me too."

"But you don't know how long ago they went."

"Yes, I do." He sniffed the letter. "I can tell from the scent. It can't be more than a couple of days old. I might be in time to help. Some of the other Nykur have to come from further away."

He went towards the door, then turned to face her again.

"Jess, you all need to go now. I have to go to the Dundee gateway."

"Dundee? Why would you go there?" Magnus stood in the doorway.

"Wolves," said Finn shortly. "My sister left me a letter. That's where my family are. They're trying to stop the wolves attacking the town. All the Nykur in the area are heading there. It's our chance to kill all the local wolves and save ourselves as well as you."

Jess noticed before Finn how pale Magnus had gone.

"My parents are in Dundee. Are they in danger?"

"Not if we can seal the gateway."

"And if you can't?"

Finn hesitated. "I won't lie to you. There are huge numbers of wolves gathering. You've seen what these wolves are like. If we can't get them back through the gateway and seal it, everyone in Dundee is in grave danger."

"I have to warn them," Magnus said immediately. "How much time do I have to get there? I have to leave now. Can I go on my own or do you have to take me back through the pool?"

Jess turned from Magnus to Finn. She could see him struggling with himself about something. He looked at Magnus's stricken face and reached a decision.

"I'll take you," he said. "You don't need to go back through the Upper World: I can take you from here more quickly. After all, it's where I'm going anyway."

Relief flooded Magnus's face.

"You would do that? Truly?"

Finn nodded.

"Thank you. Thank you. When can we go?"

"As soon as we get Jess and Freya away."

Jess opened her mouth to protest but the boys were already out of the room, striding to the front of the house, Magnus calling Freya's name.

They emerged into the shimmering air above the river. Freya was leaning out over the bridge rail dropping fallen leaves into the water. Fish shivered silver, chasing the leaves as they spun away on the current.

"What is it?" she said without looking up.

"You have to go back now," Magnus said urgently.

She turned, smiling.

"I know. I wish we didn't have to, it's so beautiful here. I'd forgotten that. Please say we can come back again, Finn? Surely we can make our families understand now that we've got things sorted out?"

"Perhaps," said Finn, not really listening. "But you and Jess have to go back right away. Come on."

He reached for her hand, but Freya pulled it away, frowning.

"Me and Jess? What about Magnus?"

"I'm staying. There's going to be a wolf attack on Dundee – a huge one. Finn's taking me there through his world, so I can warn my parents and the rest of the town."

Freya's eyes were wide. "How do you know?"

"Rowan left me a letter," said Finn. "Now come on, please."

Freya glanced at Jess, who shook her head emphatically.

"You're not sending us home," said Freya. "We want to help."

"If you want to help, then go," said Magnus shortly.

"No," said Freya, eyes blazing. "They're my family too, remember? There's nothing we can do in Westgarth or Kirriemuir, but there might be some way we can help here or in Dundee."

"It's too dangerous," said Finn.

"It's no more dangerous for us than it is for Magnus," said Jess. "Taking us back will just waste more time."

"Don't be stupid, Jess. I've killed some of these wolves, remember?" said Magnus.

She turned on him. "Do *you* remember? Freya and I were there. We saw what they can do. We helped kill them. We're not going to be sent home. Now come on, this is just wasting time."

Finn let a hissing breath out through his teeth.

"I can't look after you all. Remember that," he said.

"We don't expect you to," Jess retorted. "We'll look after ourselves. Can we go now?"

Breathing hard, Jess pulled herself up the last few metres of rock and straightened slowly, wiping sweat from her forehead. Beside her Freya stood catching her breath too, looking back towards Finn's house, now far below them in the valley. They'd been scrambling up a trail, which for the last hour had scarcely existed, hauling themselves up steep slopes, or scrabbling from ledge to ledge up crags and outcrops.

Finn had led the way, setting a ferocious pace at first, with which the others could barely keep up, but he had moderated it as his temper cooled. As it became more of a climb than a scramble, he slowed down further, so that they could see the route he took up the rock.

Magnus reached the top of the crag and pulled himself up to stand with the others.

"You may as well sit down," said Finn. "We'll have a break before we head into the forest."

Jess looked round at the forest that waited for them. Again, she had the sense that everything was more alive than it was in her world. She was sure she could hear the trees creaking, although there was no wind. She could smell the forest too: a composty smell of rotting vegetation.

It was quite unlike the woodland they'd come through on their way from the pool to Finn's home. These trees were much smaller, their trunks branching close to the ground and their scabbed greyish bark almost obscured by skeins of trailing grey-green lichen. Jess looked for any sign of wolf charms among the branches, but there were none that she could see.

Freya moved to the stream that plunged off the edge of the crag and crouched down to drink from her cupped hands, before wiping them across her sweaty brow.

"How long will it take us to get to Dundee?" she asked Finn, now that he seemed to have put his anger behind him.

"If we get through the forest before nightfall, we should reach the door by afternoon."

Jess reached a hand down to Freya and pulled her up as Magnus walked past them, grim-faced. Jess caught his arm as he went by.

"We'll get there in time, Magnus. I know we will."

He looked at her wordlessly, gave her the hint of a smile and went on.

They stared around them as they passed into the forest. All the trees were the same type, their grey bark ghostly pale, thin limbs curving towards the sky. They had long, narrow leaves the length of Jess's palm, shaped like scythe blades. Many of the leaves had already fallen, as though it were autumn here, and those still on the trees were turning from green to a translucent pinkish red.

Once again, Finn followed no path that the others could see, but chose his way without hesitation, although he seemed uneasy, constantly glancing round. The moss underfoot cushioned their steps and deadened sound as well, so that they moved in something close to silence.

Jess found her eyes starting to play tricks on her. The confusion of trunks and branches and lichen, together with the disconcerting shimmer of the Nykur world's air, began to look like bearded faces from the corner of her eye, as if the trees were watching her. She saw Freya, ahead of her, glance round suddenly a few times.

"Seeing things?" she asked.

"I hope so," Freya replied. "This doesn't feel like a friendly place, does it? I suppose Finn would have mentioned it if there were wolves in here?"

"Not friendly at all... I wonder how much further it is?"

"It can't be far. The light's starting to go and Finn said we'd be out of the forest by nightfall."

"He *hoped* we'd be out of it by nightfall," Jess corrected her.

"Then let's make sure we are," said Freya, speeding up.

As the light faded around them, Finn waited for the others to catch up.

"We'd better stay together now," he said. "It would be easy for you to get lost."

"Are there wolves in this forest?" Freya asked.

"No. No, not here. They don't like this forest any more than the Nykur do."

Just then, something fluttered between the trees just in front of them.

"I thought there weren't any birds?" said Magnus.

"There aren't. That was a bat. Come on, we need to hurry now. This is the bats' territory, and they'll defend it after dark."

"What exactly does that mean?" asked Jess, quickening her pace.

"Have you ever been bitten by a bat?" Finn looked at her. Jess shook her head.

"We're not in any danger from them, but – well, it's not pleasant. They've got sharp teeth, and if there are a lot of them…" He gave an involuntary shudder. "I've been caught in here once after nightfall; I'd rather not do it again."

There was hardly enough light to see where they were stepping now, and bats swooped, chittering, around their heads.

Jess gritted her teeth, determined not to yelp as another one zipped past her face. How long before they started to attack?

At that moment, the trees thinned in front of them and Finn gave a shout.

"That's it – we're out."

They emerged onto a bare hillside under the stars. The land rolled away beneath them into indistinct shadows.

"I suppose we have to wait until it gets light before we go on?" said Magnus gloomily.

"No. There's enough light for me to see," Finn replied.

"So, what now? We all hold hands and you lead us down the hill?" Magnus couldn't keep the frustration out of his voice.

"No. Now I take horse form, and you ride."

"But we can't leave the girls here," Magnus objected.

"That's not what I meant. You ride – all of you."

"You can't carry three of us, Finn," Jess protested.

There was just enough light to see the grin he flashed her.

"Not in your world, but here I can. Horse form is difficult for a half-blood in your world, but here it's easier, and much stronger."

Jess found it hard to believe he could really do this, but he sounded confident.

"Well, get on and change then," Freya commanded him.

Finn grew still as he had done when Jess had watched him change before. He closed his eyes and let his breath go…

… and the dark horse was there.

"We're never all going to fit," said Magnus.

The horse moved across to a boulder to make it easier for

them to mount. Freya climbed up first, then Jess behind her. Magnus looked at them doubtfully.

"This isn't going to work."

"Just climb up, Magnus," Jess urged him, "And we'll soon see."

A few seconds later, Magnus was behind her, his hands on her waist.

"This shouldn't be possible," he muttered, and Jess couldn't help but laugh.

Finn tossed his head and moved off.

As long as she lived, Jess remembered that ride. Finn moved at a smooth pace across heather moor and meadowland, through patches of woodland and across streams. Although it was too dark to see much, Jess could smell the difference between the landscapes, sense it in the way Finn ran. Freya's hair blew in Jess's face, and Magnus's arms were around her waist. There was no need to hold on; it would have been impossible to fall off. She remembered the sensation of almost becoming part of the horse from her other brief rides.

The stars seemed to stream past them. Once or twice Freya turned to Jess with a delighted smile. When Jess twisted to look at Magnus, there was an expression of baffled wonder on his face.

Dawn streaked the sky, turning the clouds shell-pink and apple-green before Finn slowed and came to a halt. Magnus, Jess and Freya slid down from his back and watched as the horse became Finn again.

He looked at Magnus and raised his eyebrows.

"I apologise," said Magnus. "That was…"

"Incredible," supplied Freya.

Finn turned to Jess and for a second, their gazes caught. She smiled at him.

"Amazing," she said. "And much better without wolves chasing us."

She realised just too late that it was the wrong thing to say, as she saw Magnus's expression change, and Finn's in turn grow serious.

"If we all walk for a bit just now, I can carry you again in a while," he said.

They walked into the rising sun, each wrapped in their own thoughts. Broad swathes of grassland stretched ahead of them, utterly empty, moving like a sea as the wind ruffled across it.

Finn called a halt and they sat down by a stream and watched the sun come properly up. Jess drank deeply, hoping the cold water would fill the empty place in her stomach. She couldn't work out how long it must be since they'd last eaten.

"Aren't there any towns nearby, Finn?" asked Freya. "We haven't even passed another house. Where does everyone live?"

Finn sat up slowly.

"There aren't many of us left around here. We never had towns – remember, when you're not here we spend a lot of time in horse shape – and we won't be passing any of the other houses the way we're going. Not until we get to the gateway."

"Don't you get lonely?" Freya asked, frowning.

For a few seconds she didn't think he would answer, then he seemed to relent.

"Yes. Of course. It must have been so different here long ago, when there were lots of Nykur. I've never known what it was like to run with a big herd, to have lots of my own people around me."

Jess's heart went out to him, hearing how sad he sounded.

"Come on," he said, getting up. "That's enough of trailing along at human speed."

They rode for another four hours or so, the grass flowing under Finn's hooves, then the ground rising again until they crested a hill and he stopped. Before them was a bowl-shaped valley, cupping a small loch of intensely blue water. Beyond it the hills rose steeply again, tree-clad and wild. On the nearest side of the loch, small figures moved, horses and human, close to another Nykur house. Like Finn's, it overhung the water and was a series of linked buildings, but it looked much older, the wood faded silvery pale on walls and roof.

Jess, Freya and Magnus climbed down, peering into the distance to try and make out more of the people beside the loch.

"At least there don't seem to be any wolves around yet," said Freya.

Changed back, Finn spoke.

"I doubt that's good news." He pointed at the loch. "That's the gateway to Dundee. They must have gone through already. He took a deep breath, looking at the figures at the lochside. "My family, and the rest of the Nykur are down there. We're in time to help."

Chapter Twenty

They stood looking down at the figures on the loch shore.

Jess turned to Finn. He had sounded nervous when he spoke; his face now was paler than usual.

"It'll be all right. Remember what Rowan's letter said. As soon as they see you, it'll be all right." She searched his eyes. "You should go down alone."

Finn shook his head.

"No, let's get it all over at once," he said. "But don't say anything until we see what sort of reception we get."

They began the long, exposed walk down the hillside, Finn a little way in front. Jess counted the people and horses by the loch as she walked. Fifteen.

"When will the rest of the Nykur get here?" she asked, raising her voice so that Finn would hear her.

"The rest? Everyone's here already," he said, without looking round.

"Fifteen? That's all of you?" Jess was shocked.

This time he stopped and turned.

"That's all of us *now*. And two of the people down there are the boys who used to live in your world."

"But there must be others," Freya insisted.

Finn stared at the three of them.

"You really don't understand, do you? These fifteen are the only people I have ever known in the Nykur world. There's no one else for over a hundred miles. Now perhaps you realise why I came to your world so often."

He turned and walked on without another word, leaving the others gaping in his wake.

Jess watched his straight back and started after him, her mind in a whirl. *Fifteen.* It was almost impossible to believe. And these Nykur were living by some agreement that no one in her world even knew about, risking themselves to protect the unthinking populations of Kirriemuir and Dundee from these terrible wolves.

The Nykur by the loch had noticed them now. Activity had come to a halt and Jess felt their eyes on her and the others as they came down the hill. At that moment she was very tempted to turn and run back up the slope. Glancing at Freya and Magnus's faces, she guessed that they felt the same.

One figure detached itself from the group of Nykur and began moving towards them: a girl, slim and dark haired. A few seconds later she broke into a run, and then so did Finn.

"It's Rowan," Freya breathed beside Jess, her face lighting up.

Finn and his sister reached each other and she threw her arms round him, sobbing. The others stopped, not wanting to intrude.

"Finn, Finn! I knew you would come back. I knew! I wished for it every night and every morning." She drew back to look at him properly. "Did you find my letter?"

"How else would I have known to come here?" Finn said with a smile.

Rowan seemed to see the others properly for the first time.

"Freya?" she said uncertainly. "And you!" She looked at Jess. "Why have you brought them here, Finn?"

"I'll explain later, Rowan. I have to talk to Mother and Father now." He took a deep breath.

Rowan took his hand. "They want you back, Finn. Don't forget that, whatever Mother says to you." And, ignoring the others, she turned and pulled Finn towards the rest of the Nykur.

Jess, Freya and Magnus hung back in spite of what Finn had said before.

Finn stopped abruptly, bringing Rowan to a halt beside him, and waited as his parents walked forward. They stopped a few paces away from him.

"I banished you," said Gudrun, "And yet, you have returned."

"And you have brought people from the Upper World," added Euan.

"Why have you defied me?" asked Gudrun, her eyes fixed on Finn's face.

"Because you are my family, and I am Nykur," said Finn so softly she could only just hear him. "And because I love you, and I cannot bear to live alone in the Upper World."

For perhaps ten seconds no one moved, then Gudrun threw her arms wide, and in a heartbeat Finn was embracing her. A second later the embrace included Euan and Rowan too.

Jess could see Gudrun speaking to Finn, but much too softly for her to make out the words. She saw him nod, his face buried in his mother's shoulder. After a moment, Finn raised his head and swiped a hand across his eyes.

Gudrun's gaze shifted to them and a frown appeared and deepened.

"Why have you brought *them* here, Finn? Surely there has been enough trouble already?"

"There has, but now I know why." He looked at Jess, then back at his family. "The others will need to hear this too, later." He took a breath.

"The people in the Upper World don't know about the agreement. The men who made it were so ashamed that they

232

had agreed to trade their children for their safety that they told no one. Humans now didn't know anything about the Nykur or the wolves, or that we've been protecting them all these years."

Gudrun, Euan and Rowan stared at Finn in astonishment. It was Euan who broke the silence.

"Is this true?"

Magnus answered.

"It's true. We knew nothing about this, until a couple of days ago. Now a few people understand. And the wolves... Some of them came out of Roseroot Pool. Your son saved us all from them." He lapsed into silence.

"The barrier at the pool needed repairing," Finn said to his mother. "I did what I could when we came through."

For the first time, Gudrun spoke to them directly.

"You truly did not know? So when you came," – she fixed her gaze on Jess, "to take Freya back, you all thought we were wicked creatures who stole your children for our own amusement?"

Jess swallowed. "Not exactly. No one except my grandmother even believed you were real." She turned to Euan. "My grandmother was your cousin Ellen in the Upper World. Do you remember her?"

Euan shook his head slowly.

"She remembers you. She spent most of her life wondering what had really happened to you. It made her happy to find that you had a family." She risked a smile and found it hesitantly returned.

"I brought them to our world so that Freya could remember properly what had happened to her," Finn said to his family. "I thought I owed her that. Then I found Rowan's letter. Magnus's family live in Dundee. He wants to warn them, and this was the fastest way to get him there. I said I would take him through this gateway."

His parents looked at each other and, after a pause, Gudrun spoke.

"We must ask the others. This is not a decision for us to make alone. It concerns *all* the Nykur. Rowan, find them some food while they wait."

They were left alone with Rowan.

"Come on, I'll get you something to eat."

She led them towards the Nykur house that overhung the loch. As they got closer, Jess noticed signs of disrepair: missing shingles on the roof and cracked boards on the walls.

Inside there were signs that the place was being used as a makeshift camp by the Nykur who were human: bedrolls in several of the rooms, traces of hasty repair here and there. Rowan led them into the kitchen, rummaged in a cupboard with a door hanging drunkenly from one hinge, and produced bread and apples.

It was a long time since they had last eaten. There was silence as they chewed. Rowan sat next to Finn, watching his every move as though he might suddenly disappear again.

Magnus turned impatiently to Finn.

"When can we go? What's happening?"

"I don't know. For now, you must be patient. We can't do anything unless the others agree."

When they finished eating, they went outside and watched from a distance as the discussions continued, until at last Gudrun waved them over.

The Nykur, all in human form now, waited silently, watching the strangers who had delivered such shocking news. They were all tall, long limbed and blue eyed, whatever colour their hair. Their silent regard was disconcerting.

Gudrun spoke without preamble, her voice tight.

"Finn, the clan has set you a test if you are to be accepted as

234

Nykur again. There are almost two-hundred wolves massed on the other side of the gateway. You must draw them back here so we can destroy them. They have been waiting for this night before they attack the town."

"Why?" Magnus interrupted.

"You have hunted your own wolves out of the hills round Dundee. The black wolves want vengeance. The full moon rises tonight. They will attack then."

"What do I have to do? How do I get them back here?" asked Finn.

"What? Finn, no, you can't do it," Jess exclaimed.

"He must," said Euan. "That is the test."

"You can take the boy with you," Gudrun said to Finn. "He can warn the town if he can get there. But your job is to take this." A black-haired man handed something to Gudrun. "This has taken us two days. We have poured all our power into it."

She held up her hand. From a leather thong hung a stone about the size of a walnut, smooth and dully gleaming, dark as a piece of midnight sky, speckled with tiny crystalline points of light.

Finn took it, handling it carefully. His eyes widened and Jess watched as understanding dawned on his face.

"The full moon," he said wonderingly.

"What do you mean?" she asked.

"Show them, Finn," said his mother. "Show us all that you can release the power we have trapped here."

Finn held the stone in his cupped hand and slowly, it began to glow. In the sky above them a pale light gleamed. They looked up at the full moon.

A mutter of approval ran through the Nykur as Finn opened his hand and the moon faded away.

"It will be brighter there," one of them said.

"You must show the wolves *this* moon before the real moon

rises in the Upper World," said Gudrun. "You must use it as a lure to bring them back through the gateway and then we will seal it and destroy them." Finn nodded, slipped the thong over his head and tucked the moonstone inside his tunic. Gudrun turned to Jess and Freya.

"You cannot go with them. Finn's speed will be their only defence. You will stay here. Someone will take you back to your own world when this is over."

There was no possibility of disagreeing with that voice. Jess and Freya kept silent.

"How soon can we leave?" asked Magnus.

"You should go as soon as possible. We cannot be sure what you will find on the other side."

Rowan's lower lip was trembling. It was clear she couldn't bear the thought that she was losing Finn again when she'd only just got him back. He noticed her distress and gave her a reassuring hug.

"I'll hardly be gone for any time," he said. "Don't do anything too brave when the wolves come." He leaned closer to her and whispered so only she could hear. "Look after Jess and Freya for me. Everyone else will be too busy."

"All right," said Rowan uncertainly.

"We'll go now," said Finn, turning to Magnus.

Magnus nodded grimly.

"Be careful, Magnus – you too, Finn," Freya said, hugging each of them quickly, then stepping back so that Jess could do the same.

Jess found herself suddenly at a loss, overwhelmed by the feelings she had for both of them that she had only half admitted to herself.

She summoned a bracing smile and somehow managed to give first Finn and then Magnus a firm embrace and a friendly kiss.

"Give my love to your parents," she said to Magnus and, to Finn, "You'd like his parents; they're good people. If it's possible to talk a wolf to death, Magnus's mother will do it."

And then they went, walking into the dense blue water, Magnus's hand on Finn's shoulder.

They were gone.

Magnus was swirled through blue water like a bubble. He held on to a breath until it became impossible not to take another, and found to his surprise that his head was not in water but in air, in darkness, his eyes shut.

He gasped a breath, then another, looking round. At first it seemed just as dark with his eyes open. Which way was the shore?

It dawned on him that he was standing, not floating, up to his shoulders in freezing water, and then that he shouldn't be alone. Where was Finn?

Magnus was about to call out, then he thought about the wolves, and kept silent instead. A few seconds later he heard a sound from the water behind him and saw Finn's dripping head appear close by, coughing and spluttering.

Now that his eyes had adapted to the dark, Magnus made a move towards the shore, but Finn caught his arm and signed to him to wait. They stood together, listening intently. There was the *kee-vik* of a tawny owl close by, then silence.

"All right," Finn breathed, stifling another cough, and they waded ashore.

"Where are we?" Magnus whispered, looking round. He'd thought they would arrive in Dundee itself, but all he could see were the dim shapes of broken ground and open country.

"Dundee's about four miles that way. You'll see the lights soon. Come on. We'll have to walk for a bit, but I'll change as soon as I can."

Five minutes later they came round the shoulder of a hill and Magnus saw the scatter of lights from Dundee and knew where he was. Speeding up, he thought longingly of the warmth of his parents' house. First things first, though; they had to get to the watchtower, convince the watchmen of the danger, and get them to alert the town.

Somewhere ahead of them, a wolf howled. Finn and Magnus stopped abruptly. The howl came again, and this time it was answered from behind them.

Magnus drew his knife. "Can you see anything?" Finn said softly.

They stood back to back, still listening.

"No," Magnus replied. "Do you think they can smell us?"

"There's no wind to speak of. It might just be coincidence," Finn said.

The knife blade glimmered in Magnus's hand. "What do you want to do?" he asked.

"Maybe they've gone. Let's give it a minute."

But just then there was another howl from ahead of them, and this time, answering wolf song from several throats. The howls were behind them and off to one side now as well.

"Let's move," Magnus said. Finn nodded agreement, trying not to cough. "Are you all right?" Magnus asked.

"Yes, fine. I just swallowed some water as we came through. It's not very clean, this close to Dundee."

They moved more slowly now, listening every few steps, constantly looking round, but now the wolves were silent.

The boys began to relax slightly. Five minutes had gone with no sign that the wolves were tracking them. And then a flicker of movement caught the tail of Finn's eye.

"They're back," he said quietly, without breaking stride. "Stop when I tell you and wait for me to change. We'll need more speed to outrun them than your legs can manage."

Magnus could see the wolves now as streaks of deeper darkness against the sky. He tightened his grip on the knife.

"Now."

Finn stopped and, with an effort, so did Magnus. It made his flesh creep to stand still, knowing that the wolves were closing on him, but Finn was right: if he ran, he'd be brought down before he had any chance of reaching Dundee.

Beside him stood the black horse. He reached for its mane to pull himself up and found himself astride its back without doing anything – the horse's stride already changing from trot to canter.

Behind them now, no longer the sound of howling, but deep, angry snarls, as the wolves realised their quarry had a chance of escape. Magnus dug his left hand deep into Finn's mane and shifted his grip on the knife.

Jess and Freya went to where Rowan was walking.

"What are you doing?" Freya asked.

Rowan paused to push a strand of dark hair out of her eyes.

"We're collecting stones to seal the gateway."

"So, can we help?" Jess asked.

"You won't be able to recognise the stones that we need."

"No... how *do* you recognise them?" Jess enquired, looking at the two in Rowan's hand. To her, they looked no different from any of the other stones lying at her feet.

"Because..." Rowan struggled to find something to say that would make sense. "They just... look *right*. They look like themselves, like they did when they lived in the loch."

Jess and Freya exchanged glances.

"Mmnn... I see," said Jess, slowly.

"Really?" Rowan's surprise showed in her face.

"No. I've no idea what you mean. Sorry."

Rowan snorted. "You can still take them down to the shore

and give them to someone to put in place." She handed the stones she was carrying to Freya. "Over there." She pointed to where two Nykur men were moving slowly around the margin of the loch, setting stones down every few paces in some precise and obscure pattern.

"All right." Freya beamed at Rowan and went off on her errand.

Rowan watched her go, then fixed Jess with a stare.

"I want to talk to you," she said. "About my brother."

Magnus watched the lights of Dundee growing closer as they pounded along. So far, the wolves weren't gaining on them, but nor were they dropping back. He could feel the effort of the horse's muscles working beneath him. This wasn't how it had been in Finn's world.

They were among the disorganised scatter of buildings at the edge of town now. Magnus let his mind stray to the fastest route to take to St Mary's watchtower. And then, without warning, he hit the ground hard, and all the air was jarred from his lungs. He hadn't even felt Finn stumble. What had happened?

He struggled to his knees, gasping for breath. Finn, back in human shape, was doing the same a few metres away.

Close now, a wolf snarled.

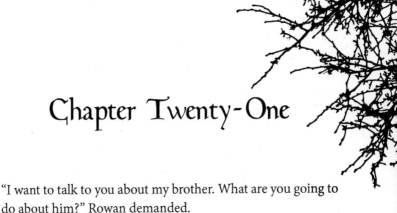

Chapter Twenty-One

"I want to talk to you about my brother. What are you going to do about him?" Rowan demanded.

"Do?" repeated Jess. "I don't understand what you mean."

Rowan's expression said quite clearly that she didn't believe a word of that.

"About him. About you," said Rowan impatiently. "About how he feels."

"I'm not sure what you…" Jess began, but the tide of heat rising in her face gave the lie to the words before she even said them.

"That's why he took Freya, you know." Rowan rushed on with what she wanted to say now, almost ignoring Jess. "It was meant to be you, but the horse senses are hopeless at telling people apart. He's been watching you for years. He's loved you for years. What are you going to do? What do you feel for him?"

Jess stood with her mouth open like a fish. A series of images reared up in her brain.

The first time she saw him, in the firelight, when she came to the Nykur world for Freya. The feeling in her chest when she saw him, white and still in the snow. The moment he had kissed her, before he went out to face the wolves at Westgarth.

"I… Magnus and I… there's nothing…" she stammered.

"What do you feel?" Rowan insisted.

"I don't know."

"Liar!" Rowan spat the word out. "He's risked everything for you, and you can't even be honest about your own feelings." She turned away and started to scan the ground, and Jess saw that Freya was on her way back. She put her hands to her hot face, trying to cool it before Freya noticed.

Magnus scrabbled his way over to Finn, looking around wildly as he moved, sure that wolves were about to erupt from the ground around him.

He grabbed Finn's arm and pulled him to his feet.

"What happened?"

Finn shook his head. "I'm not properly fit – not here, anyway," he said with difficulty, and pulled Magnus into a run. In the street behind them they could hear the wolves.

Magnus hauled Finn round a corner to the left and into a narrower street, then right into a tiny alley that ended in a flight of steps and beyond that, the backyard of an inn, empty barrels stacked waiting by the cellar door. They launched six barrels down the steps towards the pursuing wolves, and heard the sound of wood and flesh crashing into each other, and whimpers of pain.

Magnus dragged Finn off again across the paved inn yard and out through the archway where the carts came in. They had gained precious time.

"It's not far now," Magnus told Finn.

Finn nodded. "Go. I'll be right behind you."

Magnus ran.

Jess carried an armful of stones to the lochside, glad to escape from Rowan's scrutiny for a few minutes. The Nykur men looked at Jess with undisguised curiosity as she handed over the stones, but didn't speak. She walked a little way off and sat down facing the loch.

She needed to untangle her feelings. She'd been pretending for so long that there was nothing to face up to that she'd almost come to believe it, but now Rowan had forced her into honesty.

What do you feel?

Magnus made her feel safe, made her feel happy. She was comfortable with him. She was very fond of him. She hadn't quite managed to keep her imagination in check, and had pictured being older, and married to him, and it was a safe, comfortable, happy feeling. It fitted. Everyone would be pleased if they married.

It was the right thing to do.

What do you feel?

Her heart always seemed to have been beating faster when she was with Finn. *That's because there's always been danger when you've been with him,* common sense said. But she knew it was more than that. All these years he'd watched her and she'd known without knowing it that he was there. And then when she finally met him and he told her about that, instead of being angry, or frightened, it was as if a piece of her heart had clicked into place.

Jess got to her feet, agitated, afraid of what she was admitting to herself. She loved them both.

"No," she said out loud. "I can't love Finn. I hardly know him. I love Magnus."

And, repeating it over and over under her breath, she stomped determinedly back towards Rowan and Freya.

St Mary's Watchtower rose ahead of Magnus.

Reaching it, he turned the handle on one of the few doors in town that was sure to be unlocked and barrelled into the tower. He held the door ready to slam it as soon as Finn was inside.

As soon as Finn was inside.

Where was he?

Magnus could hear feet hurrying downstairs. He ducked out of the doorway into the street again to see Finn coming towards him at a laboured run, two wolves closing on him fast.

Finn half fell through the doorway into the tower. Magnus shoved the door closed with his shoulder on a rapidly advancing vision of teeth and claws, barred it, and slid down it to sit in a sweaty heap.

From the stair, two astonished men looked down at the panting figures on the floor.

"You lads had better have a good explanation," said one of them.

Rowan looked towards the crags on the other side of the loch.

"We're running out of time," she said. "The light will soon fade. We have to be ready by the time darkness comes." She handed the stones she was carrying to Freya, and bent to pick up a final one.

"Come on," she said and joined the rest of the Nykur walking to the loch.

Jess watched as the last stones were set in place. What were they for? And what was happening to Magnus and Finn on the other side of the gateway?

Gudrun and Euan had come to join Rowan. Jess went to stand beside Freya.

"Now what happens?" Jess asked nervously.

It was Gudrun who answered.

"Now we must wait for Finn to bring the wolves, then try to seal the gateway as they come through."

"And if you can't?"

Gudrun shook her head. "If the wolves are on this side, there are so many of them that we may all die. If they are on the other side, Dundee may fall to them. There are so few of us here that we cannot be sure we have enough power. And we cannot spare any to protect you as we work. You must stay in the house with the boys who used to live in your world, and do what you can to protect yourselves."

Jess glanced at Freya, seeing her own growing fear mirrored in her friend's face. Gudrun had already turned away to talk to another Nykur.

If Jess thought about what might happen in the next few hours she'd just curl up on the ground, whimpering. Instead, she gave Freya's hand a bolstering squeeze.

"I suppose we'd better do as we're told," Jess said. "I'd almost prefer to stay here though; at least there are plenty of rocks to throw."

"How's your aim?" asked Freya.

"Well, either it'll improve very quickly, or it won't get the chance."

"Then let's see what we can find to throw from inside."

They climbed the steps to the house.

"At least we've got knives," said Jess. "There can't be much difference between gutting a fish and gutting a wolf, can there?"

"Just size," said Freya, with the air of an expert.

"And you do come from a family of famous wolf killers."

"Exactly. And the head above the door needs replacing. It's far too scruffy. Maybe I'll take father back a new one."

Jess had no idea why this ridiculous conversation was making her feel better, but it was.

"Boiling water," she mused as they reached the kitchen. "They won't like that…"

"The knives are sharp, but they don't give us much of a reach," Freya pointed out. "It would be better if we could fasten them to something – makeshift spears."

"You're right. Let's see what we can find."

Magnus opened his mouth to start explaining himself, but was pre-empted by a crash against the door and the sound of furious growling from outside.

"What's chasing you?" asked the watchman, eyeing the door in alarm.

"Wolves," said Magnus, getting to his feet. "The kind that don't give up once they start hunting."

"How many?"

"We didn't wait to see once they started chasing us, but there are hundreds massing not far from here to attack the people in town. You have to sound the warning."

There was a small, shuttered window to the right of the door. One of the men went to open the shutters now, as bodies continued to thud against the door.

"Don't!" yelled Finn. "They'll get in."

"No they'll not. Not unless they can chew through iron." He threw back the shutter to expose a metal grille. The sudden source of light alerted the wolves, and in a few seconds jaws were snapping outside the window.

The watchmen looked at each other.

"We'll sound the alarm. Stay inside."

"Don't worry about that," Magnus said feelingly as the men took the stairs two at a time.

A few seconds later a bell sounded: not the continuous tolling that would have signalled a fire, but three notes and a pause, repeated over and over; the signal for people to get off the street and arm themselves, for the wolves were here.

Finn got up and peered cautiously out at the wolf-haunted street. "Let's go upstairs. We might get a better idea of what's happening."

Out on the platform they watched as lights were kindled in windows all over the city. Finn grabbed Magnus's arm and pointed.

"Look. Here they come."

A river of black bodies flowed into the streets at the southern edge of town, where they had been only a short time earlier. Magnus saw three terrified cats torn to pieces as the pack began to spread itself through the town.

"You've saved lives tonight, lads," said one of the watchmen. "If we hadn't rung the bells to get everyone off the streets…"

"What happens now?" asked Finn.

"We can't do much until it's light." He stared at the seemingly endless river of wolf fur. "How many are there? Where did they come from?"

Finn and Magnus exchanged glances, but said nothing.

Jess stood by the kitchen window, trying to convince herself that she felt safer now she was holding a makeshift wolf-spear: a knife fastened to a length of wood.

Behind her, Freya carried one as well, as the two stolen boys checked the pots of water boiling over the hearth. Jess wouldn't have recognised them as Donald and Aidan. They seemed to have grown up far more than was possible in the time since they had disappeared, and showed no sign that they remembered Freya or Jess.

The rest of the Nykur stood at intervals along the loch shore. Freya and the boys joined Jess at the window. Freya elbowed Donald in the ribs.

"What are they doing?" she hissed.

"The stones used to live in the loch. We are telling the loch that it is made of stone, not water. Then nothing will be able to force a way through it again. The gateway will be sealed."

"But what are they *doing*?" Freya persisted.

"They are joining their thoughts to the stones' thoughts."

Freya gave up, looked at Jess and rolled her eyes. "I feel much better now I know that," she muttered.

The scream made Magnus's skin crawl. The wolves had found an open window in one of the nearby houses. He wasn't sure how many had got inside. At first there had been the sound of fighting, but then the wolves had clearly overwhelmed the people. There was nothing he could do but stand here and listen to them die.

He tried to keep his mind away from his parents, but it was no good. The house would be locked up tight, surely? His mother was always careful about that, but his father sometimes forgot. He could hear his mother's voice in his head now; she always said the same thing to his father when it happened.

"You're not in Kirriemuir now, you big daft lump. Most of these people are strangers to us. We could wake up tomorrow, murdered in our own beds."

It didn't seem so funny now, stuck at the top of this tower while the wolves quartered the town. He wanted to be with his parents, to make sure they were safe.

Finn leaned out over the edge, trying to estimate how many wolves there were. *Far too many.* How long had they been coming through the doorway from his own world?

He could hear shouting down at street level now, as people tried to organise themselves from the safety of their houses, and horses screaming where the wolves must have broken into a stable. The watchmen had disappeared inside to get their crossbows, even though the chance of hitting a wolf in the near dark was slim.

Finn knew he had to go. He watched the wolves in the street below. Still too many, but he couldn't afford to wait much longer. It couldn't be long until moonrise.

"I'm going now," he said to Magnus. "There's not much time left to get them back to the loch. I hope your parents are all right."

"Once the men come back up we'll go inside, slip through the door to the stable and take their horses," said Magnus.

"But you're staying here, aren't you? And I'm going to take horse shape."

Magnus eyed Finn. "That didn't work too well on the way here. Why not use real horses to get us at least part of the way – save your breath for the tricky part?"

"You're right: I'll take a horse. But," Finn repeated, "you must make sure your parents are safe."

"There's nothing I can do to protect them by staying here," said Magnus flatly. "I can't reach them. It makes more sense to make sure you get the wolves back through that door."

Because he couldn't find the words to express how he felt, Finn just nodded.

Footsteps heralded the return of the watchmen, crossbows primed. Magnus and Finn hurried down the stairs and went straight through the internal door to the stable, where two wild-eyed horses were tethered.

"Hush now," said Finn, walking up to the first one, which backed away to the limit of the rope. "Give me a minute, Magnus. I can calm them down a bit."

Finn slid his hand up the rope to the halter, then down the animal's neck and stood quietly beside it, whispering into its ear, while Magnus went to fetch saddles. When he came back, Finn had calmed the first horse and was doing the same to the second.

As they tightened girths, Finn shook his head.

"You're crazy," he said. "There's still time to change your mind and stay, you know."

Magnus made a face. "Jess and Freya would never forgive me if I set you loose on your own, and they're even scarier than the wolves."

Finn chuckled.

"I owe you an apology," Magnus went on, turning sober, "I don't understand everything, but I believe now that you never meant any of us any harm. You've more than proved that."

"Thank you. I'm glad I'm not doing this on my own. I'd say we're about even." Finn hesitated, then went on. "Jess is lucky to have you – they both are."

Magnus shrugged.

"I'm serious about Jess. I've made my choice," he said.

Has she made hers? Finn wondered, but this was hardly the moment to ask.

They walked the horses to the outside door. Finn checked that the moonstone was safe inside his tunic, then slid back the bolt and opened the door a crack. The street outside was clear. They led the horses out, secured the door behind them and mounted. The wolves had moved further into the town. Denied human prey, they snarled and snapped at each other, the occasional one falling to a lucky crossbow bolt or arrow. Magnus and Finn ignored the torn carcasses of cats and dogs and chickens scattered here and there, and rode in silence to the broad main street that led straight out of town. They brought the horses to a halt.

Finn reached into his tunic for the moonstone and closed his hand round it.

Magnus became aware of a soft glow above them. He looked up.

There, impossibly huge, impossibly close, the full moon hung. He looked back at Finn's face, saw him smiling triumphantly.

"Not bad for a half-blood," Finn said.

And then the howling started: voice upon voice of the wolves, until the darkness hummed with the noise. For a few seconds all the sound stopped. A child cried somewhere and was swiftly hushed.

A wolf appeared at the end of the street, staring at Finn and Magnus, at the illusory moon. It began to stalk slowly towards them. Another appeared, and another, more and more, all their eyes fixed on the moon, moving together in eerie silence.

"It worked," Magnus muttered in wonder.

And then the wolves began to run towards them.

Chapter Twenty-Two

"What's happening?" Freya asked Jess. All the Nykur had turned to face the loch. They stood still, eyes closed in the failing light.

Jess shook her head, but Donald answered.

"Can't you feel it? It has begun. Finn has cast the moon at the wolves. He is drawing on the power of everyone here to help him. He is bringing them to the door. Can't you feel it?"

The girls put their arms round each other, imagining what might be happening in Dundee, sick with fear for the people they loved.

"How long will it take? How soon will they be here?" Jess asked, but she got no reply.

There wasn't a sound from any of the Nykur. A terrible, expectant stillness had descended on the lochside. Not a blade of grass stirred. Freya and Jess tightened their grip on their weapons and waited.

As the wolves sped towards them, Finn and Magnus dragged the horses' heads around and dug their heels into the animals' sides. The horses hardly needed urging anyway. With the stink of wolf in their nostrils, all that was on their minds was escape. They shot away, barely under control.

The boys gave them their heads, trying to build some distance between themselves and the pursuing pack, knowing they would have to slow down over the rougher ground that lay ahead.

Magnus glanced back. Dozens of wolves ran behind them, filling the street as they passed, and then the horses were into the straggle of buildings at the edge of town, and then clear of it altogether.

Finn didn't speak, most of his mind concentrated on keeping the moon illusion going.

They kept to the road for as long as possible, then pulled the horses up a little, and turned away from it and onto the hillocky ground they had to cover to reach the loch. At least the fictitious moon gave them light to see by, so they could keep up a reasonable speed. The wolves, unfortunately, were perfectly suited to just this sort of running; soon they would start to gain on the horses.

In the east was a hint that the sky was beginning to lighten as the real moon rose. Finn had been right to leave when he did. The illusion would fail soon.

They could see the loch ahead of them, dark between hills. The horses were almost spent, stumbling from time to time, only their fear of the wolves keeping them going.

"We need to leave the horses now," Magnus yelled. "Before one of them falls and takes us with it."

Finn nodded. "The wolves will slow a little to kill them once we set them loose. There's nothing else we can do, is there?"

Magnus shook his head, and they pulled the horses up, jumped down and started to run without looking back. After a few seconds, they heard shrieks as the wolves caught up with the exhausted horses. Grim-faced, they ran on. Only at the edge of the water did they stop and look back.

Under the moonlight, the wolves' black pelts gleamed as they loped inexorably on, drawn by the twin lures of prey and moonlight.

"This is it," said Finn. He grasped Magnus's hand. "Don't let go."

They waded out until they were hip deep and turned to face the wolves again. The leading animals had halted at the water's edge and moved back and forth, sniffing the earth and the air.

Finn cupped the moonstone in his free hand once more, and above them, the full moon blazed with an intensity that made them narrow their eyes.

The wolves howled with one voice, and then they started to walk into the water. The boys backed away, waiting for as many wolves as possible to walk into the trap.

"Come on... come on..." Finn muttered.

The water was full of wolves now, only their dark heads visible as they swam, still more moving from the shore into the shallows.

Now Finn, do it now, Magnus urged him mentally, afraid to speak in case he upset the fearful balance of the illusion. Any second now the wolves would reach them.

And then Finn dragged him backwards off his feet so suddenly that he didn't even have time to take a breath, and water and wolves and moonlight boiled and seethed around him. He closed his lungs on the little air he had, and concentrated on keeping hold of Finn's hand.

As Jess and Freya watched, the surface of the loch began to bubble and glow silver. They heard the boys beside them gasp.

"Finn's done it. He's brought the moon to the loch. The wolves are there."

Jess let go of Freya, wiped a sweaty palm across her skirt and took a firmer grip on the spear in her hand. What was going to come out of the loch?

The Nykur faced the loch, tension clear in their faces as they waited to find whether their plan would work. And then something shot to the surface near the centre of the water.

A head. Two heads.

"Finn!" gasped Jess. "And Magnus."

Without even thinking, the girls dashed for the door and started to run for the loch, leaving behind whatever protection the house had offered.

They shouted the boys' names, saw them start to swim, saw a black head appear near them, then another, as the wolves were swept through the door into the Nykur world.

"Hurry!" yelled Freya.

"Swim!" screamed Jess. "The wolves are coming."

She glanced round as she reached the water's edge, expecting to see the Nykur poised to help, but they were concentrating on their pattern of stones, waiting to spring the trap shut.

Jess and Freya watched the terrible race to the edge of the loch. They screamed at the boys to swim faster, watching the water-sleek black heads gaining on them.

They waded out until the water was thigh deep; any further and they'd be swimming for their own lives. Jess reached Finn. She grabbed his arm and hauled him onwards.

"Don't slow down. They're right behind us," she urged him.

"Jess!" screamed Freya. "Quickly."

She looked round and saw, to her horror, Freya trying to fend off a wolf that was almost level with Magnus. Magnus himself didn't seem to realise what was happening, too disorientated by the last few minutes.

She left Finn and struggled across to help, stabbing and jabbing at the black head, trying to win a few seconds for Magnus to get clear. A red stain spread in the water and the wolf twisted and headed away from them.

They cleared the edge of the water and broke into a

stumbling run away from the loch. Jess looked back and saw the first wolf reach the edge and shake a rainbow of water from its pelt.

"I thought they couldn't get out again. What's wrong? It's not working."

Finn paused to look at the loch and then at the Nykur.

"The illusion isn't complete yet," he said.

The wolves emerging into the Nykur world were disoriented. Where was the moon that they had followed? Almost a score of them milled on the shore, trying to scent it, not yet aware of the still figures of the Nykur.

The loch was full of wolves. They'd be overwhelmed in minutes. Magnus stepped in front of the two girls, knife ready, as though he could hope to defend them.

And then…

"What's happening?" gasped Freya.

Jess watched as the movement of the dozens of wolves in the water slowed and stopped, as the water grew solid around them. There were a few despairing howls that faded to whimpers and then to silence, as the loch forgot it was water.

The wolves died where they were, crushed by water that thought it was stone.

Jess, Freya and Magnus stared in disbelief at the impossibility of what they had just seen. Finn let out a shout to alert his people. And the wolves on the shore, the very last survivors of the pack, suddenly became aware of the Nykur. All their confusion and uncertainty dropped away, for here was prey, and they were wolves, and the hunt was the very core of their being.

They launched themselves at the Nykur.

One man was dead before they had any chance to react, brought down and killed with terrible ferocity. A woman screamed and then the lochside erupted into a chaos of hooves and teeth as Finn and the remaining Nykur took horse shape. Magnus, Freya and Jess shrank close together, unable even to flee to the house through the whirling fury of horses and wolves. Magnus struck at a long body as it shot past him. The knife connected, but the wolf was gone before he could tell how badly he'd hurt it.

They saw a wolf stop and focus on Euan, the only other human in the melee, scenting an easy kill. It bared its fangs and moved in, and then a horse plunged in front of it and struck again and again with its hooves until the wolf was a twitching unrecognisable mess of red and black and white.

Around them, the wolves died, whimpering. At last the world grew quiet. The horses grew still. Every wolf lay dead or dying. Magnus took a few steps to where one lay helpless, its back broken, and drew his knife across its throat.

There was utter silence, and suddenly the horses were gone and in their place, torn and battered and blood-streaked, were the Nykur, back in human form.

There were three still figures on the ground: the man who had died at the start of the attack; a woman with long blonde hair matted with blood from a terrible wound to her skull, and Finn.

The silence was broken by a scream as the survivors took in the scene around them. Jess would have run straight to where Finn lay, but Magnus held tight to her arm.

"Let me go." She tried to shake him off.

"Jess, wait. Let his family go to him."

"No." She tugged ineffectually against him.

Magnus stepped in front of her so she had to look at him.

"Jess. His family need to go to him first."

She saw the truth in what he said, and instead buried herself in his arms, aware a few seconds later of Freya's arms around her as well. She had no idea how long she stood like that before she took in that Magnus was speaking to her.

"Jess? Jess, look up. Look. He's all right."

She looked, hardly daring to hope she understood. Finn was on his feet, his whole family hugging him. "I don't think he's even hurt," Magnus said.

He couldn't stop her this time as she stumbled across the stony earth to Finn and his family and threw her arms round him.

"I thought you were dead. I thought you were dead."

Behind Jess, Magnus had turned away, and Freya put an arm round his shoulders.

"I'm all right," said Finn, still struggling for breath. "Keeping the moon illusion going was a strain, that's all. What about you?"

"I'm fine. We all are. Is it over now?"

"Yes. It's over." He looked at the broken bodies that lay on the loch shore. "It's over."

The Nykur carried the dead man and the dying woman into the abandoned house. They made the woman as comfortable as they could and her family gathered round her bed.

Jess and Freya helped to tend the other wounded Nykur. No one else was badly hurt, though few had escaped completely unscathed. They all stayed there for the night, falling into exhausted sleep where they sat or lay. No one had spoken much, too shocked by the deaths they had witnessed.

The injured woman died just before dawn.

Once the sun was fully up, the Nykur gathered to bid farewell to their dead. Jess, Freya and Magnus hung back, not wanting to intrude, but Finn came for them.

"We would like you to be part of this, as you were part of what happened yesterday."

They followed him outside, not knowing what to expect. A burial? A pyre?

The Nykur stood in a ring round the bodies. Jess, Freya and Magnus joined it, standing between Finn and Rowan. No one spoke. The families of the dead came forward to kiss them, then returned to their places. Everyone stood silently. How long would they keep vigil like this, Jess wondered, and what would they do afterwards?

Something was happening to the bodies.

Jess blinked and squinted, for she could no longer see them properly. It was as though they were wrapped in mist, red and gold and silvery grey. The mist seemed to settle to the ground. She could see the shapes under it now, but they didn't look like bodies any more: it was as though someone had painstakingly formed their detailed images from heaped autumn leaves.

A breeze came from nowhere, swirling around. It lifted the mist away from the leaf images, then moved the leaves themselves in little spurts and eddies. The leaves moved faster, spinning in a vortex that carried them high overhead and then released them in the air to be swept away by other winds.

Jess found that her face was wet with tears, and looked round to see that everyone was weeping.

It was a new day. The wolves were defeated and the dead were gone.

"It's time we went home," said Magnus.

Finn, Jess, Freya and Magnus stood beside the river near Finn's family home.

It had been a sombre journey back. They had waited until they were all well enough to travel, then left the others at the loch.

Jess knew she should worry about the reception that was likely to face them in the Upper World, but her mind and heart were here with Finn. She was desperate to speak to him alone, but somehow either Magnus or Freya had always been with her. There was no time left if she was going to speak.

"Will you come back with us for a while? Even a day or so; just for a rest, a few meals, until your family gets here."

He shook his head.

"I can't. And you need to make your peace with your father. My being there wouldn't exactly help."

Jess's heart sank, even though he was right. She tried to smile, not trusting herself to speak further.

"Ready?" Finn asked.

They joined hands and stepped into the water, let it carry them down and up and through, opened their eyes to low sun slanting through tree trunks, and pulled themselves free of Roseroot Pool.

Finn embraced Freya and Jess.

He and Magnus gave each other a long look, and clasped hands briefly.

"We'll see you again, won't we?" asked Freya. Jess couldn't have spoken if her life had depended on it.

"Maybe," was all Finn said.

He didn't dare stay a second longer, or he'd never have the strength to go. He left his heart on the shore like a gasping fish, waded out, and disappeared.

Jess felt something inside her break and go with him. She stared at the empty water until Magnus and Freya turned her round and made her start walking.

"We'll freeze if we stand here moping," said Freya, suddenly taking charge. "Come on. I wonder how much trouble we're in? I wonder how long we've been gone? Let me do the talking, you two. I'll say I made you go with me. It's true, anyway."

She kept up a stream of chatter all the way to the edge of the farmyard, covering the painful silence that hung over Jess and Magnus.

The smokehouse door opened and out came Ashe, chewing. He looked guilty for a second when he saw them, before he realised that, for once, he wasn't going to be the one in trouble.

"Where have you been? You've missed breakfast *and* lunch. Father's furious. Why are you wet?"

"We'll tell you all about it in a while," said Freya, and they walked on towards the house.

Spring

Chapter Twenty-Three

The year turned. The winter had been a hard one, but at last the final fall of snow melted, and the rivers were free of ice again. Each day grew a little longer, a little lighter. Spring was coming.

In Dundee, the Night of the Black Wolves was still the focus of rumour and tall tales. The reality had been bad enough; nine people killed, along with countless dogs and cats, horses, pigs and chickens. Some folk said there had been hundreds of wolves, but those who had stayed safe behind their closed shutters knew that must be an exaggeration, for where had they all gone so suddenly, if they'd ever been there?

And what about the boys who had raised the alarm? They'd disappeared in the middle of the night too, with the watchmen's horses, and no one could trace them. Some folk said they were spirits, though the watchmen said they were real enough.

Magnus listened to his parents' account of that night and said nothing. He hardly believed what had happened himself; why should anyone else?

At Westgarth, farm life continued its steady round, and Jess took up her part in the pattern again.

For weeks after they had come back from the Nykur world, she had gone to Roseroot Pool whenever she could, but there was never any sign of Finn. Twice she had walked into the water, trying to reach the Nykur world on her own, but that ability had gone.

An awkward constraint had fallen between Jess and Magnus when they returned, and for a while he'd avoided the farm altogether, working in Kirriemuir for Arnor, but the rest of the family had made it impossible for him to stay away for long. Slowly, step by delicate step, he and Jess recovered themselves and began to relax in each other's company again, and Magnus started to hope that everything might be all right.

Now he walked Jess to the farm cart from Arnor's shop, arms full of supplies.

"I'll see you later," he said. He was coming to Westgarth for the weekend, ostensibly to help Ian repair fences.

She gave him a slightly awkward kiss. "Don't be late. Ellen's making a huge fruit cake for you."

When she got back to Westgarth, she could smell the cake baking. The bowl was still waiting to be washed, and she wiped a finger round it and licked off the sticky mixture with relish.

"You're as bad as Ashe," said Ellen, helping her put the supplies away. "If he'd had his way there would have been nothing left to cook."

"I told Magnus you were baking. He said he'll be sure to work up an appetite."

"I'd have made two if I'd known that." Ellen stopped what she was doing. "I'm glad he's come back to us. I missed him."

"So did I," said Jess after a moment. "It took me a while to realise how much."

"So the two of you are all right?"

"Getting there."

Ellen left things at that, to Jess's relief.

After lunch, Jess went across to the dairy to churn butter.

There was a tiny roll of paper lying by the churn. Jess wiped her hands on her apron and unrolled it.

I'll wait by the pool.
Please come.

That was all. She turned the paper over and over, sure there must be more, but that was all.

How long had it been there? She could swear it hadn't been by the churn yesterday, but it was so small she could have missed it.

She abandoned the butter, pulled her jacket on and left.

Jess had tried to convince herself to accept that she wouldn't see Finn again. Now it was almost three weeks since she'd been to the pool. She'd been trying to break the habit and had been succeeding at last.

She walked quickly, resisting the temptation to run. How long had the note been waiting? How long would Finn wait?

At last, she was there. The pool lay unconcerned in front of her, the marsh marigolds just coming into bloom, glowingly golden.

"Finn?" she called.

"I didn't know if you would come," he said, stepping out from the trees.

Her heart gave a great thud.

They looked at one another, temporarily robbed of speech. Finally, Jess said, "You look well."

It was true. All the marks of his illness had gone now, but more than that, he looked at peace with himself.

"You too."

She took refuge in flippancy.

"I'd have put on something cleaner and brushed my hair if it had been a more formal invitation…"

He waited for her voice to skitter into silence.

"Have you made peace with your father?"

"More or less," she said with a rueful smile. "Some things he'll never be able to understand, but he's doing his best to convince himself they never happened." She moved towards him a little. "You and your family are...?"

"We're fine. After what happened by the loch – it made us all realise how important we are to each other."

"That's good. And the wolves are gone?"

He nodded and took a couple of steps towards her. "Those ones at least. Even if the illusion was to break now, they're long dead."

They were so close now that they were almost touching.

"Do you think any of your family would come through this door? My grandmother would love to see Euan again. And now that everything's fine..."

Finn's face clouded.

"Everything isn't fine." He looked away for a second, then turned back to face her. "That's why I had to see you."

"What? What's wrong?" She caught hold of his hand.

"You saw how few of us there were. We've been pretending to ourselves for far too long that we can survive here. We can't go on like this. We can't stay here any longer. We've all decided to leave. We're going north: there are more Nykur there. If we stay here, we're doomed. We have to leave to have a chance."

She stared at him, took a difficult breath.

"But you'll come back sometimes, won't you?"

Finn sat down, pulling Jess down beside him. He looked at the pool for a few seconds, then turned back to her. "This gateway will have to be sealed when we leave, or the wolves that are left in the Nykur world might find a way through eventually. It can't be opened once it's been sealed."

"But that would mean I wouldn't see you again," she said slowly.

Surely that wasn't really what he meant? She waited for him to tell her she'd misunderstood.

"That's right." His voice was barely more than a whisper. "Once I leave I can't come back. So I'm asking you to come with me. To be with me. For good." He stroked her cheek. "You know I love you. I've loved you for years. I know you love me. Come with me."

For a long time, Jess was silent. She looked into his blue eyes.

"You could stay here," she said hesitantly.

He shook his head. "I can't, Jess. It nearly destroyed me to be separated from my family before. I can't do it. I can't abandon the part of me that is Nykur. If you come into my world, you'll forget this one. You won't miss it."

"I can't do that," Jess said in a small voice. "I don't want to forget them. I can't leave my whole life behind. I'm sorry. I love you, Finn. You know I do. But I can't leave behind all the other people I love."

They had moved into each other's arms. They stayed like that for a long time, not speaking, until at last Finn said,

"I should go now."

Jess tried to wipe away the tears that wouldn't stop falling as they got to their feet.

"Say goodbye to Ashe for me, and to Ellen," Finn said. "I know she never liked me, but she was very kind. And tell Magnus – no, probably best to tell him nothing. He's a good man, Jess. The two of you make a good team."

She swallowed hard, sniffed, and looked Finn in the eye.

"I know. And I do love him."

"And so you should."

They stepped away from each other a little.

"Goodbye then," he said.

"Goodbye."

And because neither of them could bear any more, he turned and walked into the water, looked back at her once, and was gone.

Jess stood there until the final ripples had died and she could see her reflection lying still again in the water. She wiped the last tears from her face and turned away.

For a long time she stood there, blind to her surroundings, following her thoughts as they spiralled away from this moment along the different paths the future could take.

Finally, she started to walk.

Magnus saw Jess coming and went across the yard to meet her.

"You're early," she said.

"Freya threw me out."

He could see the marks of tears on her face.

"You shouldn't let her boss you around, you know."

They walked together towards the bright warmth of the kitchen door.

"Where have you been?" He was almost afraid to ask.

"Just for a walk." She pulled him to a halt. "Before we go in, I've got something to say to you."

Magnus took a deep breath, trying to prepare himself.

"What?"

"I love you. I don't think I've ever told you that properly before."

"No, you haven't… not like that."

Jess put her arms round his neck and gave him a kiss that wasn't awkward at all.

"I went for a walk to Roseroot Pool, and now I'm back. For always."

Clouds of sparks danced in front of her eyes. The pressure in her head, her arms, her hands was unbearable. She couldn't stop it…

"You're a witch."

"No!" She slammed her hands flat on the table. There was a loud crack as it burst into flames.

Callie Hall is a real-life witch with incredible powers she can't control. Witchcraft might seem hard, but lighting candles with her fingers and casting protective spells can't prepare her for what's coming.

In the tunnels beneath St Andrews, something is lurking: a dark and dangerous presence that threatens everything. Callie needs help, but can she trust best friend Josh with her secret? And, together, can they defeat the darkness?

Also available as an eBook

Gill Arbuthnott was born and brought up in Edinburgh but escaped briefly to study in St Andrews and Southampton. She couldn't stay away, however, and now lives in Edinburgh with her family and Leonard the cat. When she's not writing, she works as a biology teacher. She has written several novels for children and young adults: *Chaos Clock*, *Chaos Quest*, *Winterbringers*, *Dark Spell* and *The Keeper's Daughter*, as well as non-fiction books that make science fun.

Visit Gill's website at gillarbuthnott.com